THE COVER-UP

Book 2 in the Clarke Pettis Series

Christine Pattle

Chapter 1

Clarke Pettis hated being late. She was supposed to be at the Carjon Pharma offices ten minutes ago for a briefing about the new contract. Silently, she cursed the train for being delayed, then walked faster.

If Clarke hoped for a quiet start to the Carjon Pharma contract, she was soon disappointed. Even from a distance, she spotted the large group of people milling around the building's forecourt. As she got closer, she realised it was some sort of demonstration. The demonstrators, a scruffy collection of people, were deliberately blocking the entrance. Most of them carried placards. When she got close enough, she started reading them: *Save Our Animals, Stop Animal Testing, Kill Chemists-Not Mice,* and a particularly nasty, *Death to the F***ing Animal Killers.*

Despite being aware that Carjon Pharma developed and sold medicines and drugs, it hadn't occurred to Clarke to expect trouble. She supposed protests like this must be inevitable, given the company's line of business.

The demonstrators chanted some of the slogans on the placards, their fervent shouts lending a menacing vibe to the whole performance. The vicious tone added to the actual words sent chills down Clarke's spine. She worried that a few of them really believed the vile rubbish they were spouting.

There appeared to be only one way into the building. Clarke searched for a friendly face with whom she might walk past the demonstrators. Carjon Pharma's employees must have been warned about the demo in advance and arrived at work early today, or even taken the day off if they possessed any sense of self-preservation. She took out her phone and tapped in Evan's number. Evan Davies would be her manager for this job. Maybe he would show up to escort her in. She quickly realised that wouldn't happen as the phone went straight to voicemail. No doubt Evan was safely ensconced inside the building already, probably in the meeting she should now be attending, with his phone switched to silent.

"Evan, I'm outside. I'm not happy about trying to get past these demonstrators on my own. Phone me." Clarke doubted he would pick up the voicemail anytime soon. He might at least have texted her to warn her what she would be walking into.

She couldn't stand out here all day. Taking a deep breath, she clutched her laptop tightly, and positioned her bag securely over her shoulder. They surely wouldn't do anything stupid in broad daylight in a public place. She decided to walk straight past them, trying her best to look confident. Ignore them. Power-walk straight ahead without catching anyone in the eye. She couldn't come up with a better plan on the spur of the moment.

"Excuse me." She ducked to one side to avoid the marching protestors, whose circular route made her plan of marching straight up to the front door impossible.

"Animal-Torturing-Scumbag," one of the protestors shouted directly at Clarke. His wild black curls tossed as he moved towards her.

"Oh, no," Clarke said. "I don't work here." So much for her resolution not to engage with them. She wondered if there ought to be a police presence, or perhaps these people weren't considered a risk to anyone's safety. She hoped that was the case.

The curly-haired guy stood directly in front of her, blocking her route. "Then why are you going in?"

Clarke tried not to be intimidated by his threatening manner or the size of him, but he glared at her with pure hatred. For a brief moment, she considered whacking him in the balls with her laptop and running for the entrance, but that would be madness. Beyond him, she got a good view of the front door. A flash of uniform behind the glass caught her eye. She wondered if the security guard would come to her rescue, but he stood safely inside the door. He gave no indication that he might venture outside to help her, no matter what happened.

She willed herself not to get into an argument with Mr Curly Hair. He probably wanted a fight. "I don't approve of animal testing either," she said. Her first rule of dealing with confrontation: always agree with everything they say. That way, they've got nothing to argue with you about. Sometimes that strategy worked. Sometimes it got her into trouble.

"Then come and join us."

Clarke's face dropped, unsure how best to respond.

"No, I thought not." Curly Hair sneered at her. He spat at her feet and moved aside. "You're either with us or against us," he said.

Clarke took her chance and powered on towards the entrance. The door was locked. She waved at the security guard on the other side. He shook his head. Clarke fumbled in her handbag, trying to find her Tebbit & Cranshaw employee pass. She supposed she would need to prove her identity before they would let her in. The protestors behind her made multi-coloured reflections in the glass door, distracting her from her search. Turning her back on them worried her. In such close proximity, if anything happened, it would be so quick, and she would be powerless to stop it. She desperately needed someone to open the door for her now. Clarke stared at the reflection in the glass, trying to spot the curly-haired man. His final words, that she was either with them or against them—he'd made that sound like a threat. The sooner she got safely inside the building, the better.

The shouting grew louder. They'd moved on to a different slogan now. Clarke still hadn't located her pass. She must have left it at home, as she didn't plan to go to Tebbit & Cranshaw's head office today. Again, she knocked at the door, wishing her miming skills were vastly better, good enough to convey to that stupid security guard that he should let her in immediately. No way did she want to fight her way back through the crowd of protestors. She didn't want to stay here either. She really didn't feel safe trapped in this small space by the door.

Suddenly, the security guard appeared to have a change of heart. He unlocked the door and ushered her inside quickly. Clarke didn't need any further encouragement. She slipped through the doorway like greased lightning.

"You must be Clarke." A well-dressed man rushed up to meet her. "I'm so sorry. I saw you from my office upstairs. We should have arranged for you to come in the back entrance. Are you all right?"

"It's ok. I'm fine," Clarke said, still trying to compose herself. She took a deep breath. At least this contract wouldn't be boring, although she really didn't want to go through that experience ever again.

The man smiled at her. She quickly read the name on the security pass dangling from his neck. "Thank you, Mr Carver-Jones." She recognised the name. This must be the company chairman.

"Please, call me Henry. We don't stand on ceremony here. We're like one big, happy family." Henry bade her to follow him up the stairs. "Our *friends* outside don't show up too often, you'll be pleased to hear. They're a bit lively today, but they're normally pretty harmless."

Normally? Clarke wondered what he meant by that. The implication being that sometimes they *weren't* harmless. She would definitely check out that back entrance before she left for home today.

"Is my colleague Evan Davies here yet?"

"Yes, indeed. He arrived before the protestors did. They don't generally get up early."

Henry gestured towards a door in front of him. "I've put you in the boardroom for the duration. Shall I make you a cup of tea before we start? It's the least I can do."

"Do you have coffee?" Clarke asked. She hated tea and needed gallons of strong coffee to function at her best.

"Of course. We have a proper percolator and a particularly fine Costa Rican blend. I'll put the machine on."

Clarke opened the boardroom door. Perhaps she would enjoy working here after all.

Evan greeted her without looking up from his laptop.

"I've just been doing battle with a gang of animal rights activists outside," Clarke said. "Security didn't even want to let me into the building. Thankfully, Henry Carver-Jones rescued me. Why didn't you warn me?" She put her laptop on the huge table and unzipped the bag.

"Wow. I'm sorry, Clarke. I had no idea. I got the impression they were peaceful and, well, you're a pretty ballsy lady, not one to get freaked out by a bunch of losers."

Clarke grimaced. She'd worked with Evan on several jobs since she'd joined T&C. Like most people, he assumed she must be super brave because she used to be a firefighter. That was a few years ago now. Three years at Briar Holman, and now nearly a year working for T&C.

Briar Holman. She shuddered at the memories the name recalled. That was why she'd applied for the job with T&C, training to be a forensic accountant. The fraud she'd discovered at Briar Holman gave her a taste for more investigative work. And, although forensic accountancy wasn't all glamour and intrigue, the work suited her analytical brain and inquiring mind. She'd wanted to leave Briar Holman. After what her colleague there had done, once they got arrested, it wasn't the same anymore. A dark cloud hung over their once joyous office, rapidly making the decision to move on very easy.

Henry returned. "Coffee's on its way." He sat down opposite them.

"I'll get straight to the point." Henry Carver-Jones fiddled nervously with his bright blue silk tie, pausing while his brain seemed unable to spit out the promised *straight to the point* explanation.

Clarke stared at him across the huge mahogany table, waiting for him to continue.

Evan quickly filled the silence. "Clearly you believe there's a problem at Carjon Pharma, or you wouldn't have called us in. Perhaps it would be best to start at the beginning."

Clarke poised, ready to type into her laptop, a considerably more secure storage facility for her notes than the pen and paper option she preferred. Encrypted to within an inch of its life, protected by a series of three ultra-strong passwords, and fitted with a top-of-the-range tracking device, standard issue laptops for all employees of Tebbit & Cranshaw.

Henry gave a small cough. "I don't want to accuse anyone," he said. "We're like a family here."

Clarke sensed a big *but* coming.

"It's the bank, you see." Henry twiddled with his perfectly knotted tie again. "They won't extend our credit anymore. The thing is, our last set of accounts shows the company is financially extremely healthy. We should be rolling in cash, but we're not. It doesn't make sense."

"Have the accounts been audited?" Evan asked.

"Oh yes. And the auditors didn't find a thing wrong with them. They gave a clean report."

"Is it possible that one of your employees has been stealing money from the company?"

Henry shook his head. "I really don't want to believe that. As I said, we're like a family here. Three of us founded the company, myself, Patrick Polkinghorne, and Frank Varley. Many of our employees have been with us from the start, and I don't want to believe any of them are responsible. But the company must have been haemorrhaging money somehow. I can't imagine how else that would have happened."

"Then we need to do a full investigation," Evan said.

Henry nodded enthusiastically. "Yes, of course. Let's get to the bottom of it."

"Are Patrick and Frank still with the company?" Clarke asked.

"Yes. Patrick's the finance director, and Frank's our head research scientist."

Clarke wanted to question their absence. Patrick, at least, in his role as finance director, should be the expert. "We'll need to meet them," she said.

"Yes, of course. But..." Henry hesitated. "I thought it prudent not to tell anyone about the investigation. Best that nobody knows what you're doing."

"I understand." Clarke didn't understand at all. If Henry didn't want to tell his finance director and co-founder of the company about this, that must surely mean he suspected him.

"We will need full access to everything and everyone," Evan said. "And don't worry, we'll keep this between the three of us. We don't want to put anyone on their guard."

"How do we do that?" Henry asked. "They'll ask why you're here."

"You can tell them we're producing a report to determine whether the company should float on the stock market," Evan said.

Henry raised an eyebrow quizzically.

"We've done this many times," Evan explained. "That explains perfectly why we need to do a deep dive into every area of the business. It's the most believable cover story for your particular case."

Clarke nodded. She'd done all the research into the company for Evan before this meeting. She'd also checked out the value of the company's assets. Worst-case scenario: if Carjon Pharma really was haemorrhaging cash, there would be plenty of money to ensure that T&C got paid for their work, even if it meant applying for a liquidation order.

"Don't worry," Evan said. "We'll find out what's going on."

"Thank you." Henry exuded relief at handing over all responsibility for this mess to someone else.

Clarke knew things didn't quite work like that, and there was no guarantee they would find all the answers, but if it made him feel better...

"It's imperative that no one, absolutely no one, knows the real reason why we're here." Evan held out his hand to Henry. "We can investigate much more effectively if no one gets suspicious about us."

"Do you think he suspects anyone in particular?" Clarke asked as soon as Henry left the room.

Evan considered for a moment. "He probably would have told us if he did. In any case, we ought to suspect everyone until we get some hard evidence."

Clarke smiled. Evan liked hard evidence, usually dismissing her gut feelings about people. Gut feelings, he always told her, didn't stand up in court, even if they were right.

"So, what do I do first?" Clarke switched on her laptop and waited for Evan to explain the plan. She held no great illusions. As a trainee, she got the grunt work and Evan did the interesting stuff, but she still loved the excitement of never knowing what they might uncover on any job. Sometimes, she felt like a cross between a number-cruncher and a superhero. And she learned new stuff constantly from Evan.

Her laptop pinged. "I've sent you the plan," Evan said. "Bank reconciliations, and debtor and creditor checks. Find the money. Is the cash missing, or did it never exist in the first place? The auditors gave the company a clean bill of health, so you need to be super thorough, and examine everything right up to date."

"Does Carjon Pharma do a lot of animal testing?" Clarke didn't know why she had changed the subject so dramatically. Mr Curly Hair giving her the evil eye earlier had definitely unsettled her. She'd been contemplating the subject for the last few minutes.

Evan steepled his fingers in the way he always did during a serious conversation. "Yes, of course they do. They develop drugs to use on humans. Testing on animals is a legal requirement."

"Yes, I guess so. But surely the protestors out the front are aware of all that. Why don't they protest outside cosmetic companies instead? Why here? Are pharmaceutical companies an easy target?"

"I've got no idea, Clarke. Have you got principles to worry about here? I can get you replaced with someone else if it's giving you a moral dilemma."

"I'm fine," Clarke said. Henry had given them access to all areas. She would make it her business to enquire about animal welfare and numbers, just out of interest.

A knock on the door interrupted them, and a young woman entered.

"Henry asked me to bring you coffee." She set down a tray on a side table. Two steaming cups of black coffee, a jug of milk, and two small bowls of sugar cubes, brown and white. She took a couple of drinks mats from a pile on the side table and placed them on the larger table, one on the right-hand side of each of them.

"Thank you," Clarke said. "Sorry, you didn't tell me your name."

"I'm Kerry."

Clarke smiled at her. Henry mentioned Kerry earlier as being one of the people they should talk to. "What do you do in Carjon Pharma, Kerry?"

Kerry paused and put her hands on her hips. "I'm not a tea lady," she said. "I'm an accounts assistant. I work with Patrick. Henry only asked me to make coffee because his PA is on leave this week."

Clarke smiled again, trying to disarm Kerry's aggressive stance. She never intended to patronise the girl. "That's great. We're having a good probe into everything here, so I'm sure we'll need to call on your expertise at some point."

"You mean like an audit?" Kerry said. "We've only just been audited."

Evan stepped in. "We're putting together a case for floating the company on the stock market. So, we'll be looking at all the work the company does. It's an exciting time to work here." He gave her a warm smile as she handed him a coffee. "I'm sure we'll be coming to pick your brains later."

"Don't forget the cover story," Evan said to Clarke as soon as Kerry left the room.

"I haven't forgotten." Clarke sipped her coffee. Wow, it tasted good, although the twenty-minute wait for it to percolate might be a problem. Maybe she'd keep a small jar of instant in her handbag for when she needed immediate gratification. "I'm well aware of how sensitive this job is, but I wanted to get her on side and more relaxed. Didn't you notice how defensive she was, like she's got something to hide?" Clarke was slightly annoyed at Evan for managing to disarm Kerry so quickly, with nothing more than a charming smile.

Evan laughed. "Now who's getting defensive? I'm sure you wouldn't say anything stupid, but it never hurts to remind you."

"So anyway, Carjon Pharma is about to start human clinical trials on their new wonder drug. It's supposed to be the cure for a particularly aggressive form of cervical cancer. Ironically, it would actually be an interesting time to float the company on the stock market. They'd probably make a killing if they did."

"Henry seems to pride himself on it being a family company."

Evan laughed. "Carjon Pharma was never really a family company, although Henry's late brother worked here for a while. Henry flat shared with Frank and Patrick at uni, so they consider themselves as family. That, and the fact that the company is still small enough for Henry to be familiar with all his employees, gives the place a family feel. He likes to perpetuate the myth about it being a family company. It's good for their image, particularly when the media confronts him about events like this morning's demo."

Clarke was impressed. "You've done your homework," she said.

"Always."

Clarke walked over to the window. Working with Evan was a great learning experience. His forte was strategic thinking about the business and analysing a company's strong and weak points before they even started each job. That gave them vital clues about where to search for issues.

The demonstrators continued to march around outside. Clarke stepped back, not wanting any of them to spot her if they glanced up at the first-floor windows.

"Have these animal rights protestors given any trouble before?" she asked. "Henry says they're not dangerous, but they seem quite aggressive." Maybe being in the thick of things, surrounded by shouting people, had made her feel vulnerable earlier. The curly-haired man, who was particularly tall and muscular, would be a frightening opponent if he decided to get nasty. She wondered if her imagination was running away with her. Perhaps they merely wanted to draw attention to their cause peacefully.

"Henry's been dealing with them for years, so he's the expert."

"I hope so."

"I'll make sure you get a pass for the staff car park and the back entrance," Evan said. "If you drive in every day, you won't get any trouble. Henry says they always stay at the front of the building. I guess there's no publicity in demonstrating out of sight round the back."

Clarke nodded. She would drive in tomorrow and start earlier, too. She saw no point in asking for trouble.

Chapter 2

Patrick arrived late at the hospital. He hated to keep Martina waiting. His twenty-minute traffic hold-up on the ring road meant that Martina's sister would have already left to get to her job on time, so Martina would be on her own until he showed up. The guilt weighed him down, slowing his steps when he should be walking faster so Martina wouldn't be waiting any longer than necessary. It was tough enough for her enduring chemo, without having to go through any of it alone.

He proceeded straight up to the Chemotherapy Suite. It seemed almost cruel calling it a suite, as if it was a penthouse hotel room on the French Riviera. Martina simply laughed at the name, calling it the Chemotherapy Sweet, as these were the only days she broke her incredibly healthy diet and allowed herself two squares of Cadbury's Dairy Milk, her favourite chocolate, as a reward for putting up with several hours of hell.

Patrick crept in while Martina was engrossed in her Kindle. She liked reading romances. Not the sexy, erotic stuff, but clean, sweet romances that provided perfect escapism from the cancer that ravaged her ever frailer body. She didn't notice him come in. He wondered if he should pretend he'd been here for ten minutes already, but after twenty-three years of marriage, she read him as well as the book on her lap, so lying would be pointless.

"Hi, darling." Martina glanced up as Patrick called out to her. Did he detect a brief flash of annoyance on her face? "I'm so sorry. I got held up in traffic." He sat down next to her and took her hand. "Did Sonia come this morning?"

Martina smiled. "Of course she did. The hospital doesn't like me coming on my own. I'm lucky I've got such a good sister." She pulled her hand away from his to switch off her Kindle.

Patrick wondered if she was making a comparison between him and her saintly sister, who doubtlessly showed up on time this morning.

Or did Martina seem a bit off because she'd got to a good point in her book and didn't want to stop reading? Or, then again, it wasn't any fun having chemo. That alone would make anyone a bit cross or miserable. He reached over and took her hand back, caressing it gently because he wanted her to appreciate, whatever his failings compared to Saint Sonia or the heroes in her romance novels, he did love her very, very much.

"How are you feeling today?" he asked. Her face appeared completely drained of colour. Chemo always took so much out of her. The doctors weren't even sure the treatment would work, but they offered no alternative options right now.

"The usual. Tired but bearing up. At least it's only another hour or so, then we can go home." She smiled. "You're cooking dinner tonight."

Patrick smiled back. "You bet I am." Not that she would eat much of it, but he was becoming rather skilled at making exciting things with vegetables, probiotic yoghurt, and all different varieties of beans. He'd even started to dabble a bit with tofu.

Martina had stage four cervical cancer. They'd discovered the cancer quite late and were treating it aggressively, so much so that sometimes the cure made her feel worse than the illness did. The doctors warned that she might not survive it, but Patrick steadfastly refused to entertain any such negative thoughts. He was doing everything possible to get her through this. Everything. Every time he looked at her, he searched for any tiny signs of improvement, despite it being still early days yet. She'd endured three rounds of chemo to date. This was the fourth, so Patrick assumed the effects would start kicking in soon, maybe tomorrow, when today's treatment had been given a few hours to start working its magic.

He squeezed Martina's hand gently. "Frank's making great progress. He'll be ready to start clinical drug trials soon. If we can get you on that trial, it will make a massive difference."

Martina gave a weak smile. "Perhaps. Maybe when he's tested it further. The chemo might have worked by then."

"Yes, I'm sure it will." Patrick didn't want to argue with this woefully weak version of Martina. He tried to avoid anything that might raise her stress levels by even the tiniest amount. But, so far, the chemo proved to be a bit of a dead loss. He must talk to the doctors again. Surely it should be making a difference by now. Perhaps not. He wasn't an expert.

"Frank's achieved amazing results when he's tested the drug on the rats in his lab," Patrick said. "Dramatic improvements."

"I'm not a rat," Martina pointed out indignantly.

"Of course not. I didn't mean to suggest that. But Frank is brilliant, and he really believes in this drug."

"Didn't a girl die a couple of years ago in one of his clinical trials?"

"Yes, but..." The coroner had delivered a not guilty verdict for both Frank and Carjon Pharma. "There must have been something wrong with her." They were supposedly signing up healthy twenty-somethings. She must have lied on her application form and slipped through the screenings.

"But the coroner didn't find anything."

"Well, what about Frank's other achievements? He is brilliant. The new drug is amazing." Patrick began to realise why Martina had been less than positive every time he mentioned the new drug trial. She must have been researching it on the internet. That was the trouble with being ill—too many long hours to while away. And everybody knew you should never, ever Google your own illness. The internet was full of sensational horror stories. Reading them only served to frighten people and make them shy away from a drug that might potentially save their life. Somehow, he would convince Martina. If the cancer got any worse, if the chemo didn't work, Frank's drug trial might be her only option.

The nurse came in. "Time's up, Lovey. I'll disconnect you and you can go home shortly, as soon as you feel up to it." She deftly removed the catheter from Martina's arm, performing each step in the process automatically, as if she'd done it a million times. He wondered how the nurse managed to stay so cheerful when she spent most of her time dealing with extremely sick people, some of whom, sadly, wouldn't make it.

"I'll sit here a little longer," Martina told Patrick. "Then we can go home."

Patrick couldn't wait to leave.

Chapter 3

"Henry, what's going on? Why didn't you tell me you're planning to float the company?" Deborah Glayton flew into Henry's office in a whirlwind.

Henry got up and shut the door, so no one would accidentally overhear their conversation. In this volatile mood, Deb might let anything slip out. He needed to be careful, even if she didn't. If his wife found out... well, she couldn't. That simply must not be allowed to happen.

"Shall we calm down?" he said.

"I don't know," Deborah said, "shall WE? Why didn't you tell me before?"

"Deborah, you aren't one of the company's owners. So, it's perfectly reasonable that you won't be the first person I tell." It annoyed Henry how Deborah so often confused business with pleasure. If she understood him at all, she would appreciate that he liked to keep the two things completely separate, and that business always came first.

Deborah continued to pace around the room. "But I'm the managing director," she said. "I should at least be consulted. I do have an opinion."

Henry sat down. No doubt she was about to voice that opinion. Somehow, he needed to get the situation under control before she started shooting her mouth off. He should remind her that she was only *acting up* in the managing director's job, and, if she gave him any trouble, he would demote her back to sales and marketing director in less time than it took for her to open a bottle of prosecco. Deborah scowled at him, almost as if reading his thoughts, and he decided to leave that course of action for another day.

"It affects my career." Deborah finally sat down. "I have plans in this company. Will I even get to keep my job? It's always the people at the top who get replaced first, isn't it? Have you thought about that?"

Henry conceded to himself that he hadn't. But it was always *All About Deborah*. "I'm sure, if you do have to go, you'll get a handsome payoff." *If the company had any money left by then.*

Deborah reached her hand across the desk until she touched Henry's fingers. He snatched his hand away as if he'd been scalded.

"We need to remain professional in the office," he said coldly.

If anyone found out, if news of the affair got back to Sarah, his wife, she'd boot him out. That would pain him far more than Deborah could possibly imagine. His and Sarah's was a rather unequal marriage. Financially, at least, he'd been punching well above his weight when he'd married her. She came from old family money, loads of it. The house: eight bedrooms, stables, a swimming pool, and a fabulously large reception room that hosted some splendid parties, all belonged to her. And, although Henry drew a small salary from Carjon Pharma, if the cash situation proved to be as bad as it seemed, he might be forced to rely totally on Sarah's money simply to put food on the table every day, not to mention paying Imogen's school fees. He refused to even contemplate divorce. Maybe he'd been stupid getting into this relationship with Deborah in the first place.

Henry decided it would be prudent for now to try to keep Deborah calm, although she was damn sexy when she was angry. "I'm sorry. Perhaps I should have asked for your opinion. Anyway, I'm telling you now, aren't I?" He smiled at her, tilting his head to one side in a way he'd been told looked irresistible.

Deborah ignored his smile. "Who exactly are these people in the boardroom?"

"Evan Davies and Clarke Pettis." He decided not to mention that Evan and Clarke worked for Tebbit & Cranshaw, in case Deborah Googled them and discovered what sort of work the accounting firm really specialised in. Best that she didn't find out that they were forensic accountants, experts in investigating financial abnormalities. Evan Davies had made the situation quite clear. Anyone might be a potential suspect, so it made their investigation much easier if everyone in the company remained oblivious to the real reason for their visit. "I've hired them to do a detailed report into the company, then write a prospectus if they agree we should float the company on the stock exchange. I've given them permission to talk to everyone and access to everything."

"But—"

Henry decided it would be best to quash her objections before she voiced them. "Anyway, that wasn't why I wanted to see you."

Deborah's face lit up.

"No, not that," Henry said. "At least, not in the office." He coughed. "We need to make some changes... cutbacks. The bank won't extend our credit at the moment, which leaves us with a temporary cash-flow problem."

"How? I mean, I've looked at the annual accounts and all the monthly reports. I didn't notice a problem."

"We've been over-spending very recently," Henry lied. "Anyway, you'll have to tell Frank his research budget is being cut."

"But his results are amazing. We can't halt the testing programme now."

"Yes, I agree. It's a pity, but I'm sure it will only be temporary." Henry crossed his fingers under the desk. "We simply have to concentrate our resources on the proven sellers, to bring in more income. You need to brief the sales team too. Get them working harder."

"You can't postpone Frank's testing. He's not going to be happy." Deborah folded her arms, as if setting up for further confrontation.

"Yes, but we won't earn any income from the new drug for at least another couple of years. We need to focus on increasing income now." If only he could tell Deborah how much they needed this, but he daren't press the point.

"But..."

Henry ignored her. "I have a spare couple of hours tonight," he said, eager to change the subject. "Shall I come over?" Sarah would be out, watching Imogen in a school play. He ought to pretend to be the perfect father and go with her. Imogen would be disappointed if he didn't. Acting was not Imogen's strongest talent. In fact, she was unbearably bad, although he hated to admit it about his own daughter. Lord knows how she'd actually managed to get the part—probably something to do with the large donation the company made last year towards building the new science block. Anyway, he'd already told them he needed to work late this evening, so they wouldn't be expecting him.

Deborah's face lit up. "That would be great. I'll get some food in."

"See you about seven then," Henry said. Deborah wasn't much of a cook. It didn't matter. There wouldn't be much eating going on.

Chapter 4

Frank Varley loved his rats. Definitely more than many people. Sometimes even more than his wife. He gave Delilah, his favourite, a cuddle before returning her to her cage. He would love to feed her a titbit, but she, like all the others, was on a strict diet. They all needed to be fed exactly the same to avoid messing up the test results.

"Frank." Deborah poked her head around the door.

Frank shut the cage. "Come in." Deborah rarely visited his lab. He hoped she hadn't been loitering by the door long enough to catch him fussing over Delilah. He didn't even let Ollie see him get soppy with his rats.

Deborah stepped inside the door.

"It's ok. They won't bite." Frank knew she didn't want to come in because the rats scared her. At least that guaranteed she wouldn't stay long. "What can I do for you?"

"We need to discuss your budget." She took a tentative step towards him, then seemed to change her mind and reversed.

"Not much to discuss. I'm not over-spending."

"That's good, but we need to make some cuts."

"Why?" Suddenly, Frank became suspicious. Deborah hated visiting his lab. This must be bad if she felt obliged to break the news in person. Normally, she would simply have sent an email. She looked a bit pale too. Something was definitely wrong. "How much?" May as well get the painful bit over with. They were scheduled to start clinical trials on the Fexizon drug next month. As long as he had the money to run those, he'd be happy.

Deborah hesitated. "Carjon has some cash-flow issues," she said. "You'll need to stop all spend on testing and research for a while."

"But..." Frank's mouth hung open, with his lower lip flapping gently as he tried to get the words out, but couldn't decide what to say. He wasn't expecting it to be this bad. "But surely you realise the Fexizon clinical trials start next month. It will cost a fortune to postpone them."

"I'm sorry, Frank. You may have to cancel them altogether for the moment."

"What?" Frank stared at her. Cancelling altogether would be far worse. He did a few lightning quick sums in his head. Cutting the budget would be disastrous.

"How much?" Frank assumed Deborah's reticence meant bad news. And why cut his budget now? Suddenly, he wondered if he would get paid this month. But surely Henry would have told him by now if the company was in serious financial trouble. He suspected Henry might be planning to spend the money on something else instead and resolved to talk to him later.

Deborah clung to the doorframe with one hand. "No new spend on research at all. Same goes for testing. We need to focus on the money earners for a little while. I'm sure if we all do our bit, we'll be back to normal in no time at all." Her voice began to falter by the time she finished her speech.

Frank only half noticed Deborah's uncharacteristic loss of confidence. "But the test results of the drug so far are outstanding. We can't delay testing now. We simply can't." Patrick was counting on this trial for Martina. When Frank last visited Martina, she'd looked awful. If the trial got delayed for a few weeks or, God forbid, months, it would be too late for her.

"Is Patrick aware of this?" It seemed odd to Frank that this directive didn't come from Patrick. After all, he was in charge of finance.

"Henry's discussing the issue with Patrick now."

Frank's heart plummeted into his shoes. If this decision came directly from Henry, there would be nothing either Frank or Patrick could do about it. Easy-going, affable Henry possessed balls of steel when it came to making difficult business decisions and sticking to them. Again, Frank wondered what lay behind this directive.

"How long?" Frank felt a sudden dread of hearing the answer and wished he hadn't asked.

"A few weeks," Deborah said. "Might be longer. A few weeks won't hurt. We're still years off of being able to sell the drug, so a few weeks won't make any difference at all."

Frank decided, in the event of him ever becoming seriously ill, he would want Deborah to stay as far away from him as possible. "It's all about money to you, isn't it?" It baffled him how she could be so completely lacking in sensitivity. He wondered if she'd experienced some dreadful childhood trauma to make her this way. "What about the people? We've spent a long time already carefully selecting our sample for the trial. In a few weeks, some of them will be at the wrong stage in their illness to be able to take part."

"Then you can select some more."

Frank shook his head in disbelief. Deborah was a piece of work. "Some of them might die. Don't you care about that?" He cared. He cared very much. That was why he had got into this business in the first place. The money didn't matter. His whole raison d'être was to save people. "Some of them are counting on this trial. We've given them hope. We're their last hope, their only hope, and you expect me to pull the rug out from under their feet and tell them they don't count." He cared about everyone, except in this case, he knew he wasn't referring to every single person who had signed up for the trial. He knew he was talking about only one person, Martina. Patrick would be devastated.

"I'm sorry."

"Yes, you already said that. *Sorry* doesn't save lives." She didn't even sound as if she meant it. Her lack of sincerity really riled Frank.

"Sorry, Frank, but I can't magic cash out of thin air. We can't find any money for this. Get over it. If you've got a problem with that, talk to Henry." Deborah turned around and marched out, slamming the door of the lab behind her.

That was more the Deborah he recognised, bolshy cow. But what was all that crap about there being no money? Yes, he would definitely be talking to Henry. And while he was doing so, he would put in a complaint about Deborah's attitude.

Chapter 5

Kerry brought Clarke and Evan coffee soon after they arrived the next day.

"Henry asked me to show you round properly," she said, "and introduce you to everybody."

"That's great. Do you want to come back in about half an hour? We'll make a plan while we're drinking our coffee."

"Who do we need to talk to?" Clarke asked as soon as Kerry left.

"Definitely Patrick Polkinghorne. He's the finance director, so if anything's going on with the money, we need to find out what he knows. But anyone might be involved. If we start with the biggest players: Patrick and Deborah Glayton, and both interview them together, then for the rest of the week we'll split up and interview everyone else between us."

"That's a fair few people." Clarke sipped at her coffee. The Costa Rican blend tasted as divine today as it did yesterday.

"I'm sure some of them will be extremely short conversations. The tricky bit will be getting the information we want without them suspecting why we're really here. But at least we might get a feel for who has the knowledge and opportunity to pull off something like this…"

"Something like what?" Clarke interrupted. "We're not even sure what we're dealing with yet."

"No, but if it's fooled the auditors, it will need to be something clever. Worth finding out if anyone's got a chip on their shoulder about something the company has done, or if they've got money troubles."

"Doesn't everyone?"

Evan laughed. "Yes, granted some of the smaller fry people you'll be interviewing don't get paid enough to afford themselves, but that's not enough to drive them to commit major financial crime. At this stage, I simply want us to get a grip on who everyone is and what they're like."

"How come we haven't done this before?" The other times she'd worked with Evan, Clarke had only been analysing figures.

"I always talk to the main people involved," Evan said. "Numbers don't happen on their own. They're made by the actions of people, paying an invoice, for example, or deciding which supplier to use. You were too junior to get involved with all that."

"Ah, I'm being promoted."

"Don't get excited. You don't get any more money. Not yet. But you've got a bit of experience now, and you're good with people. Time to let you loose on the clients. You'll be great at it. You remind me of a terrier. Once you get started on a problem, you keep worrying at it and won't let go until you've found the answer. If anyone's hiding something, you'll find it."

Evan handed Kerry a list of people he wanted to meet.

"All the really important people are on the first floor," Kerry said, glancing at the list.

Clarke smiled. The first-floor offices were all arranged around the boardroom, Clarke and Evan's base for this assignment. She wouldn't need to walk far, for a change.

None of the offices were huge. The biggest housed only five desks, with a private office in the corner. Kerry made a beeline for the corner office, ignoring everyone else in the room. Clarke followed her and Evan, although she would much rather stop to chat with some of the people sitting at their desks. No doubt Kerry would get to them shortly.

Kerry tapped on the door of the corner office, opening it tentatively.

"Not now, Kerry." A male voice.

Kerry jumped back as if she'd been stung and closed the door.

Clarke eyed the nameplate on the door. Patrick Polkinghorne, Finance Director. He didn't seem too friendly.

"Patrick's busy," Kerry said. "We'll go downstairs and meet Frank." She headed stridently towards the door, again ignoring the office's other occupants.

So much for not having to do any walking. Clarke remembered Henry telling them earlier that Frank Varley's research facility was situated in the basement.

Kerry seemed put out at Patrick's rejection, undoubtedly taking it personally. Clarke wondered if anything was going on between them, some history, an argument, a recent telling-off from the boss. It might be worth prodding things, to see what came out. Kerry certainly didn't want to hang around here. Fear of Patrick? Or embarrassment of a rebuttal in front of her and Evan, or in front of her colleagues? As Clarke already surmised, it might be anything.

"How long have you worked here, Kerry?" Clarke asked as they walked down the stairs to the basement.

"Long enough."

Clarke wondered if Kerry was always this rude. She really wanted to labour the point and push for an answer. But Kerry obviously considered it none of Clarke's business. She would somehow find a way to make her open up another time. Kerry definitely had issues, although Clarke considered it unlikely that they would have any relevance to their investigation. Even so, she didn't like being defeated, and her natural curiosity made her want to find out more.

By the time they'd walked down both flights of stairs, Kerry seemed slightly more amenable again.

"Frank is our senior research scientist. He develops new drugs. Without him, Carjon Pharma would have no new products to sell. We're very proud of him." She said the words with little enthusiasm, as if reciting some textbook company spiel.

"I've heard a lot of good things about Frank," Evan said. "I'm looking forward to meeting him."

Kerry dispensed with the knocking this time, opening the door to Frank's lab and barging straight in.

"Frank, these people have come to meet you. They're the people Henry has brought in, Evan Davies and Clarke Pettis."

Frank took off his big plastic safety glasses and placed them neatly on the table in front of him. He held out his hand.

"We won't take up too much of your time," Evan said, shaking it.

"Sorry, just in the middle of something now, but please come back another time. I'm sure Ollie can help you for now."

Frank excused himself, grabbing his safety glasses. Clarke wondered if there were any dangerous substances in the lab, whether they should all be wearing protective gear. Perhaps she was becoming too cautious. Surely a scientist of Frank Varley's reputation wouldn't put them at risk.

Kerry led them over to a bank of two desks. "Hi, Ollie."

One of the big office chairs swivelled round to face them. A nice-looking young man stood up.

"This is Ollie Jenner," Kerry said. "He's Frank's number one assistant."

"She means I'm his only assistant, unless you count Carmen, but she's only part-time and non-technical."

Kerry smiled. The first proper smile Clarke had seen from her today. Were she and Ollie an item? They must be a similar age. The romantic in Clarke wanted to pair them up, although, from what she'd seen of Kerry so far, she wouldn't want to inflict her on anybody.

"How long have you worked here?" Evan asked.

Ollie scratched his head, as if it was a difficult question. "About a year. I joined straight from uni. Carjon Pharma is small enough that I get to do lots of exciting stuff, instead of just rubbish boring work all the time. I love it."

"It's great when you enjoy your job." Clarke felt a brief nostalgic pang for the fire brigade before pulling herself together and reminding herself that she enjoyed her current job almost as much.

"Yes," Ollie said. "Don't you agree, Kerry?"

Kerry scowled and stepped away from Ollie, almost as if his enthusiasm might be catching. Ollie ignored her.

Clarke reappraised the situation, ruling out the possibility of a budding romance. Kerry and Ollie had no chemistry together whatsoever.

A woman appeared through a door in the far corner of the lab, carrying two steaming mugs. She walked towards them. Her black hair, twisted into a neat bun, together with her white lab coat and stern expression, made her look every inch the scientist. A pair of black-rimmed glasses would have completed the ensemble perfectly.

"Ollie, I've made your favourite Earl Grey tea exactly the way you like it and coffee for Frank." She turned to Clarke and Evan, the stern expression replaced with a weak smile. "I'm sorry, I didn't realise Ollie had visitors. Can I get you anything to drink?"

"We're just leaving," Kerry snapped.

Carmen glared at her before turning away to address Clarke and Evan. "Nice to meet you," she said.

"We should go back upstairs." Kerry turned around and headed for the door, clearly expecting to be followed.

"We can come back later without her," Evan whispered.

"Patrick may be available now," Kerry said, her footsteps clattering angrily on the stairs.

"Actually, it might be better if we met everyone else after lunch," Evan said. "Do you mind?"

Kerry shrugged. "Fine."

"Wow. She was prickly. I'd rather cuddle a cactus," Evan said as soon as he shut the door of the boardroom.

"Yes. She got a bit touchy when Patrick told her to go away. She obviously doesn't handle rejection well."

"My guess is that Ollie's turned her down before," Evan said. "She wasn't in any better mood with him."

"I doubt that Ollie was the problem. He seemed nice enough." Clarke craved coffee now and wished she'd asked Kerry to bring them some, but probably best to give her time to calm down. "Did you notice, as soon as Carmen showed up, she positively bristled with anger? What's going on there? Carmen seemed ok."

"Could be Kerry's just a moody madam," Evan said.

Clarke laughed. From what she'd seen so far of Kerry, she realised that, for once, Evan may actually be right.

Evan decided to crack on with interviewing Patrick. He was interested to find out how much Carjon's finance director really knew about the company's true financial position. Clarke had listened to Evan explain everything twice before the meeting with Patrick, so she'd planned exactly what she wanted to ask him.

"How long have you worked for Carjon Pharma?" Evan dropped his notepad on the table in front of him.

Clarke knew he wouldn't use the notepad. She took notes on her laptop. If Evan wanted to note a particular point, he would nod at Clarke and she would attempt to type twice as fast to keep up, without making too many typos. It would be so much easier to record the meeting and use a voice-to-text app to convert the recording afterwards. Unfortunately for her, the strict privacy laws about recording meetings meant getting permission, which lots of people weren't comfortable granting.

"Henry, Frank, and I started the company about eighteen years ago," Patrick said.

Clarke wondered, if the three men had been business partners for so long, why Henry hadn't confided his suspicions to them. Did that mean he suspected either Patrick or Frank?

With the small talk out of the way, Evan quickly moved on to bigger things. "Who has access to change anything in the online accounting system?"

Patrick gave off an air of calmness—considerably more calmness than Clarke had expected if the rumours were true about his wife's terminal cancer.

"I do, of course," Patrick said. "Kerry does a lot, then we have a couple of girls who make all the payments and do the monthly billing, but they can't change anything else."

Evan nodded. Clarke typed in the names of the other staff, making a note to talk to them later.

"Do you have bank reconciliations and cash-flow analysis?" Clarke asked.

"Kerry does all of that," Patrick said. "She can give you everything." He reached to open a drawer behind him, pulling out a sheet of paper. "Here's the latest one. I signed it off this morning." He passed the piece of paper to Clarke. "Can you take a copy, please, and give the original back? Kerry can provide you with all the previous ones. She does them twice a month."

"Thank you," Clarke said. "Have you had any other staff working in accounts during the last year? Anyone who has left?"

"No," Patrick said. "My team have all worked here for a number of years now. We don't get much staff turnover. People seem to like working here."

"That's good." What a shame. A disgruntled ex-employee may have been responsible for embezzling some of Carjon Pharma's cash before they left and would give Clarke and Evan an easy win. Never mind. Clarke kind of liked doing things the hard way. It provided more of a challenge.

After lunch, Clarke and Evan met with Deborah.

"I haven't got much time," Deborah said as soon as they sat down. "I'm covering the managing director's role as well as the sales and marketing director job until Henry finds time to recruit. It's a massive amount of work, but someone has to do it."

Clarke had recognised Deborah as soon as they were introduced. She'd seen her earlier coming out of Henry's office. It had been a very different Deborah to the serious woman who sat in front of them now. As she'd been saying goodbye to Henry, Clarke could have sworn she'd been flirting with him. She wondered now if there was anything going on between them, and if that would have any bearing on their investigation.

"Acting up is always a good career move," Evan said.

"Exactly," Deborah agreed.

Clarke opened up her laptop, ready to take notes. Deborah did seem flustered. She wondered if Deborah might be so over-worked doing two jobs, that she'd made mistakes. "How long have you been covering both roles?" She wanted some context to ascertain if Deborah's exhausted state might be relevant to anything.

"Only a couple of months so far. But the longer it goes on, the better it is for me."

Clarke typed the information into her laptop. The accounts would have been finalised before then, so, although that didn't rule Deborah out of anything, it certainly didn't provide an easy explanation either. It seemed that Deborah wanted the MD's job permanently. Clarke resolved to talk through the implications of that with Evan later.

"Henry tells me you've got an MBA." Evan smiled at Deborah.

"Yes, I did it at Manchester Business School."

"That's a prestigious course," Evan said. "High flyer. Carjon are lucky to have you."

Deborah beamed at him.

Clarke ignored it. She'd seen Evan buttering up clients before. Deborah would be eating out of his hand any minute soon. At that point, he'd start asking more difficult questions.

Evan smiled, flashing dazzling white teeth at Deborah. "You must be an accountancy expert then."

"Of course." Deborah returned the smile. "I came top of the class in the accountancy modules of my MBA."

"Definitely a high flyer." Evan's teeth flashed again, ready to bite.

Clarke suppressed her smile before it turned into a fit of giggles. Evan had Deborah exactly where he wanted her now. And she'd confirmed indirectly that she would probably be very capable of manipulating the company's finances if she wished. Now they simply needed to find out what had happened, and if Deborah had a motive.

"This year's annual accounts look good," Evan said.

"Yes, the company's doing well."

"That's great," Evan said. "But did I hear something about freezing expenditure due to cash-flow problems?" Evan kept his tone casual, but Clarke guessed he would go in for the kill, discovering how much Deborah knew.

Deborah couldn't hide her surprise. "Yes, but... who told you that?"

Clarke stopped typing into her laptop, keen to observe Deborah's reaction. Clearly she was aware of the company's money problems. But she hadn't expected Evan to have that information.

"Henry's been very open with us." Evan turned his chair round to face Deborah directly. "I always find that's the best way. We can help the company so much more if there are no hidden surprises. Don't you agree?"

"Er, yes, yes, of course." Deborah sounded unsure of what to say next.

Evan prompted her. "Do you want to run us through your take on the issues? I'd really value your opinion." Evan smiled again, although it looked like its effects were beginning to wear off.

THE COVER-UP

Deborah paused. Evan waited for her to speak.

"Are you ok?" Clarke asked. Deborah seemed very pale, and she'd sort of glazed over, as if something was distracting her.

"I'm fine," she said. "Yes, we do seem to be a bit short of cash at the moment," she said. "I'm sure it's only temporary. You really need to talk to Patrick. He's the finance director. He'll be able to tell you exactly what's going on."

Clarke was pretty certain Patrick Polkinghorne didn't have a clue. With major issues at home to deal with, he'd lost his grip on what was happening in the company. She agreed with Deborah. It *was* Patrick's responsibility. But that didn't change the fact that it might have been somebody else who had either committed a pretty big financial crime, or made a serious mistake, without anyone noticing. And she wanted to find out if that person had been Deborah.

"I'm sorry." Deborah got up and walked shakily towards the door. "I need to go." She speeded up but didn't quite make it to the door before throwing up all over the carpet.

Chapter 6

"Can I have a word?" Patrick poked his head around the door of Deborah's office. He'd meant to confront Deborah yesterday, but she'd gone home, feeling unwell. Yesterday, he'd been all psyched up to go into battle. Today, he had calmed down and he was exhausted from tossing and turning all night, worrying about it. He was in no fit state to confront anyone, but he thought of Martina and steeled himself to fight.

Patrick shut the door behind him, taking Deborah's lack of response as a *yes*. He pulled out a chair and parked himself in it.

"About Frank's research budget cuts," he said, not seeing any point in sugarcoating things. May as well get straight into the issue.

"There's nothing I can do about it."

"Nothing you can do? I'm sure there must be something. And why didn't you involve me in the decision?" Deborah looked very pale today. Patrick wondered if she still felt ill. He couldn't afford to catch anything, for fear of passing the germs on to Martina. He pushed his chair back, away from Deborah's desk. "Frank's latest test results are incredibly promising. It's sacrilege to hold things up."

"Patrick, as you're well aware, it takes ten to fifteen years to develop a new drug from start to finish. So, in the scheme of things, a delay of a few months won't make the slightest bit of difference. Frank can probably catch up that time and be back on schedule in six months."

"But we don't have six months." Martina didn't have six months. Patrick was sure of that. They needed that drug trial. They needed it now.

"Patrick, I'll be honest. The company has a cash-flow problem. You're already aware of that. The only way for the company to survive is to prioritise manufacturing drugs that are already in production, ones that are making us money now. Unless you don't want your salary paid this month. A few months won't hurt the new drug development at all."

"At least let me find another way to save the money." Freezing spend was a knee-jerk reaction to the problem. Clearly Deborah hadn't considered all the options thoroughly. She'd simply taken the easiest way out.

"The quickest way to solve the immediate cash-flow problem is to stop spending. It's a temporary postponement and it won't affect anything in the long run."

"But it can't be postponed. Martina needs that drug. She needs to be on that drug trial. Please, I'm begging you." Patrick looked at Deborah's face and immediately regretted telling her that. He wanted to retract the words or make Deborah forget ever hearing them. But both options were impossible.

"Patrick! Martina can't be on the drug trial. It's unethical. She's too close. Besides, there's a fifty-fifty chance she'd end up in the placebo group, anyway. She's better off continuing with tried and tested treatments."

Patrick wondered if he should plead further with Deborah now that he had started, admit that Martina's chemo wasn't working. Deborah's medical knowledge was scant, to say the least. He could probably feed her a load of bull to try to convince her. But he appreciated how bloody-minded Deborah could be. And Martina meant nothing to Deborah. Why would Deborah go the extra mile for her when she never went out of her way to help anyone except herself?

Patrick left feeling despondent. Deborah was right about the company's cash flow. They needed to do something drastic. Even he couldn't magic up money from thin air. He would have to find another way to fix this.

Frank appeared to be kissing a rat when Patrick barged into his lab.

Patrick wondered for a moment if Frank's wife, Kas, minded coming second in his affections to a big white rodent. "I trust Deborah's told you about cutting your research funding."

Frank grunted.

"Have you given any thought to how you're going to get round that little problem?" Patrick asked.

"I've promised Deborah I'll find some other costs to cut. When I get time." Frank put the rat back in its cage. It made a squeaky noise and scuttled to the back of its house to talk to its friend next door.

"Frank! You'll need to do more than that if we want to stay on track." Patrick put the pile of papers he'd been holding on Frank's desk and shuffled through them. "I've got a grant claim form here," he said, handing a thick wedge of papers to Frank. "You'll need to fill in the details, but if you make the project sound good, we should be able to obtain a substantial amount of funding, enough to run the first couple of stages of the Fexizon trial." That would be enough. It pained Patrick to admit it, but if Martina didn't get completely cured by then, it would be too late for her. And then he would stop caring about Frank and the new drug. He would probably stop caring about anything.

"Ok. I'll take a look."

"Please, Frank, can you make this your top priority? Martina..." Patrick's words faded. Frank realised how desperate they were, how little time Martina might have.

"How is Martina?"

Patrick shook his head. "The chemo doesn't seem to be working. You're our only hope, Frank." He ignored the minor issue of Deborah forbidding him to enrol Martina in Frank's drug trial. There were plenty of ways round that. Martina and Kas were good friends. Frank wouldn't be allowed to stand by and let Martina die.

"I'm sorry."

"Don't be. Just do your magic. And get those forms filled in," Patrick said. He would check back with him tomorrow to make sure he'd sent them off. "I'm meeting with a potential investor this evening," he said. "If he's interested, you may need to present something to him next week and discuss the whole project in depth. In the meantime, I need to pitch something to him. I've got all the basic blurb to give him. I need something more. I need an angle, Frank. Give me something I can work with, something sexy that I can dangle in front of my investor to get him to bite."

"Ok, so how about telling them that I'm going to win the Nobel Prize," Frank said. "Is that sexy enough?"

Patrick smiled. "That's damn sexy. Can you really do it?"

"No guarantees," Frank said, "but the results of the animal testing are amazing, and Fexizon is a really innovative breakthrough in cancer treatment. There's got to be some chance. Probably the best chance I'll ever get."

"Maybe this will be the big one for both of us. Don't forget the form either, Frank. We can't afford to waste a single minute, neither of us."

Patrick walked back up the stairs, beaming. He'd never seen Frank this excited. He may or may not be in the running for the Nobel Prize. He certainly possessed the ability and Fexizon seemed to have tremendous potential. But those dreams would turn to dust if Frank's research didn't get adequately funded. And Martina? Would she turn to dust as well? They simply couldn't risk any delays.

Chapter 7

"We need to go through everything with a fine-tooth comb." Frank put two cups of coffee on the desk, one for him, the other for Ollie. "Sorry, I forgot to get tea bags." Frank felt guilty about that. He'd promised Ollie he'd buy some more tea bags at lunchtime. Ollie loved his tea.

"It's fine." Ollie picked up his coffee mug, then plonked it straight back down again as the steaming liquid remained far too hot to drink. "What are we looking for?"

Frank sighed. *A pot of gold at the end of the rainbow.* They definitely needed one of those, the sooner the better. "We're looking for any way we can cut costs, so root out anything over-spec-ed, any supplies we can buy cheaper, any wastage, any tiny thing." Every last penny would help, although those pennies would need to add up to a hell of a lot to persuade Henry to let him continue with his testing programme. He needed to find something soon. Frank resolved to stay late tonight, however long it took for him to find an answer.

He picked up the grant claim form that Patrick left him. That route certainly wouldn't provide an instant solution. The wheels of government quangos turned painfully slowly, and these bodies allocated grant funding at a much more leisurely pace than Patrick realised. One glance at the onerously thick pile of paper in his hand told Frank that even filling in the form would probably take hours, or even days if he needed to dig out additional information, or write a full proposal. He tossed the paperwork in the waste paper bin by his desk.

Perhaps it would be easier, and quicker, to cut costs. There might be some scope there. Frank always spec-ed his testing programme way above the legal minimum. He liked certainty, as far as that was possible with scientific experiments. Sometimes, he'd actually considered that he might be in the wrong job because of that. But he was passionate about what he did. He wanted to save lives, not risk them. He needed to be as certain as possible that there would be no danger to anyone who trialled his drugs.

"You should probably start by checking the specifications," Frank said. Best to delegate that task to Ollie, who would be much more impartial than Frank. Cutting some of the specifications on his testing, after he'd spent forever designing the perfect programme, would be, for Frank, like cutting the head off of one of his children.

"Ok. I'll get cracking on it now. Got a date tonight, so don't want to be here all evening."

Frank smiled. "How many is that?" Ollie's attempts at computer dating so far had produced little success. It was a shame. Ollie was such a lovely lad, albeit a bit geeky. Frank wondered why the women of Brackford didn't appreciate his charms. Ollie was slim and fit too. Frank looked down at his own stomach, which had started overflowing his trousers several years ago. He would love to have a body as good as Ollie's, but those days were long gone.

"It's nineteen so far, but this one's a second date. She might be *the one*."

"Nineteen!" Frank lost count weeks ago. He didn't realise it was that many.

"You need to sift through a lot of gravel to find a diamond," Ollie said. "Loads of people go on far more dates than that before they find *the one*."

"Well, let's hope this is *the one*, or you'll bankrupt yourself buying them all dinner."

"Oh, I don't do dinner on the first date anymore. We just meet for a quick drink, or a coffee, except I don't like coffee, but it doesn't sound the same asking a girl out for a cup of tea."

Frank felt sure Ollie hadn't deliberately meant to reinforce his guilt over forgetting the tea bags. He resolved to buy a big box of Ollie's favourite Earl Grey on his way home tonight.

Delilah squeaked from the other end of the lab, reminding Frank that it was feeding time for her and her friends. He got up and found the bag of triangular-shaped pellets in the cupboard. He began tipping carefully measured scoopfuls into the feed hoppers that hooked onto the side of every cage, then neatly sealed the bag and replaced it in the cupboard. A bag of sultanas called to him as he shut the door. He steeled himself to ignore it. He kept them to feed to the rats as treats. Delilah, especially, loved them. But, in the middle of testing, any changes in feed would affect the results, which forced him to be really strict about it. He would spoil all his little darlings in a couple of days when this round of testing finished. He'd be spoiling them a lot more if Henry wouldn't allow him to continue testing after that.

He returned to his desk. His stomach twinged as he sat down. It had been grumbling all week, not enough to bother seeing his doctor, but enough to be annoying. If it still troubled him by the weekend, he would book an appointment for next week, but he would probably be fine by then. He'd heard Deborah had thrown up yesterday. Maybe there was a bug going round.

Reaching down, he fished the grant application form out of the bin, hoping Ollie wouldn't spot him and ask what he was doing. Ollie was concentrating hard on his computer screen. Frank secretly hoped Ollie wouldn't find any way of cutting the test specifications, because he would have to ignore it if he did. He smoothed out the creases in the grant application form. He couldn't possibly cut any corners in his testing process. It would ruin everything.

This latest cancer drug, Fexizon, promised to be the most important breakthrough of his career. He couldn't risk screwing up any part of the process. He hadn't been joking to Patrick about wanting to win the Nobel Prize. For once in his life, he had a minuscule chance. He'd be up against some of the best scientific brains in the world. But it was a chance, probably his best one ever. He'd dreamed of this for years, and he intended to do whatever it took.

A knock on the lab door startled him and a woman's head poked around the partially open door. "Can I come in?"

"Yes. Clarke, isn't it? Do you want a coffee? I've just made one. Sorry, there's no tea. I forgot to buy the teabags."

Clarke sat down in the chair he pulled out for her. "I've not long ago had a coffee upstairs," she said, "so I'll pass on that, thanks."

Frank sat down next to her. It would be rude to drink his coffee if Clarke wasn't having one. He would make a fresh cup when she'd gone.

"I just wanted to get an idea of what you do here," Clarke said. "Henry's asked us to investigate floating the company on the AIM market."

Frank nodded. "Not sure what the AIM market is."

"It's simply a smaller sub-section of the stock market, a bit less regulated than the main one, for smaller companies."

"I see."

"Anyway, we need to investigate everything the company does, so we can come up with the best-selling points, and put all the necessary information into the brochure."

"Yes, of course," Frank said, wondering how long this would take, and if it would screw up his plans. He couldn't simply break off his work halfway through. He needed a three-hour clear slot. He ought to tell Clarke to come back tomorrow, but Henry had been adamant that he expected full cooperation with these people. Frank decided to get it over with. He would work late to finish if need be.

"So, can you please explain what your role is here, in layman's terms, so the share-buying public can understand? Although I expect most of the shares will be bought by pension funds, but they're not pharmaceutical experts either."

"We're probably the smallest team in the company but definitely the most important. We develop new drugs." Frank loved talking about his work. Maybe he would carry on talking all evening. Perhaps it would be a good thing if they sold the company, then there would be plenty of money to fund his research. He wondered how long the process would take.

"That's interesting," Clarke said. "How many people are in your team?"

"There are only three of us. I'm the chief research scientist. Ollie Jenner here is my assistant. He joined the company as a graduate trainee, but I've given him a lot of experience since then. He's become invaluable. Then there's Carmen de Silva, who is part-time and is mostly involved with looking after the animals but helps me with some preparation work too."

"You keep the animals to experiment on?" Clarke busily typed notes into her laptop.

Frank sighed. Clarke's expression made it obvious that she didn't approve. She'd better not be one of those animal rights hippies. "Sadly, it's a legal requirement," he said. "We have a vast number of regulations to comply with before we get anywhere close to bringing a new drug to market. The legislation forces us to test on animals before we can start human trials." Personally, Frank had always been of the opinion that testing on convicted serial killers would be a far better option than risking his beloved rats, but apparently that was frowned upon by the authorities.

Clarke nodded, continuing to type.

Frank stretched to see what she'd written. It probably wouldn't be anything complimentary at this stage. "We mostly use rats, and they do get the very best care," he assured her. He spent much of his time hugging the rats and making them feel loved to assuage his guilt, when he should be working.

"How many drugs are you testing now?"

Frank sighed with relief that Clarke hadn't pursued the animal testing angle. He always dreaded getting into an argument about it with anyone who didn't understand. "At the moment, we have five new drugs at various stages in the development process."

"Five?" Clarke seemed surprised. "That sounds like a lot for such a small team."

"Developing a new drug usually takes ten to fifteen years," Frank said. "There are so many stages of testing to go through, to ensure every drug is as safe as possible, and to make sure they actually work. But much of the fifteen years might be spent waiting for various approvals to come through." *And filling in infinite numbers of forms.* "The delays and the red tape are ridiculous. The government departments involved are understaffed and, quite honestly, grossly inefficient. We also have to put each drug through a lengthy testing process, to determine if there are any longer-term side effects. Even if the process could be speeded up to, say, one year, we wouldn't be able to tell if a drug produced any serious lasting side effects with just a few months of testing."

"Yes, that makes sense." Clarke stopped typing for a few moments. "Tell me about these five drugs. I guess they're the future of Carjon Pharma."

"Yes, they certainly are. Where shall I start?"

"How about the one that's progressed the furthest? Then we'll work back from there."

"Ok. That's Fexizon. It's possibly our most exciting drug ever. We hope it's going to be the wonder cure for cervical cancer. That's one of the deadliest cancers there is, so this is potentially a real breakthrough." Frank waved his hands about, trying to get across the immense excitement that coursed through him every time he even thought about the progress he'd made on this, excitement that he couldn't possibly expect Clarke to understand. "We've been developing the drug for several years already, but the most recent tests have shown amazing results. The next stage is human trials. There's still a long way to go before we get it licensed and ready to sell, but you need infinite patience in this game."

Frank couldn't possibly convey to an outsider just how much patience he needed in an average week. He'd been brimming with excitement every day for the past year, wishing the red tape would all fall away so he could get the drug into production and start saving lives. But red tape was the least of his worries right now. Since Henry had frozen all research and development spend, he would be treading water on the project until Patrick found him enough money to continue. And who could predict how long that would take.

"And the other four drugs?"

Frank suppressed a sigh. "They're a mix of painkillers and palliative treatments for cancer." They would be bread and butter earners for Carjon Pharma in due course. But none of them were groundbreaking, nothing like Fexizon that he could get really excited about. "We're a lot further behind the curve on these. We've been putting more resources into Fexizon. That's our superstar." Stupid of him to concentrate all his eggs into one tiny basket, but the basket also contained the glittering attraction of a Nobel Prize. It was calling his name, and he couldn't ignore it.

Frank's mobile rang, blasting out an embarrassingly upbeat boy band tune that Kas had put on his phone for him. He grabbed it, immediately rejecting the call when he saw Kas's name showing on the screen. He would phone her back as soon as Clarke left.

"Sorry," he said, "the wife. I'll call her back later."

"It's ok. You should call her now," Clarke said. "It might be important."

Frank pushed the phone away. "Let's finish this," he said, wanting to get it over with as quickly as possible to concentrate on his work. "I'm sure she can wait." He was dying for a coffee. The hardly touched cup on his desk was stone-cold.

No sooner than he finished speaking, the phone rang again. He supposed he would have to answer it this time. "I'm in a meeting."

The voice on the other end of the phone was a mixture of high-pitched hysteria and tears.

"Calm down," he said, "and tell me what the problem is."

"I'm sorry," he said to Clarke a couple of minutes later. "Someone broke into our house while my wife was out shopping. She's in a real state. I'll have to go home." He supposed Clarke would want to come back and finish off tomorrow. He would try to fob her off with Ollie to answer any of her remaining questions.

"Of course. We'll touch base again in the morning," Clarke said. "Really, it's no problem."

Frank went over to Ollie's desk. "Will you be able to finish off that work before you go home? I'll pick it up in the morning."

Ollie nodded. "Of course. I'll stay a bit later."

"Mind you're not late for your date," Frank said. He didn't want to ruin Ollie's evening or wreck his chances of finding the perfect woman.

"Don't worry. No way am I going to miss that."

"Thank you." Frank picked up his stuff and headed for the door, silently dreading going home. If the state of Kas on the phone was anything to go by, the house would be in a mess. He'd better get home fast and try to calm her down. Hopefully, the burglars hadn't taken anything important.

Chapter 8

Patrick checked his watch. He'd promised Martina he'd be home by eight, but it was gone ten already. He'd met a potential investor, an old school friend, Simon, who'd done rather well for himself and now owned a successful chain of garden centres. Of course, one thing had led to another, and he couldn't say no when Simon suggested dinner. After all, when Patrick had told him that Frank might be a serious contender for a Nobel Prize, Simon all but offered to write him out a blank cheque. Three bottles of rather good wine later, Patrick was confident he would be able to seal the deal.

It was too late to phone Martina. She went to bed early these days, and he didn't want to wake her, not now when she needed her sleep so badly. Just as well she would be in bed. Patrick needed to drop into the office to pick up a couple of things so he could email Simon the information tonight, as he'd promised. With the extra journey, and having to take the train and a taxi, as he had drunk way more than the limit for driving, it would likely be midnight by the time Patrick arrived home. Anyway, the late night would be worth it. And, he had to admit, he'd enjoyed a fun, relaxing evening for a change. Since Martina became ill, they didn't get out often, and he certainly didn't ever get drunk.

Patrick let himself into the Carjon building by the staff entrance and went straight upstairs to his office. It wouldn't take long to find what he needed, then he could head for the station and get home to bed.

Chapter 9

Deborah got into work early. She didn't sleep well last night. The discovery that she was pregnant had come as a total shock. At least it explained why she'd thrown up in the middle of the office. That had been a mortifying experience, but this... this baby... She didn't think she'd ever sleep again for worrying about what to do about this baby situation. It should have been an easy choice. She was naturally a decisive person. She made decisions all the time in her job, granted, not always the right ones. And perhaps that explained her problem. If she got this decision wrong, there would be consequences. Whatever she decided, at some stage, she would reach the point of no return and her choice simply wouldn't be able to be undone. The inability to make the right choice crippled her.

She looked at her *To Do* list, which reminded her that she still needed to finish her conversation with Frank. She picked up the phone. Frank always got in early. He would definitely be in by now.

No answer. He was probably busy with those dreadful rats. She looked at her diary. Back-to-back meetings all day. If she didn't speak to him now, it would drag on for yet another day. By then, all sorts of rumours might be floating around the company. She didn't want him finding out from anyone else that they were seriously considering making Ollie redundant, as a quick way of saving some money, and in any case, with the testing programme postponed, Frank really wouldn't need him. She decided to walk down to his lab. She wouldn't go in. If she just poked her head around the door, she could easily check his availability for later, then make him come upstairs to her office to discuss things. If Ollie was there, they'd need to talk in private, anyway.

Her abdomen spasmed as she got up. Probably a guilt pain, for what she planned to do to Ollie, or maybe something she'd eaten. It was far too early in the pregnancy to be the baby kicking... wasn't it? Truthfully, she didn't have a clue. She should ask someone who knew about these things. But then they'd try to influence her decision, and this decision was far too important to let someone else force her down the wrong road.

Frank's lab was unlocked. That must be a good sign. She pushed the door open. The lights were off, although a fair bit of daylight came through the windows on the far side of the room. She wouldn't go in. The germs worried her. She didn't want to set one foot inside Frank's lab with God-knew-what floating around in the ether. Not now. Because what if anything in that lab harmed the baby? Deborah shrank back into the doorway. What nasty diseases were present in the lab? What had he injected into those awful rats? Whilst she was still struggling over how much she really wanted this baby, she knew that, if she did decide to keep it, she would want it to be fully healthy, not made sick by some deadly disease that Frank might carelessly inflict upon it.

She'd made a mistake coming down here. She should have held out to make Frank come to her office, but she was here now. Best to get it over with quickly.

"Frank," she shouted through the open doorway. The room seemed gloomy without the lights on. Deborah called out again, breaking her promise to herself not to enter the room. "Frank." Had he gone into the little kitchen to make a coffee?

She walked over to his desk. Perhaps she would leave him a note to phone her mobile. If she was in a meeting when he phoned, it would make a good excuse to leave. She stumbled as she tripped on something on the floor and just managed to keep her balance by grabbing at the desk in front of her.

Cursing Frank for being so untidy, she turned to see what she had tripped over. He'd left a shoe on the floor, poking out from under Ollie's desk. She bent down to pick it up, but as soon as she touched it, she realised the shoe was firmly attached to a foot and a leg.

"Frank?" Had he collapsed and fallen under the desk? Quickly, she went to the other side of the desk to check on him.

THE COVER-UP

He hadn't fallen. He was curled up under the desk, so she still didn't have a good view of him. "Frank. Oh my God, Frank." Deborah pulled at his shoulder to turn him over. He fell heavily onto his side. Not Frank. Ollie. And his arm felt so cold and stiff. Was he dead? She let out a whimper, then pulled herself together and stood up, reaching for the phone on Ollie's desk. She would phone for an ambulance. He might not be dead. People Ollie's age didn't die that easily.

Her hand shook as she began to dial the emergency services. A sudden scuffle behind her made her jump. She spun round quickly. A huge white rat scampered towards her.

Deborah dropped the phone. Instantly, she scrambled onto the desk and screamed and screamed and screamed.

Chapter 10

Clarke's head was all over the place this morning. As she walked from the car park towards the rear entrance of the Carjon Pharma building, she could barely remember what day it was. The letter she'd received yesterday had really unnerved her, and she hadn't even dared to open it yet. Right now, it was burning a hole in her pocket. She touched it quickly to check it was still there, then snatched her hand from her pocket as if it had been scorched as well.

She knew who had sent the letter. The HM Prisons logo on the envelope gave it away. Even seeing that took her back to last year's dreadful experience working at Briar Holman. She thought she was over it, but clearly she wasn't.

As soon as Clarke opened Carjon Pharma's staff entrance door, loud screams rose up from the basement stairway. Without a second's thought, she ran towards the stairs. As far as she remembered, Frank's lab took up the whole of the basement floor. Maybe he'd had an accident with some chemicals and needed immediate first aid. The screaming sounded like a woman. She racked her brains to remember the name of the woman on Frank's team. Carmen. Perhaps it was her.

The screams grew louder as Clarke got closer. She dived through the half-open door, unsure what she would find.

Deborah stood on one of the desks, still screaming.

She stopped when she saw Clarke. "Help," she said breathlessly. "Help." She pointed at the floor.

Clarke took a step back. Someone lay under the desk. Deborah was still pretty hysterical. She would deal with her in a minute. She hurried to check the person on the floor.

It looked like Ollie. Clarke had only met him briefly a couple of times. She crawled under the desk and reached for his arm, searching for a pulse, desperately trying again when she failed to find one. Still nothing. His hand felt ice-cold.

THE COVER-UP

Deborah whimpered as Clarke rummaged in her handbag for her phone. The poor woman must be in shock.

"Ambulance, please." She moved away from the body, away from Deborah. In a moment, she would have to tell them that she thought Ollie was dead. She didn't want Deborah to hear that, not in her traumatised state, although, judging by the amount of screaming, she may have already come to the same conclusion.

"Try not to touch anything," the operator on the other end of the phone said. Clarke guessed they would send the police. They'd already asked Ollie's age, so the death was suspicious, and they hadn't even seen the irregular location of the body.

Clarke turned her attention to Deborah, who still stood on the desk. "We should get out of here." They couldn't help Ollie and it was important that they didn't contaminate a potential crime scene.

Deborah pointed to the floor and tried to speak, but nothing more than a small whimper came out.

Clarke looked around the room for the first time and saw Deborah's problem. A large white rat sat on the floor behind her. A couple more scurried along the skirting board. Clarke picked up the large rat and carried him across the room. One of the cages was open. She placed the rat carefully inside and fastened the door. His two friends had disappeared and Clarke didn't fancy her chances at finding them quickly. Best if she took Deborah out of the lab and closed the door, then at least they wouldn't escape.

"Come on, I'll help you down." Clarke extended her hand to Deborah.

Deborah shrank back. "You've touched a rat. I'll get myself down."

She sounded horrified, as if the rat had come straight out of the sewer, instead of being a well-cared-for, healthy, domestic rat. Clarke would wash her hands as soon as possible, but her priority right now was to get them both out of this room.

"Did you see anything?" Clarke asked as Deborah made an ungainly descent from the desk.

"No. He was like that when I came in." Deborah's gaze darted around the floor, searching for the remaining loose rats. She hurried towards the door.

Clarke followed her. "Where's Frank?" she asked.

Deborah voiced what Clarke was considering. "He's not here," she said. "Do you think he killed Ollie?"

Chapter 11

Clarke tried not to jump to conclusions. She'd only just met Frank, and she had no idea what might have happened. Ollie had seemed like a sweet guy and she couldn't imagine anyone wanting to kill him. Maybe it was simply an unfortunate accident. Either way, the police would arrive soon. Best to leave it to them to find out.

Clarke wasn't thrilled when Detective Constable Kevin Farrier showed up, accompanied by another detective constable who Clarke didn't recognise. As soon as she saw Kevin, it reminded her of the problems at her last employer, Briar Holman.

"Trouble seems to follow you around," Kevin said.

"Deborah found him," Clarke said. Deborah was still very distressed. She needed to sit her down somewhere more comfortable with a drink and a box of tissues. "Nothing to do with me." How dare Kevin Farrier insinuate whatever he was trying to insinuate? She would tell Paul about his attitude. Paul always said Kevin was an idiot.

"What are you doing here?" Kevin asked.

"I found Deborah. She screamed, and I came to find out what was going on. I'm working here. The company hired us for a project." She kept things deliberately vague, not wanting to elaborate on the precise nature of the project in front of Deborah, although Clarke doubted that Deborah would take in anything she said, not in her current state.

"Bit of a coincidence you showing up."

Clarke ignored the jibe. "His name's Ollie," she said. "He's Frank Varley's lab assistant."

"Who's Frank? Can I speak to him?"

"He's not here." Deborah spoke for the first time since the police arrived. "I came down here to find him. He's always in early. But he's not here."

"Frank phoned in." Henry walked into the middle of the conversation. "Frank's house got burgled yesterday. He said he'll be in later this morning. He's got to sort out the insurance and all that stuff. Now, will somebody please tell me what's going on?" The tendons in Henry's neck stood out taut with worry. "Why are the police here?"

Deborah started to cry. "Ollie's dead."

Clarke put an arm round her. "Kevin, this is Henry Carver-Jones," she said, nodding at Henry, whilst congratulating herself on making Kevin scowl by introducing him using his first name. "He's the Chairman of Carjon Pharma. Henry, this is Detective Constable Kevin Farrier."

"We'll need to talk to all three of you," Kevin said. He asked his colleague to get the details for the deceased. "I need to examine the body." Kevin entered the lab, shutting the door behind him.

Clarke wondered if they would call the Murder Investigation Team. Paul frequently told her that was standard procedure if they suspected murder. Would Paul show up if MIT got called in? Probably not, she assumed, not if Kevin told them she was involved. Suddenly, she longed for Paul to appear and give her a hug, not that he'd be able to do that if he was working.

"What happened?" Henry asked.

"Deborah found Ollie's body under his desk." Clarke still considered it an odd place for him to be. Did someone put him there, or had he been scrabbling under the desk for something he'd dropped and succumbed to a heart attack? He was young and pretty slim too, but heart attacks happened even to young people sometimes.

"I came to look for Frank." Deborah started to sob again. "There were rats, everywhere. Rats running around the room."

Clarke wondered if Ollie had been chasing a loose rat. Perhaps he banged his head on the desk whilst trying to catch one. She wasn't sure which would be worse, dying because of a stupid accident, or being murdered.

"Can we get Deborah a cup of tea and somewhere to sit down?" Clarke asked. "She's in shock." Clarke didn't fancy the chances of Kevin Farrier getting any useful information out of Deborah at the moment.

"Let's go to my office," Henry said.

"We should wait for DC Farrier," his colleague said.

"Really, the poor woman's upset, and you expect her to stand in the middle of a corridor waiting for God knows how long? I'm taking her to my office. You can come with us if you're worried we might talk to anyone else."

"I'll stay here and show DC Farrier up when he's finished," Clarke said before anyone tried to protest.

"That's settled then," Henry said, taking Deborah's arm and walking her towards the lift with the detective tagging on behind.

Clarke leant up against the wall. She didn't want to wait in the corridor for too long, but she didn't want to leave Kevin alone in Frank's lab either. He probably should have locked the door and waited for MIT to arrive.

After a few minutes, Clarke had nearly made up her mind to knock and ask Kevin what was happening, when the door opened.

"What's going on?" Clarke asked.

"Waiting for SOCO and MIT to get here. They won't be long. Are you sure you had nothing to do with this?"

Clarke glared angrily at him.

"Is there a key to this door?"

"I'll ask Henry if he has a spare." Clarke didn't want to wait around keeping Kevin company. Although Clarke wasn't at all violent, if she stayed here too much longer, she'd really want to punch him in the face.

Paul was the last person Clarke expected to bump into as she rounded the corner towards reception.

"I thought you weren't allowed..." Clarke trailed off as Paul made a shushing sign to her. Of course, it would be best not to let on that she and Paul had been seeing each other for the last few months. They should be professional while he was working, although she longed for a hug after the stress of seeing Ollie's dead body.

She led him towards the stairs. "His name's Ollie Jenner," she said. "Deborah Glayton, the company's managing director, found him, and I found Deborah."

"So, what are you doing here?" Paul asked.

"Evan and I are working on a project for the company."

Henry stood outside the lab door talking to Kevin when they got down the stairs.

"This is Detective Sergeant Paul Waterford," Clarke said. It still seemed strange referring to Paul as a detective sergeant. He'd only recently passed his sergeant's exams and got promoted. She introduced him to Henry with a glow of pride.

Paul wanted to examine the body. Kevin remained talking to Henry, keen to interview him before the rest of MIT showed up and took over. Clarke volunteered to wait for Paul and show him upstairs when he'd finished.

As soon as they'd gone, Clarke opened the door to the lab. "Can I come in?"

"Stay there," Paul said. "Forensics are on the way here." He came over to the door.

"What happened?"

"Too early to say, and, in any case, I can't tell you."

"Paul!" She feared this would be a repeat of when Paul had investigated her colleague Tammy's disappearance at the last company she worked for. Clarke had done most of the work to solve the case, but Paul flatly refused to tell her anything useful whenever she'd asked.

Clarke had even been a suspect herself for a while when another colleague there had been murdered. She gave Paul a particularly black look as she recalled that detail. At least that time, she and Paul hadn't actually been in a relationship, but it had still taken her a long time to forgive him for that.

"It doesn't seem like an accident, ok?"

Clarke gave him *the look* again.

"Clarke, stop it."

"You never tell me anything," she said. "And how come you're even here? I gave my name when I phoned for an ambulance. Surely, they must be aware we're seeing each other?"

Paul looked sheepish. "I may not have mentioned it."

Clarke felt thoroughly quashed. A lot of things made sense now. Like her not being invited to the police station Christmas party.

"It was difficult. We got together soon after Tammy's trial and, with you being a key witness, I worried it might look bad."

"So, you should tell them now."

"They'll take me off the case. Please, Clarke, it's my first murder case as a DS."

"What about Kevin Farrier? He remembers me."

"He doesn't know anything."

"He's a detective. He'll find out."

"He's an idiot. We just need to act professional."

Clarke half expected Paul to tell her they should cool it between them for a while. He'd always put his career first. She reached out a hand to touch him. He shrank back. He may as well have kicked her in the teeth.

"Deborah is upstairs in Henry's office, and DC Farrier has gone with them, in case you're wondering," she said. "Deborah's upset. I don't suppose she's ever seen a dead body before."

"I'll need to interview her as soon as SOCO arrives. And I'll need to inform Ollie's next of kin. Will Henry get me the address?"

"Kevin and his colleague are organising that," Clarke said, not really wanting to be around Paul at this precise moment. "When you're ready, go back to reception and ask for Henry." Would she and Paul ever be a serious item? Yesterday, she would have said a big fat *yes*, but now she doubted everything.

Chapter 12

Erica, Paul's favourite SOCO, finally arrived, carrying an armful of kit.

"I expected you an hour ago." Paul still needed to inform the next of kin and hadn't begun questioning anyone, although Kevin Farrier had started interviewing before Paul arrived, which worried him a little. Now that it was MIT's case, Kevin would have no further involvement, much to Paul's relief.

"Sorry, there's been an accident on the roundabout. Traffic's completely snarled up. What have we got here?"

"Ollie Jenner, twenty-two years old. He worked as a lab assistant here. One of his colleagues found him under the desk. Looks like he's been there for some time."

"Working late?"

"Probably. I haven't spoken to anyone yet." He should have started interviewing people, left Farrier to guard the lab until SOCO arrived. First murder case as a DS, and already he'd made a bad call. It didn't say much about his management abilities. He would have to get better rapidly if he was going to solve this case and impress the DI.

Erica bent down to examine the body. "Not easy to get at. But he's definitely showing all the signs of being dead for some time."

Paul knew better than to bother asking Erica for a time of death at this stage. A squeak behind him reminded him of the other problem. "There are rats running loose," he said.

Erica got up. "Have you got any food?" she asked. "There might be some over by the cages."

Paul found a bag of feed. He tipped out a handful.

"Give me some of that." Erica held out her hand. She knelt on the floor. "Come on, my lovely," she cooed, holding out her hand with the feed in it.

The rat came to her instantly. "You must be hungry, poor dear." She picked it up. "My brother used to have a pet rat when we were young.

I was the only one who could actually catch him." She put the rat back into one of the cages. "How many more are loose?"

"I've only seen one more," Paul said, impressed with Erica's handling of the rat, a stark contrast to what Clarke told him about Deborah's hysterics, although, to be fair, Deborah was probably traumatised at discovering a dead body.

"We need to find it," Erica said. "Don't want it eating the body. That's tampering with the evidence."

Paul searched for the missing rat, while Erica took photos of the body. There was no sign of the rodent. It could be anywhere in this big room, probably curled up in some little nook, waiting to venture out when they'd all gone. He shook the feed bag, hoping that would entice it out, but that didn't work. Perhaps it slipped out the door when it got left open.

"It looks like the drugs cabinet has been broken into," Paul said. "We'll need to check what's missing."

"Could be a motive."

"I'd already thought that." Paul didn't need Erica telling him how to do his job.

"I need to go and inform the next of kin," Paul said. "Are you ok here?"

"Just leave me to it. I've got another couple of the team on their way over. Probably got caught in the traffic hold-up too."

"Calm down, Frank." Henry sat down. "Getting worked up isn't helping anyone."

"Calm down? How can I calm down? Ollie's dead." Frank still struggled to believe it. First the break-in at home yesterday, and now he'd arrived at work in the middle of the morning to be confronted with this, although he would rather deal with a hundred break-ins than have Ollie lying dead in the middle of his lab.

"The police will want to question you, Frank. Best that you're thinking straight. You were probably the last person to see Ollie alive."

"I didn't kill him. Is that what they're insinuating? He was fine when I went home yesterday."

"No one's accusing you. Not yet. I'm sure the police will realise you didn't do it once they've interviewed you," Henry said.

"Interviewed? That's a bit formal, isn't it?"

"Stop worrying, Frank, and tell me what happened."

"I can't tell you what happened. I wasn't there."

"But before that?"

Frank considered for a minute, trying to remember. "Ollie was going through the testing procedures to find anywhere we might be able to cut costs," Frank said.

"Go on."

Frank glared at Henry. This was all his fault. Without Henry's damn budget cuts, Ollie wouldn't have needed to stay late to go through those costs. He would have left much earlier and would still be alive. "Clarke was there," Frank said. "She asked me a load of questions about what the company does for the brochure. No one's going to want to buy shares in the company now, are they? You may as well save the money and send them both home."

Henry ignored him. "When did you leave?"

"Kas phoned. She'd been out for the afternoon and, when she got home, someone had broken into the house. She'd got herself into a right state. I had to go and sort out everything. Clarke went back upstairs, and Ollie said he'd work late to finish off the task. He wants, wanted, testing to resume as much as I do."

"And he seemed ok when you left?"

"He was absolutely fine." Frank wished Henry would stop this interrogation. He would have to endure more questions from the police soon. He didn't need the third degree from Henry as well. "Ollie was happy. He had a date later." Frank wanted to cry. Did that poor girl even know about Ollie yet? Had she waited for him last night?

"When will I be allowed into my lab?" Frank asked. "My rats will need feeding."

"You'll have to wait for the police," Henry said. "I expect they'll need to move the body first, if they haven't already."

"Has anyone told Ollie's parents?" Frank had met them a couple of times. They'd be devastated.

"The police are doing that. I understand you were fond of Ollie, but we should leave everything to the professionals," Henry said.

Fond! Henry had no idea. When you worked day in, day out with someone, you couldn't help getting close. He saw Ollie almost as a son. They were all close, all three of them in the lab. He often joked that Carmen was his work wife and Ollie their work son. Carmen never quite saw that as a joke, but Ollie saw the funny side of it. And it was true. Sometimes, even though Carmen only worked part-time, Frank spent more time with her than he did with Kas. And he spent many more hours every week with Ollie.

"Does Carmen know? She'll be upset." Frank tried to wipe a tear from his eye without Henry noticing.

"Do you want me to phone her?" Henry asked.

Frank nodded, still totally shocked by what had happened to Ollie. He wondered how long this awful feeling would last. "I'd really like to go home."

"Yes, of course," Henry agreed. "But I'm sure the police will want to speak to you first. You should sit in my office with Deborah for a while."

Frank couldn't imagine anything he'd rather do less. "I'll be ok." He would have to be.

Chapter 13

"What's going on? Where have you been?" Evan was already in the boardroom when Clarke got there. It looked like he'd been working for some time. "I saw the police arrive earlier. I'm pretty sure I saw your other half too."

Clarke sat down. "Please don't mention that to anyone, Evan. It turns out Paul hasn't told anyone he works with about us. It might get tricky if he's working on a case here."

"Trickier still if they find out and he hasn't mentioned it."

"Yes, but, even so, I'd appreciate it if you would keep it to yourself."

Would she appreciate it? Clarke had already asked herself that several times, while still seething about Paul not telling anyone at the station about her. If he had a problem with commitment, then it would be game over for her. She shouldn't doubt him. It wasn't healthy for their relationship.

"Ok," Evan said, "I promise not to tell." He opened his briefcase and pulled out a large bundle of letters. "So, what case is Paul working on here? No one's reported any fraud, I trust. We're not out of a job yet?"

"Ollie's been murdered," Clarke said bluntly, wondering if she should be more upset about that, even though she barely knew him, than she was about Paul's lack of commitment.

"Murdered? Who's Ollie? What happened?" Evan focused his full attention on Clarke.

"Ollie is Frank's lab assistant. You met him briefly yesterday, remember? He seemed like a really nice lad." He seemed like a lovely lad. She grieved for his parents. What a tragic loss to lose someone so young.

"What happened?"

"I've got no idea." Evan's excitement to hear about the dreadful event, overriding any care about the victim, reminded Clarke that Evan was still young himself, younger than her anyway. "Deborah found the body. She was screaming her head off when I arrived this morning, so I rushed down to find her."

"Hang on, where did this happen?"

"In Frank's lab, in the basement."

"And what was Deborah doing down there? Maybe she killed him."

"I doubt it." Deborah wasn't a killer. Clarke was sure of that. Pretty sure anyway. "She said she went to find Frank. Seems feasible. Her, Patrick, Frank, and Henry are the senior management team here."

Evan nodded. "How was he killed?"

"I don't know, and I'm sure neither do the police yet. There'll be a post-mortem. Paul seems sure it's murder. Ollie's only twenty-two, and he's very slim and fit, so it's unlikely to be natural causes." *He was so young.* That's what got to her.

"How exciting."

"Evan! There's nothing exciting about a young man being murdered. Deborah's traumatised, Henry's upset, and Frank is in a right state. And the poor man's parents must be heartbroken. It's really not exciting at all."

"Sorry, I meant—"

"It doesn't matter what you meant. You need to show some sensitivity. Carjon Pharma is a small company. Everybody knows everybody. They're bound to be upset."

"Of course. I'm sorry. Let me get you a coffee." Evan got up. Clarke let him go. She needed a coffee, a very strong one.

When he got back, carrying two steaming mugs of coffee, Evan aimed straight for the pile of letters on his desk. "These are for you," he said. "I picked them up from the T&C office on my way home last night. It looks like some of the results from the debtors and creditors audit."

Clarke took the bundle of envelopes reluctantly. How was she supposed to concentrate on work today? It wouldn't be easy, but it might help to take her mind off of Ollie.

She had sent out letters last week, asking Carjon Pharma's customers and suppliers to confirm directly to her how much they owed the company, or were owed by them, on the date of Carjon's last annual accounts. It was standard procedure to obtain third-party evidence to compare to the figures in the accounts. She had picked a sample of customers and suppliers. Judging by the size of the bundle of envelopes, most of them had replied. Yes, this was exactly what she needed. Something to take her focus off of this morning's events, but not too brain-taxing.

An hour later, Clarke had opened all the envelopes and logged the results. She set about comparing them against the list of debtors and creditors provided by Patrick that made up the figures in Carjon Pharma's accounts.

Clarke was about to discuss it with Evan when a knock on the boardroom door disturbed them. Quickly, she scooped up all the letters and pushed them into her briefcase, not wanting to risk any of Carjon Pharma's employees accidentally seeing any confidential information.

Henry poked his head round the door. "Clarke, one of the police officers wants to talk to you. Nothing to worry about. I'm sure it's only because you found Deborah in the lab. He's waiting in my office."

"Thank you." Clarke smiled at him and got up. If only Henry knew, it wasn't her, but Paul, who should be worried about their imminent conversation.

Chapter 14

"What happened to Ollie?" Clarke asked Paul as soon as she stepped into Henry's office.

"I'm supposed to ask you that," Paul said. "Why don't you tell me everything, right from the beginning."

Clarke sat down opposite Paul. "I've already told you. I got here this morning and heard Deborah screaming as soon as I walked through the door, so I ran down to the basement." Running hadn't helped her ankle at all, especially going downstairs. Her bad ankle ached like crazy. She'd take another paracetamol as soon as she got back to the boardroom.

"And then what?" Paul asked.

"Deborah was standing on Frank's desk, and Ollie was underneath his own desk." Paul stared at her intently. Clarke wondered what might be going through his head right now. Did he regret putting his career before her? Sadly, she was willing to bet he didn't.

"I checked Ollie in case I could help him." Initially, Clarke was hopeful he had just banged his head lightly on the desk and would come round at any moment. But she'd found no sign of a pulse. She recalled spending ages double-checking, reluctant to give up trying until she was absolutely certain, but as soon as she realised how cold and stiff he was, she knew it was hopeless. "I couldn't work out why he was jammed under the desk like that. I wondered if he was trying to catch the loose rats, but how did they get loose in the first place?" The more everything churned round and round in her brain, the more unsure she became. "Did someone put him there?"

"We don't have all the facts yet," Paul said.

"I can't believe he's dead."

"Death seems to follow you around," Paul said.

Clarke glared at him. That's exactly what Kevin Farrier had said. Had they been talking about her, making jokes? She didn't find it funny.

"I'm sorry," he said. "I realise it's been hard for you, dealing with what happened at Briar Holman. I shouldn't have said that."

"It's ok," she said, not meaning it at all, but now wasn't the time or place for an argument. One colleague murdered, another convicted. "I got a letter from the prison," she said.

Paul looked surprised. "What did it say?"

"I haven't opened it yet."

Paul squeezed her hand briefly, although Clarke noticed he kept one eye on the door, presumably in case anyone came in.

"I'm sure Ollie died last night," Clarke said, eager to change the subject.

Paul nodded. "I wondered about that."

"Frank left early yesterday, so Ollie said he'd stay and finish some work for him." She kicked herself for not realising earlier. "He was wearing the same clothes."

"Are you sure?" Paul scribbled something in his notebook.

"It was definitely the same shirt and tie," Clarke said. She remembered Ollie saying he had a date. Did he stay with the girlfriend last night? Either way, he hadn't gone home. She hadn't noticed any stubble on his face. If he'd not been home and had died this morning, he would be showing some stubble. Unless he kept a razor at his girlfriend's house. But then why didn't he also keep a clean shirt there? She stopped herself, not wanting a repeat of Briar Holman. That had been far too traumatic. She wouldn't get involved this time.

Paul wrote it down.

"How did he die?" Why had she even asked that? She really didn't intend to get involved, but the question had slipped out. And now that it had, Clarke wanted an answer. She stared at Paul, daring him to ignore the question.

"I can't tell you that," Paul said.

Clarke stared at him some more.

"There's no obvious sign of any wound, but we'll have to wait for the post-mortem."

The door opened. DC Barry Medway entered the room, carrying three mugs. Drips of coffee spilled over the edges as he struggled to keep them upright and open the door at the same time. He plonked them down on Henry's desk, leaving a ring of coffee on the table around each one.

Clarke grabbed some drinks mats and a box of tissues and began wiping the desk, anxious that the hot coffee might leave a stain. Neither of the men moved to help her.

"Have you noticed any tension between Ollie and anyone else in the company?" Paul asked before she had finished cleaning up Barry's mess.

"I only met him yesterday."

"What about Frank? He worked closely with him. Did they get on?"

If Paul was asking questions like this, he clearly assumed it was murder, not just a heart attack. "Yes, they certainly appeared to," Clarke said. As far as she remembered from yesterday, they got on great. Frank almost seemed to treat him like a favourite nephew.

"What about Frank? Does everyone like him?"

"Yes," Clarke said. "Yes, they certainly seem to. Why are you asking that? Nobody's tried to hurt Frank."

"No," Paul said, "but is it possible that someone mistook Ollie for Frank?"

Clarke smiled, the first smile she had cracked so far this morning. "You haven't met Frank yet, have you? Ollie's young and slim. Frank's much older and, well, a bit more portly, shall we say?"

Paul smiled. "Ok, so it's not likely then. Just asking."

THE COVER-UP

"Have you solved the murder yet? Who dunnit?" Evan asked before Clarke even got a chance to sit down. He frequently teased her about her experience in her last job at Briar Holman, where she solved the case of a missing colleague, a murder, and a big fraud.

"Evan, it's not funny. A young man is dead." Even though she only met Ollie very briefly, his death had upset her more than she imagined it would. Maybe because she'd seen the body. When she'd been a firefighter, she'd seen dead bodies. It had always saddened her, and they hadn't even been people she'd met.

"Sorry."

"Anyway, never mind about that. I need to talk to you."

"Shoot."

"I've analysed all the debtors' and creditors' confirmation letters we got back." She'd been so worried about the results, she'd checked everything twice. "The thing is, hardly anything matches."

Evan looked up, paying attention now. "How so?"

Clarke scrolled down the screen of her laptop. "It's mostly the dates," she said. "A lot of the amounts are correct, but the timing's wrong. Someone's altered the dates to make the company appear to have more debtors and fewer creditors at the date the accounts were made up."

"Well, obviously something was going on," Evan said, "or we wouldn't have been called in."

"Yes, but..." Clarke thought Evan would be more surprised, or shocked even, but he took it in his stride, like he'd seen it hundreds of times before, which he probably had.

"So what do you plan to do about it?" Evan asked.

"Me?"

"Yes, you. What do you think we should do?"

"Do a bigger sample." That would confirm the validity of their theory. That's what Evan had taught her.

"How big a sample?"

Evan was putting her on the spot. Would she seem stupid if she said what she thought? "There are so many errors, I'd extend the sample to absolutely everything," she said.

"Wow. That bad?"

"Yes." Clarke started to doubt herself now. Maybe she was being over-cautious.

"Ok," Evan said. "Miss out the really small stuff. Set a lower limit. Then get it done. Let's find out what we're dealing with."

Clarke smiled for the first time that morning.

"It makes sense," Evan said. "It would explain why the accounts look healthier than the bank position suggests. What we need to find out now is who and why. That's the trickier bit."

Chapter 15

Patrick had barely sat down at his desk this morning when the two detectives showed up demanding that he accompany them to the police station. But then they'd left him sitting in this godawful room for an hour. Despite the chill in the room, his whole body oozed sweat. He took out a handkerchief and surreptitiously tried to wipe the beads of sweat from his brow, so the police officer standing by the door wouldn't notice. He didn't want the detectives to assume he was guilty, but the stress of the whole situation made him perspire like crazy. He had nothing to feel guilty about, did he?

"Sorry to keep you waiting." The more senior of the two detectives proffered a cup of coffee. Patrick held out his hands and took it, then changed his mind, placing it on the table in front of him and pushing it away. Hot coffee wouldn't help the sweat problem. Besides, he wasn't yet desperate enough to drink machine rubbish out of a plastic cup.

"Do I need a lawyer?" Patrick immediately regretted asking, worrying that it might make him appear guilty.

"That's your prerogative," the detective sergeant said. "We can arrange one if you want."

Patrick shook his head. He didn't need legal representation. He hadn't done anything wrong.

The detective sergeant sat down next to his colleague, who had already made himself comfortable opposite Patrick. He tapped his fingers on the table and smiled.

"I'm Detective Sergeant Waterford," he said. "You can call me Paul. And this is Detective Constable Medway."

Patrick remained silent. Surely it must be a good sign that Paul was smiling. Perhaps this would all be over soon and he could get back to work and stop worrying.

"Where were you yesterday evening?" Paul asked.

Patrick relaxed. This would be easy after all. Simon would give him an alibi. That would prove he didn't have anything to do with Ollie's death.

"I met an old friend for a drink. Simon Edmonds."

"Where did you go?"

"The wine bar in Brackford marketplace, *Cheers And Beers*." The bar staff would probably remember them, Patrick reassured himself. They'd been there a while. They must have been, to get through multiple bottles of wine and a meal in their restaurant too.

"We'll check that out. What time did you arrive and leave?" Paul glanced over at his colleague.

"I got there at six fifty-five p.m." Patrick was certain of that. Even if he couldn't remember, he would have guessed the time. He'd arranged to meet Simon at seven, and he wanted to be sure not to be late, so he'd arrived five minutes early, like he always did for any important meeting. Simon had shown up shortly after him.

"And when did you leave?" Paul stopped smiling.

Patrick considered for a minute. "I'm not sure." He had been very drunk, hence getting the train home. He still had a bit of a hangover now. It could have been nine or nine thirty. Or had it been even later? He simply couldn't remember. Hopefully, Simon would be able to tell them.

"Come on, you must have some idea." Paul tapped his fingers on the table impatiently.

Patrick could feel sweat dripping down his forehead. He wiped his hand across his brow. "Nine thirty," he said, trying to sound as decisive as he could.

"Ok, so where did you go when you left?"

"I walked to the station. I'd had a bit to drink." It must have been three bottles of pinot noir between them. He was sure he'd drunk more than Simon too. Patrick never drank that much, but Simon insisted they carry on and he couldn't risk offending him. He needed Simon's investment too much. "I took the train home." It was a real pain getting into work this morning without his car, but thank God he hadn't driven home drunk. That would be difficult to explain.

"Really?" Paul glared at him.

Patrick avoided his gaze, which he found unnerving. He turned towards the other detective, who also stared at him in disbelief. What had he forgotten? Had he been wrong about the time?

"Where did you go before you went to the station?" Paul demanded.

The question confused Patrick. He didn't understand what they were getting at. "Nowhere."

Paul stood up, towering above Patrick. "We've got CCTV of you entering and leaving Carjon Pharma's offices," he said. "Nine forty-five p.m. entering, and ten eleven p.m. leaving. What did you do there? Did you kill Ollie Jenner?"

"What? No." What were they talking about? He couldn't have gone into the office. He'd have remembered. Whyever did they think that?

Paul pulled out a TV screen from the corner of the room and clicked on a remote control. The screen flickered to life.

"Is this you?" he asked.

Patrick stared at the screen. It showed a poor quality image. But the coat looked like his, and he recognised his favourite polka-dot tie that he'd been wearing yesterday. He felt numb. How could it be him? There'd be a simple explanation. It must be someone who looked like him because surely he would have remembered. But he didn't even remember walking to the station. He recalled leaving the bar and getting off the train at the station near his house. But he couldn't for the life of him remember anything about the bit in between.

"Is that you?" Paul shouted at him.

Patrick nodded, almost imperceptibly.

"For the tape, please."

"Yes," Patrick said. Why couldn't he remember? How much did he drink? It must have been even more than he'd recalled. Had it been enough for him to go back to the office and completely blank out the whole of that time? The realisation hit him like a bullet to the brain. Had he drunk so much that he killed Ollie and hadn't even remembered? Had his brain blanked out the horror of it all?

"Interview suspended, twelve thirty-six." Paul flicked off the recording.

"I'd like a solicitor," Patrick said.

Chapter 16

Frank still couldn't get his head around everything that had happened. Ollie murdered. The burglary at home. And Selwyn and Effie both dead.

The police had found Selwyn and Effie during a thorough search of the lab. They'd taken away the bodies of the dead rats. Apparently, they were evidence. Frank struggled to process the events. He'd like to kill whoever did that to his rats. He'd like to kill whoever had murdered Ollie.

The police still wouldn't allow him back into his lab, so Henry had sent him home. In an effort to occupy his mind, he'd logged into his network account from his home office. He still needed to check all his costs, in case he could find anywhere to cut corners.

He needed this sort of tedious work now—something that didn't require too much brainpower, because his brain didn't seem to be working at all today. None of this made sense. He'd spent a lot of money on equipment earlier in the year, but he couldn't find the spend anywhere on his codes. Perhaps payment hadn't gone through. But it must have done. He'd definitely signed off the invoices for payment, and if that supplier hadn't been paid, they'd have been on the phone with Frank personally multiple times by now.

There weren't many chemical costs logged either, normally a high spender. And rat food. The same thing. All in all, it looked like he'd barely spent any of his budget so far this year. It made no sense.

He queried the accounts system by the name of one of the suppliers. The big equipment invoice he remembered signing off had definitely been paid, nearly three months ago. Eventually, he found it, but on completely the wrong code, mixed in with all the drug sales proceeds.

Searching for his other regular suppliers, he found the same thing had happened. The spend was mis-coded to the drugs' income codes.

He needed to talk to Patrick in the morning to get these errors corrected.

And another thing. The police took Patrick away this morning. Not actually arresting him, but firmly insisting he should go. What was that all about? He couldn't imagine Patrick would have anything to do with Ollie's death. But Patrick still hadn't come back by the time Frank left the office, which was before lunch. Did the police have any evidence?

The more Frank considered it, and the more he tried to convince himself there was no way that Patrick would have killed Ollie, the more he started to have doubts. Maybe Ollie had provoked Patrick. But Ollie was so sickeningly nice. Frank doubted he'd ever upset anyone in his entire, all too short, life. Perhaps it had been an accident. These things happened. Perhaps Patrick had unintentionally knocked him over, and Ollie hit his head. Except that Henry had told him Ollie's body was found wedged under the desk. He would have never fallen there by accident. Something must have happened. But Patrick simply wouldn't have killed Ollie deliberately, would he? If he had, then Frank would personally do everything in his power to make sure he rotted in prison forever.

Chapter 17

Patrick was cooking lunch. He did a lot of the cooking now, and he'd taken to producing a full roast dinner every Sunday. He peered through the glass oven door. The chicken, corn-fed, of course, was roasting nicely, turning a beautiful golden brown. He needed to be so careful with what he fed Martina. Everything was fresh, organic, and the best quality, healthiest option available.

He started peeling some carrots. Cooking was quite therapeutic. After his dreadful experience with the police, he suddenly appreciated the simple things in life. He was lucky to even be here, at home.

Martina came into the kitchen. He'd forgotten how frail she'd become lately, walking like someone twenty years older. He resolved to tackle Frank again tomorrow. There must be something he could do.

"Don't cook too much for me." Martina sat down.

Patrick sighed. He spent most of every mealtime with Martina gently cajoling her to eat a little more. She needed her strength and good nutrition to help her heal. Ok, so her cancer wouldn't be cured by a plate of organic veg, but she sure as hell would struggle to recover if she starved herself.

"I'll give you a small portion," he reassured her. "You can always come back for seconds."

She smiled at him, and his heart melted. "Thank you, Paddy Bear," she said.

The carrots came to a boil and Patrick turned down the gas. "Ready in five minutes."

Frank stood outside Patrick's front door, hesitating. It had seemed like a great idea to show up at his house on a Sunday, on the pretence of finding out if he was ok. He'd already heard from Henry that the police had let Patrick go. Now Frank itched to find out what happened, and what they'd asked him, and, most of all, if any of it shed any light on who might have murdered Ollie.

But now, standing on the doorstep, it worried him that Patrick, one of his oldest friends, might take it the wrong way, and that he might appreciate some time to himself to get over his ordeal. Having recently experienced police questioning himself, *ordeal* was the only way to describe it. It was a harrowing experience, one that Frank never wanted to go through again.

Well, he was here now. He pressed the doorbell before he could change his mind.

"Frank." Patrick seemed surprised to see him.

"I wanted to check how you are." A delicious smell of roast chicken wafted out of Patrick's house, reminding Frank it was nearly lunchtime. He noticed Patrick's colourful plastic apron and kicked himself for coming at such an inconvenient time. Of course, he would be cooking lunch for himself and Martina.

"That's good of you." Patrick stepped outside the door, closing it behind him. "I need some fresh air," he said, checking his watch.

Frank wondered exactly why Patrick hadn't invited him in. "Is Martina ok?"

Patrick ushered him down the driveway and indicated for him to turn left. "She's bearing up, thanks."

"And you?" Frank struggled to keep up with Patrick's long stride. This conversation would be so much easier if they were sitting down, preferably with a civilised glass of whisky in his hand.

"I'm ok."

"What happened? With the police, I mean." The police let him go, so he must be innocent, thank God. He'd never believed Patrick would do anything like that, not really.

"I don't want to talk about it." Patrick wiped a bead of sweat from his brow.

Frank noticed the bags under Patrick's eyes, evidencing a total lack of sleep. He wondered how long Patrick would keep up the abrupt, uninformative answers. They were getting further from the house now, making Frank suspicious as to why Patrick didn't invite him in. Frank had been in his house loads of times over the years, and he and Kas counted him and Martina as good friends. If Patrick was so innocent, why didn't he want Martina to overhear their conversation? Because that seemed wrong to Frank right now.

"I'm sorry about Ollie, by the way."

By the way! Frank was annoyed at Patrick simply mentioning his catastrophic loss as an afterthought. Like Ollie didn't really matter very much. Like Frank wasn't in pain at losing someone he'd worked closely with every day for the last year, who he considered a friend. No, if he was honest with himself, Frank considered Ollie to be a surrogate son. If the police were wrong about releasing Patrick, and he turned out to be responsible for Ollie's death after all, Frank swore to himself, he'd kill him.

Frank bit his tongue. "Thank you. I'm still very shocked, to be honest." He ought to give Patrick the benefit of the doubt. The police had released him for a reason.

"What did the police ask you?" Frank needed some answers. He needed something that would make these doubts about Patrick disappear.

"Nothing."

Frank stopped abruptly, grabbing Patrick's arm to make him stop too. "Listen, Patrick. I cared about Ollie, and honestly, I'm struggling to come to terms with this whole sorry mess. It will really help if you tell me what's going on." Patrick looked ridiculous in the middle of the pavement in his plastic apron. Frank almost laughed. He would have if he hadn't been welling up with tears.

Patrick sighed. "The police made some totally untrue accusations. They obviously thought better of it because they let me go. I'm really sorry about Ollie. He was a nice lad. But I've got enough to worry about with Martina. I don't need you harassing me like this."

"Sorry, I realise you're upset, but I need the truth. What did the police question you about?" They surely wouldn't have taken him to the police station and kept him for so long without a good reason.

"Nothing," Patrick snapped. "It was a misunderstanding."

"But what sort of misunderstanding?" Frank was determined not to let Patrick fob him off that easily.

Patrick hesitated. "They said I might have been in the office when, you know..."

"When Ollie died? You were there?"

"No," Patrick interrupted firmly. "I wasn't there. It wasn't me."

Frank stared at Patrick. Droplets of sweat beaded on his forehead. And the way he'd been so adamant in denying everything, did that mean Patrick was hiding something? No way would he admit anything to Frank now, not by the looks of him. Well, Frank could be sneaky too. He would ask Henry later. If Patrick confided in anyone, it would be Henry.

"It's a sad loss," Patrick said.

Hot tears stung Frank's eyes. Everyone was being so nice to him, but it felt false coming from Patrick. He wiped his eyes with the back of his hand.

"You should get back to cooking lunch before Martina misses you." Frank knew he wouldn't get anything more from Patrick today. And, far from allaying his suspicions about him, he still vacillated over Patrick's innocence. He wanted so much to be wrong.

Patrick ran back into the house. A burning smell came from the kitchen. He hurried to the stove and snatched up the saucepan of charred carrots. Sod Frank. Quickly, he took some more carrots out of the fridge and started to peel them before checking on the chicken.

Martina came in. "I smelt burning."

Patrick pulled out a chair for her. "Only the carrots. I got sidetracked." He finished peeling the replacement carrots, putting them in a clean saucepan, and chopping some broccoli.

"What did the police say? You never told me."

Patrick shuddered. Martina's question came like a bolt out of the blue. That was all he needed, more questioning. He'd had as much as he could take from Frank. "It was all a misunderstanding." He shrugged his shoulders, summoning up some extra patience that he didn't even realise he possessed, and turned his back on Martina to get some cutlery to lay the table. Even thinking about it caused him more stress than he would have imagined possible. Of course, he couldn't tell Martina anything, not with her in such a frail state. What would it do to her to find out that the police actually accused him of murder, that they still might believe he did it? Worse still, that he might actually have done it. He'd agonised over it for the last two days. Those hours between leaving the bar and arriving home had vanished. Had he subconsciously blocked them from his memory because something dreadful had happened? Could he really have killed Ollie?

"Yes, of course," Martina said. "These things happen all the time. The police have to be thorough and investigate every possibility."

"Yes, that's right." Patrick tried to sound upbeat, but conscious of the waver in Martina's voice. Was she simply feeling tired and frail, or did she doubt him? Martina wasn't stupid. The police would have never detained him for so long over a simple misunderstanding. Frank doubting him was one thing, but Patrick simply wouldn't be able to bear it if Martina stopped believing in him.

He took the chicken out of the oven. It smelt delicious. Hopefully, that would encourage Martina to eat more than usual.

"You could never do anything like that," Martina said. "Kill that poor boy, I mean."

Patrick concentrated on the chicken, taking it out of the roasting tin and placing it on a plate, ready for carving. He didn't quite trust himself to look at Martina yet. Her support meant a lot to him. She genuinely believed he didn't do it, and he thanked God for that. The trouble was, he wasn't sure if he fully believed it himself. The doubt was eating him alive.

"Thank you." He finished carving the chicken and dished up, piling his own plate high and putting as much as he could on Martina's plate without overwhelming her. She wouldn't even eat half of it. He smothered her food in gravy, the way she liked it, and placed the plate on the table in front of her.

"I'll never manage all that."

Patrick smiled at her. Mealtimes were always the same these days. No matter what he said, she would never eat enough, but lately, she'd been eating even less. He hoped the cancer wasn't getting worse.

"Frank's drug is nearly ready for the trial," Patrick said. He hadn't told Martina about the budget cuts, or about Frank being forced to put all testing on hold.

Martina forked up the tiniest mouthful of potato. "I've been wondering about that."

"So have I," Patrick said. "It really could make the difference." He would try harder tomorrow to persuade Frank to give Martina the drug now. He was prepared to do whatever it took to convince him.

"No, I mean, I don't believe it's going to work."

"Nonsense. The test results are amazing. It's the best chance we've got."

Martina stopped eating, her fork suspended in mid-air while she gazed oddly at Patrick. "But it's not *we*, is it? It's just *me*. I've had enough. I'm tired of being poked and prodded and given endless drugs that make me feel worse afterwards than I did before."

"But, darling, the end result will be worth it. You don't have to do this on your own. I'll be with you all the way."

"It's too late, Patrick. This horrible disease has already gone too far. It's too late to stop it now. I've come to terms with it. Now you must do the same."

Patrick dropped his knife. He sat stunned as it clattered onto the floor. Surely, Martina couldn't be giving up? Not now. How could he have missed the signs of her starting to feel like this?

"I can't lose you." The words came out so quietly he wondered if she even heard them. Everything was going wrong. Maybe he would lose her, anyway. If he really had killed Ollie, he would go to prison for a long time, perhaps for the rest of their lives. That didn't bear thinking about. But, if he had to lose Martina, he was determined it wouldn't be to cancer, not while a potential cure existed. That would be worse than anything, worse than going to prison for sure. Somehow, he needed to persuade her to take Frank's drug.

Martina reached across and took his hand. "I'll always love you, Paddy Bear. I just won't always be here."

Patrick felt a tear escape one eye. Martina using her pet name for him made it even worse, reminding him of what they had together. "Please, for me, Martina, please don't stop fighting this. Please." Patrick was aware that his pathetic begging didn't come across as he'd intended, but he didn't see how else to get through to her. "Please, just try this drug. If it doesn't start working really quickly, you can stop." Martina had stopped eating. Patrick knew he should wait and have this conversation later, concentrate on trying to get some food into his wife. "Please, will you think about it? Please." He couldn't stop himself. And it wasn't as if he had even managed yet to persuade Frank to give Martina the drug. He needed to shut up.

"Sorry," he said quietly. He reached for the gravy jug. "Shall I pour some more? It will warm your food up." Her food must have gone cold by now, and she'd hardly eaten any.

Martina shook her head. She looked scared. They were both scared. Somehow, Patrick needed to fix things.

Chapter 18

Frank had intended to avoid Patrick today, so he was annoyed to run into him as soon as he arrived at work on Monday morning.

"How are you?"

Frank nodded. Patrick's concern was touching, but he felt awkward being around him after yesterday's confrontation. He wondered if he should tell Patrick about his costs, or lack of them, but he was having second thoughts on that subject. He'd tossed and turned all last night trying to decide what to do.

The lab was still a crime scene, so Frank was forced to work upstairs. Pretending to be in a hurry, he strode along the corridor in search of a spare office where he wouldn't keep bumping into Patrick all day. Best for him to concentrate on work—the only thing that helped take his mind off of Ollie. And if he concentrated hard enough, maybe the answer about how to handle his mis-coded costs problem would come to him subconsciously, or perhaps in a flash of blinding light. He willed his subconscious to tell him he should show Deborah his ultra-low spend so far and beg her to reinstate his budget so he could resume his testing programme. Because if the testing programme got postponed for any longer, Martina stood no chance. How could he shatter her hopes? He had hopes too, and Fexizon had also been important to Ollie. They'd both worked endless hours on developing it and spent many more hours discussing their dreams for when they finally released Fexizon to the world. It meant a lot to both of them, and Frank had come too far with this to give up without a fight.

Finding himself outside Henry's office, Frank realised he had to confront him. He couldn't give up. He would do it for Ollie.

Chapter 19

"Henry, what is going on?" Frank was in no mood to observe social niceties, like knocking on doors or making polite small talk.

Henry put the phone down. "Frank, you can't come barging in here without knocking. What do you think you're doing?"

"Sorry." Frank wasn't really sorry at all. "But I need some answers. Why have you frozen all spend on research and testing?" He'd already tried to talk to Henry last week, but Henry kept fobbing him off. Well, Ollie's death had steeled something in Frank. He wouldn't put up with being fobbed off again, not when it was this important.

"Sit down." Henry gestured to one of the chairs in front of his desk.

Frank obediently sat. Extracting answers from Henry would be just as easy sitting. "This is a critical time for the Fexizon drug. I've got people lined up to start the trial next week."

"I'm sorry, Frank. It's a cash-flow problem. You'll simply have to postpone things."

"But all the people we've selected are at exactly the right stage in their illness to benefit from the drug. In a few weeks' time, they won't be, then the test results will be totally skewed." Frank sighed. Henry really didn't understand. But then Henry wasn't a scientist. Nothing more than a glorified salesperson, really.

"So find a new group of people."

"That's crazy," Frank said. "Do you have any idea how long it took to find the right group of people? And, if you're worried about money, setting up a whole new test group will cost us much more. It makes no sense economically." Not only that, but someone would need to waste extra time on the gruelling task of contacting everyone in the current test group, explaining why they were shattering their hopes and effectively sentencing some of them to death with a single phone call. He dreaded that task. Absolutely dreaded it.

"Frank." Henry glared at him. "Read my lips. We have no money."

THE COVER-UP

"That's ridiculous." Frank snorted. He read the monthly management reports that Deborah wrote. Well, he skimmed through them anyway. The company was doing well, wasn't it? Doubt started to set in. Did he miss something? Perhaps he needed to read the reports again. "What are you spending my budget on, Henry? You'd better not be buying another new company car. This drug testing is important."

"No, I'm not buying a car," Henry snapped. "And you're biased. All that matters to you is covering yourself with glory when Fexizon gets launched."

"If Fexizon succeeds, it will cover the company in glory too," Frank said. Was he being self-centred in his desperation to finish developing the drug as soon as possible? No. He reminded himself he did this job to help people. And it would help the company too. "Carjon's profits will go through the roof when this drug takes off."

"Frank, you're not listening. We need money now, not in a couple of years' time. The bank won't extend our credit any more. We need to pay our employees. I'm simply not authorising any more spend. And that's final." Henry stood up.

"But—"

"Final." Henry glowered at him.

Frank got up, recognising the futility of trying to reason with Henry in his current frame of mind, but he couldn't resist a final parting shot as he stepped out of Henry's office. "And you need to sort out Deborah," he said, slamming the door behind him. Perhaps Henry would take his bad mood out on Deborah now. She deserved it.

Chapter 20

"Hey, check this out." Clarke walked round to Evan's side of the big boardroom table, waving two sheets of paper at him.

Evan looked up. "If you stop flapping them around, I might be able to read what's on them."

Clarke laid both sheets of paper on the table in front of him. "Last month's bank reconciliation," she said. "This is the one Patrick gave us." She pointed to the one on the right. "And this one I got from Kerry."

Evan took a few seconds to examine them. He whistled. "Wow."

"They're not the same at all, are they? The one Patrick signed doesn't even tie back to the balance on the bank statement. He can't have checked it properly."

"Patrick appears to have signed them both."

"Yes, but if you examine them closely, the signatures aren't quite the same." She pointed. "See, this one's got a lot more pressure on the Ps, and the tail of the G slopes more."

Evan stared at it. "Maybe." He didn't seem sure. "Or, perhaps Kerry got him to sign both documents. I bet he signs anything that's put in front of him when he's busy."

"We should get them checked out by a handwriting expert," Clarke said. "It must have been Kerry who produced the fake bank reconciliation. It might help prove that she's involved."

"I agree. It has to be her. But why? Why could she possibly want to alter the annual accounts, then cover up the cash position? What's in it for her?"

Clarke sat down. "I've been trying to work that out myself. Perhaps she made some really big error in her work, and she's been trying to cover it up ever since so she doesn't get sacked."

"That's plausible," Evan said. "And once something like that goes on for a while, she'll have got sucked in by all the things she's done since to hide the evidence, so now there's no way she can confess to the original mistake."

"I suppose we need to find that original error," Clarke said. That sounded like a lot of work. "How far back should we search?" She was disappointed that, instead of an exciting fraud case, this might turn out to be just a stupid error on the part of a junior member of the staff.

"How long has she worked here?" Evan asked. "You should talk to Kerry some more. Make friends with her. See if you can find out what's really going on. It may not have been a mistake. If she altered something deliberately, we need to find out."

Getting close to Kerry, with her bristly personality, wouldn't be easy. Clarke wondered if Evan would have better luck. Kerry seemed to be more susceptible to a good-looking man smiling at her, but one glance at Evan told her he wasn't about to volunteer to talk to the bolshy madam anytime soon. He'd delegated the task to her, and she would do it, somehow. But Clarke was sure that asking Kerry too many questions, would rapidly put her on her guard. She would need to consider this very carefully.

"Now that you've interviewed the main people in the company, do you have a theory on who did it?" Evan asked.

Clarke put her half empty coffee mug down on the table. "Are we discounting all the manufacturing staff then?"

"They're at a different site. They probably wouldn't have got the opportunity."

"And are we talking about Ollie's murder or doctoring all the year-end invoices?" Clarke was already convinced that the two events may be connected. It was too much of a coincidence otherwise. But, so far, she hadn't worked out what the connection might be.

"Both, I suppose," Evan said. "Do you have any theories? Because I'm stumped on this one."

Clarke reflected for a minute. "As far as the invoices go, it's got to be either Henry, Patrick, Kerry, Deborah, or possibly Frank. It's a small company. No one else would have had enough opportunity or the expertise to do it."

"I'm not sure that Frank's got the technical knowledge," Evan said.

"He's highly intelligent."

"Yes, but as a scientist. He isn't an expert on the finer details of accountancy. Whoever did this knew what they were doing."

"Ok, we'll discount Frank, for now." Frank remained one of the obvious suspects for Ollie's murder, despite him seeming to adore the lad. If the two events were connected, she wouldn't take him out of the equation yet.

"It's unlikely to be Henry either." Evan flipped his laptop open. "He would hardly call us in to investigate himself. And he doesn't seem to like getting his hands dirty with actual work. He seems much happier in high-level meetings and sucking up to hospital reps. This sort of thing isn't his style."

"That narrows it down a little." Clarke put a question mark against Henry's name on her list. It might be a brazen double-bluff on his part or simple stupidity.

"So that leaves Patrick, Deborah, or Kerry. Kerry's fairly junior. Would she have enough knowledge to do something like this? It's been very well executed," Evan said.

"She's in a junior position, yes, but she may be more clued up than you give her credit for." Evan annoyed Clarke by discounting Kerry because of her relative youth and inexperience. She hoped not because Kerry was a woman.

"Now Patrick's a possibility," Evan said. "He's got motive."

"Oh yes, his wife. If Carjon Pharma goes bankrupt, the drug trial goes down the pan with it. I gather his wife is in a bad way, and she's counting on that new treatment."

"He's probably got the strongest motive and the most experience to pull off the accounts manipulation."

"But he would hardly kill off Ollie, would he? Murdering the research assistant would surely slow down the test programme." Nothing about Ollie's death made sense to Clarke.

"The two things may not be connected. We could be looking at two completely separate people, or it may have been an accident. The police have certainly taken an interest in Patrick. You should ask Paul."

Clarke didn't believe in coincidences. "I'm staying open-minded," she insisted, ignoring Evan's suggestion. Paul wasn't being too cooperative in passing on confidential information to her.

"So that leaves Deborah. She's got an MBA. That probably gives her enough finance knowledge to pull this off. But why? She's got no motive," Evan said.

"We must be missing something here." Clarke was certain of that. She disagreed with Evan about Deborah, who could have any number of reasons to want to make the company's finances look better. For a start, she would lose her job if the company filed for bankruptcy. And Clarke was pretty sure that something was going on between Deborah and Henry. Deborah might have done it to help Henry. Love could be a powerful motivator.

"What about the murder?"

"I have a theory on that."

"What's that?" Evan asked.

Clarke hesitated. It was actually Paul's theory, and she laughed at him when he told her yesterday. But now she believed he might be right. "It's possible that the killer meant to murder Frank," she said at last.

Evan looked up at her. "You could hardly mistake Ollie for Frank, Ollie's young and slim. Frank's much older, and, well, somewhat larger."

Clarke laughed. Evan's recent equalities training taught him it was rude to say the F word. "You mean he's fat."

"Yes."

"It might have been dark," Clarke said.

"Frank went home early."

"That's my point. Someone expected Frank to be there late but got Ollie by accident."

"But why would someone want to kill Frank?" Evan asked.

"It wouldn't be Patrick. He needs him alive." Clarke had heard Patrick talking about his wife. She had no doubt that he loved her and would be devastated if she died. On the other hand, that meant he would do anything for her. That put him right back in the top spot for manipulating the company accounts.

"So, who else?"

"Who has he upset?" Clarke asked. Frank seemed pretty affable. She couldn't imagine him having a long list of enemies.

"That, I don't know."

Clarke didn't know either. "Anyway, I've sent the next batch of debtor and creditor confirmation letters. Now we just put our feet up and wait for the replies."

Evan laughed. "You won't be putting your feet up anytime soon. I've got loads of other work for you to do in the meantime. We need to explore every angle of this. If they've falsified the debtors and creditors, they may have tried other things too."

Clarke laughed. "You realise I was joking, right?" If anything, Evan was the lazy one, not her. She longed to unravel what was happening here, and the more work Evan gave her to do, the longer she would get to stay here. She hated loose ends, and she didn't want to leave any when they finished this job.

Chapter 21

Paul worked late, so Clarke had already eaten when she met him for a quick drink in their favourite pub in Brackford.

"How's the case going?" Clarke asked as she sipped at her glass of Sauvignon Blanc. "Have you found out yet how Ollie died?" She'd been wondering if it was murder or natural causes. She'd put money on murder.

"Clarke." Paul put his beer down, spilling some of it on the table. "I'm not supposed to tell you."

Clarke took his hand and squeezed it, looking into his deep brown eyes. They would inevitably both end up at his place or hers later. He should have come straight to hers and saved her the bother of going out.

Paul caved in sooner than she'd hoped. "Ollie was poisoned, but keep that information to yourself. Everything we found in that lab is being analysed. We aren't sure yet where the poison came from. It may not even have been anything in the lab. If it turns out to be a longer acting poison, he may have picked it up from anywhere. We'll have a better idea when Erica pinpoints exactly what the poison is."

Clarke suppressed a smile, her joy at getting what she wanted from Paul overshadowed by Ollie's death. "I've got something for you too," she said.

Paul grinned at her.

"No, not that. Some information."

"What?"

"Someone at Carjon Pharma has been falsifying the accounts, making it seem as if the company is doing much better than it really is."

"Why would they do that?"

"Any number of reasons," Clarke said. "We're still investigating. Let us get on with it for a bit longer. The thing is, I wondered if it might have some connection to Ollie's murder."

Paul nodded. "It's possible. It's a big coincidence."

"And I don't like coincidences."

"There's definitely something going on," Paul said. "I'm worried about you working there." Paul gave her hand a quick squeeze before letting go to pick up his pint.

"I'll be fine."

"Be careful."

"Stop worrying. I'll be fine." It was sweet that Paul cared, but she had to do her job. "Did you find anything else? What about the rats?" she asked, trying to steer the subject away from her personal safety.

"Ollie must have been trying to catch the loose rats, then the poison kicked in when he was under the desk. One of the rats was dead when we found it. The other one died soon after."

"Did you test them?"

Paul looked blank. "I suppose Erica will do that. She's testing everything. I'll ask her tomorrow."

"Don't you get it?" Clarke said. "They were probably poisoned by the same thing that poisoned Ollie. That means it must be something in the lab."

"Of course. Why didn't I think of that?" Paul slammed his hand down on the table in frustration, making his beer slosh in its glass. "It's so obvious."

"Sometimes you need a fresh eye on things, which is why you should always tell me everything." Knowing the poison came from the lab didn't narrow things down much. The cupboards in a research laboratory were probably jam-packed with toxic substances.

Clarke wondered how best to check who had access to Frank's lab. Whoever poisoned Ollie must have left something in there that he would eat or touch. That narrowed it down a lot, as the lab was kept locked when no one was working. Frank must be the top suspect, but Clarke couldn't understand why he would want to kill Ollie. She planned to talk to Frank tomorrow. They never finished their previous meeting, which gave her the perfect excuse to visit him again.

Chapter 22

Frank wrung his hands together in despair. This was all going wrong. The lab was still a crime scene, so he'd started going through all his calculations from the cancer drug testing to keep his mind off Ollie.

He worked on the calculations again. He'd been right the first time he'd checked. One of the decimal points was in the wrong place, which made the results appear much better than they really were. It made the difference between being in contention for the Nobel Prize and saving millions of lives, and an average drug that needed more development to be anywhere near ready for human testing.

He rechecked the figures, in case his current emotional state was causing him to imagine things. But, no matter how many times he checked, the answer came out the same.

Frank wondered how such a fundamental error slipped through unnoticed. He was always so careful. Then he remembered he had entrusted this part of the results analysis to Ollie. Ollie had shown tremendous promise and made great progress. Frank tried to involve him as much as possible, teach him new stuff all the time, give him more responsibility. Indeed, in a research department this tiny, he had to. He couldn't take on all the work himself. Had he put too much pressure on Ollie, pushed him too much, failed to supervise him enough? Had he been so excited at the results that he'd failed to check Ollie's calculations in his euphoria?

Patrick came over with a steaming mug of coffee. "Are you ok?" He put the coffee on the desk in front of Frank. "Figured you might need this. You look done in. You should go home."

"Thanks." What a pity that a cup of coffee and an afternoon off wouldn't solve this problem.

"Seriously, Henry won't mind. It's been a terrible shock, and we need to take care of you."

THE COVER-UP

Frank caught the slight hesitation in Patrick's voice, as if he intended to say something else. As if he intended to say that he needed Frank to be at the top of his game and working on the drug that might save Martina's life. Well, that scenario seemed highly unlikely now.

"Yes, I will go home." Frank couldn't sit in the same office as Patrick all afternoon, not knowing what he now knew. He would have to tell him, find some way of explaining it that would let him down gently. He needed some time to consider this properly. This would hit Patrick hard. He glanced at Patrick, not quite wanting to meet his gaze. He'd been friends with Patrick for nearly thirty years. Surely the Patrick he knew could have never killed Ollie. He really wanted to accept what Patrick said. He really wanted to stop doubting him.

Patrick patted him on the shoulder. "Go home."

Frank felt bad. If his despair showed in his face, Patrick probably attributed it to grief over Ollie. Frank picked up his coffee and sipped it. His time would be better spent trying to work out how to get the drug back on track. If he didn't come up with a brilliant idea, he would need to find a way to break the news to Patrick. Tomorrow.

Chapter 23

It hadn't been such a great idea working at home. Frank struggled to concentrate with Kas constantly fussing over him.

"I'm trying to work."

"Frank, I realise you're upset about Ollie, but don't take it out on me."

"Sorry." He didn't mean to snap, but he couldn't stop himself.

"You still haven't talked about Ollie. It really would help if you did." Kas sat opposite him. "Frank?"

"Yes, I'm sorry. It's just, he was so young." Frank didn't want to tell Kas that Ollie had been like a son to him. Kas couldn't have children, so it would hurt her to find out that. It would hurt Frank's two children from his first marriage too, not that he ever saw them. His ex-wife had taken them to live in New Zealand with Frank's replacement. He hadn't realised how much he still missed them. Had he used Ollie as a substitute child?

"Tell me about Ollie. How long did he work for you?"

"Not much more than a year," Frank said. It seemed much longer than that. "He was very intelligent. He got a first in Chemistry from Cambridge." Frank had wondered at the time why Ollie wanted to work for such a small company. He would have earned a much higher salary with one of the big pharmaceutical companies. Ollie always said he got a much better experience at Carjon. He liked being in the thick of things, involved with every part of the process, rather than being one of many junior trainees in a big organisation.

"I only met him a couple of times. He seemed really nice." Kas sat down next to Frank.

"Ollie was great." His sense of humour brightened up the lab. But he could be serious too, and ambitious. Too ambitious to stay for long. At some stage, Frank knew he would have to push him out of the company for his own good, to work somewhere bigger. His eyes welled up. This wasn't the way he'd planned for Ollie to leave.

"Did he have a family? A wife?"

"He lived with his parents in Brackford, but he'd just met someone. In fact, he was supposed to go on a date the night he died, but he never got there." Ollie had been so excited about it. She was gorgeous, according to Ollie. Had they tracked the new girlfriend down? Poor girl. Had she been told what had happened to him? Or did she still believe he was a lousy bastard for standing her up?

Probably.

Kas put her arm around him. "Patrick said you can take more time off if you need to."

"You spoke to Patrick?"

"He phoned when you left the office. He sounded worried about you. I'm worried about you."

"I didn't want to stay in the office with Patrick."

Kas looked surprised. "Why ever not?"

Frank paused, unsure how much to tell Kas. But she would keep it to herself, and he needed to get things off his chest. "It's the drug trial."

"I'm sure he'll understand. The police will let you back in the lab soon and you can continue. Will you be able to manage everything without Ollie?"

"I hadn't even considered that." Yes, it would be hard without Ollie, and Henry wouldn't pay out to recruit a replacement anytime soon, not with the budget cuts he'd imposed. Frank wondered if they'd be able to float the company on the stock market after this. The murder would be bad publicity.

"Then what?"

"The drug trials are flawed. The drug's not nearly as effective as I first thought."

"But Martina..."

"That's why I can't face Patrick. I haven't told him yet." He felt a little better already, talking it over with Kas. He debated with himself whether to tell her his suspicions about Patrick possibly killing Ollie. He quashed the thought. Patrick couldn't have done that. He couldn't. And putting doubt into Kas's head about it wouldn't help anybody.

"But you were so sure about the drug. You've been getting excited for weeks."

"I made a mistake in the calculations." He couldn't blame Ollie, couldn't sully his name now that he was dead.

"But you never make mistakes."

"Well, I did this time." Frank silently rebuked himself for snapping at Kas, but he simply had to take the responsibility for the error. He could never confess the truth. Not only would that ruin Ollie's reputation, but it would do Frank himself no good either. He'd already been questioned by the police for what seemed like hours. Initially, they'd accused him of killing Ollie, even though he had an alibi, even though he loved the boy. If he blamed Ollie for this, the police would be all over him again. They would see it as a motive. In his current emotional turmoil, he might actually break down and confess to something he didn't do and would never do. Taking the blame for the mistake himself was the lesser of the two evils. He wouldn't even tell Kas the truth. Suddenly, he found more sympathy for Patrick. Remembering how he felt when the police questioned him, it must have been like that for Patrick too. How could he have doubted him for a single second? Some friend he was. Well, he would be a better one from now on.

Kas shook her head, as if she didn't really believe him. "What should I do, Kas? How am I going to tell Patrick?"

"He'll understand."

"No, he won't. Martina will probably die. I'm her last hope."

"So, can you fix it? Can you make the drug work?"

Frank was touched by Kas's faith in his ability, that same blind faith that had propelled him throughout his career. The saying was true, that behind every successful man is a woman. Kas had always pushed him to achieve more, encouraged him, made life easier for him. Sometimes he hadn't appreciated that enough. "I hope so," he said.

Chapter 24

Deborah was about to make a cup of tea and wallow in front of a daytime soap when the doorbell rang.

She considered ignoring the visitor, but the doorbell rang again. The caller clearly wasn't going to go away.

"Henry, what a nice surprise," she lied, wishing she hadn't opened the door. Normally, she'd be delighted to see him, especially when he came bearing flowers, chocolates, or jewellery. She was a bit peeved he'd turned up empty-handed this time. Even more annoying, now she would have to make conversation and she really wasn't in the mood. And she certainly wasn't in the mood for anything more than that.

"I came to check how you are."

"I'm ok," she said. He could have picked up the phone and asked her. But he still wouldn't have got a more truthful answer. She was not ok. Not ok at all. What with finding Ollie's body, those dreadful rats, and her pregnancy, something she still hadn't been able to make a decision on, she remained very un-ok. "Come in." She stood aside to let him pass.

Henry sat down. "The police say someone poisoned Ollie."

"Poisoned?" Immediately, Deborah wondered if the poison came from the lab, and if she might have inadvertently touched some of it, and if that tiny exposure would have harmed the unborn baby. The damn baby, like her subconscious kept telling her she wanted to keep it. Except she definitely didn't. Looking after a baby would be hell. It would screw up all her plans. She really didn't want a baby. So why did she keep putting off doing anything about it?

"Did he pick up something accidentally in the lab?" She knew that lab was dangerous. She always hated going in there. She'd been right.

"It could have been an accident," Henry said. "But the police don't seem to think so. They're getting in a right tizzy about it, interviewing everybody as if they'd done the deed."

THE COVER-UP

"They came here too," Deborah said. The two detectives had stayed for ages, asking question after question, until she'd wanted to scream at them to go away and leave her alone.

Henry came over and put his arm around her. Deborah snuggled into it, knowing Henry didn't do emotion or sympathy—something to do with his boarding school education. He certainly wasn't one of the new breed of upper-class men like Prince Harry, who wasn't afraid to talk about feelings and mental health in public. Prince Harry had practically made mental health trendy. But Henry was no Prince Harry in any way. It wouldn't get any better than this. She started to cry.

"Deborah, whatever's the matter? Surely you can't still be upset over Ollie."

Deborah sobbed some more. Henry's time limit on how long it might be reasonable to feel upset over finding a dead body seemed insensitively short.

Henry pulled away from her grasp. "Let me get you a drink," he said. "That will make everything seem better."

Henry returned a couple of minutes later with a half empty bottle of gin and two glasses.

"No, really." Deborah put out her hand to wave him away with the glass. "It's too early in the day." She needed to make some sort of excuse that wouldn't alert him to the real reason for her abstinence.

"Nonsense. Exceptional circumstances," Henry insisted. He poured her a large glass, then a much smaller one for himself. "Sorry, I didn't find any tonic."

"I don't want it." Deborah pushed the glass away. She considered knocking the glass on the floor, but he'd only pour her another one, and she'd still be left with cleaning up the mess.

"It really would help you to relax." Henry pushed the glass back towards her.

"I said NO." The words came out sounding so fierce that Henry jumped back.

"You should see a doctor or a grief counsellor or someone. I understand you've had a dreadful experience, but you're overreacting." Henry began edging towards the door.

Good. She would get her peaceful afternoon in front of the telly after all.

"And perhaps you should have that drink."

Something snapped inside Deborah. "I don't want an effing drink," she shouted. "I'm not drinking anything. I'm pregnant." Damn. She didn't mean to tell Henry that, not yet.

"Pregnant?" Henry fell into a nearby armchair. He looked a bit dazed. "You surely don't mean...?"

"Yes, I do mean... it's yours. You're the father."

"That's impossible."

"What sort of slut do you take me for? Of course it's yours. There's nobody else," Deborah said. "It's definitely your baby." She hadn't wanted to tell him for worry that he might try to influence her decision. But this denial, this total rejection of her, this desire of Henry's to suddenly get as far away from her as possible, was much worse. She wished she'd never opened her big gob.

"But..." Henry's mouth gaped open.

Deborah debated with herself whether to laugh or cry. She desperately wanted to cry. But Henry's face... he was more shocked than she had been when she'd discovered Ollie's body. Maybe she should tip some gin down his throat.

"Just go," she said. It was all over. He'd made it clear where he stood, even without actually saying so. She'd been a fool if she'd ever imagined that things would work out differently.

Chapter 25

Clarke arrived at the office early. As she went in through the staff entrance, the woman who worked with Frank in the lab came through the front door. Clarke immediately recognised her. "Carmen, isn't it? I'm Clarke. We met a few days ago, in the lab."

"Yes, I remember."

"I'm so sorry about Ollie. You must have known him well." Poor woman. She must be grieving.

"Yes. He was a nice young man. He didn't deserve to die."

"No. Of course not."

"I am so sorry for his parents. No one should lose a child. It's the worst thing that can happen." Carmen began to cry softly. "I'm sorry," she said. "I lost my daughter a few years ago. She would be Ollie's age now. She was such a gift. It took years before I managed to get pregnant. I was thirty-five when she was born. It was the hardest thing to lose her."

"I'm so sorry." Clarke wished she could come up with something deep and meaningful to say to help Carmen, but no mere words would change anything. "Are you all right?" Carmen was trying not to cry, and Clarke noticed she was twisting her wedding ring frantically. "Do you want me to call your husband?" Clarke asked.

"I'm a widow."

"I'm sorry," Clarke said for the millionth time. This was getting worse.

"My husband couldn't cope with losing our daughter," Carmen said by way of explanation.

Clarke understood Carmen's distress now. Ollie's death must have brought back some dreadful memories. She wondered if Frank noticed how much Carmen was struggling. Probably not. Frank was in a pretty bad way himself. Ollie's murder had come as a massive shock to everyone in the company. She resolved to keep an eye on Carmen herself, check in with her every day to make sure she was ok. Carmen looked like she needed a friend.

Carmen headed downstairs to the basement where the lab was situated. Clarke watched her go for a moment, then walked upstairs, planning to grab some coffees for her and Evan on the way.

The kitchen door was half-open. As Clarke rounded the corner, she overheard Frank and Patrick talking. Something about the tone of their voices made her hang back.

Patrick was becoming quite heated. "When will the new drug be ready for testing?"

"Not yet, Patrick, not while Deborah has frozen my budget. There's nothing I can do without funding."

"So, when? Martina is deteriorating every day. She can't wait."

"There's nothing I can do," Frank said. "I wish there were. And, with Ollie's murder, I can't even get into my lab at the moment."

"Can you just give her the drug, anyway? Please, Frank. You're our only hope. She's dying." Patrick glanced towards the door.

Clarke shrank back against the wall, hoping he wouldn't spot her.

"No. It's illegal. The drug hasn't been tested properly yet. Do you want me to end up in prison?"

Clarke noticed that Patrick didn't answer. She suspected he wouldn't care what happened to Frank, as long as Martina survived.

"I couldn't even if I wanted to. Whoever killed Ollie broke into the drugs cabinet in the lab. Emptied it out. I'd have to make some more, and that takes time. And I'd need to get back into the lab to do it."

"Who would do that? Steal the drugs, I mean."

"To be honest, Patrick, I thought it might have been you. Probably some junkie got into the building out of hours, but the police aren't even considering that theory."

Clarke wished she could see Patrick's face, but he'd turned away from her. She would really like to see his reaction to Frank's statement because she had considered the exact same thing, that Patrick might have stolen the drugs. Frank may be right.

"Whoever took the drugs might be dead by now," Frank continued. "Some of them are pretty strong. If they're used at the wrong dose, they can cause organ failure."

Clarke sneezed. Both men looked towards the door. She walked confidently in their direction, trying to act casual and hoping they would assume she'd only shown up at that moment. "Any coffee going spare?" she asked. Damn. She would have liked to listen to that conversation for a lot longer.

Chapter 26

"Do you want to hear my latest theory," Clarke said as she watched Paul tip a tonne of spaghetti into some boiling water. They were at his flat, on the outskirts of Brackford.

"Go on." Paul stirred some mince in the frying pan and poured over a jar of Bolognese sauce.

Clarke wished Paul would let her do the cooking when she visited his place. She shouldn't be discouraging him really, except that she would have made the sauce from scratch, and it would taste a whole lot better. Perhaps she should teach him to cook properly.

"Well, the company does drug testing on animals," she said. She reached over to the wine rack for a bottle of red. That would make the ready-made sauce taste much nicer.

Paul nodded.

Clarke passed him the wine, barely needing to stretch her arm out to reach Paul in his tiny kitchen. It would make more sense for him to move in with her. Her flat was bigger and nicer. He was paying a fortune in rent too. No one anywhere near London could afford to buy their own place these days. She'd been lucky, receiving a large compensation payout when she left the fire brigade after she got injured.

"It's possible that one of the animal rights activists murdered Ollie," she said. "They're always demonstrating outside the building." Yes, it would make sense for Paul to move in with her. But she kept holding back, wanting to hold on to her independence. Perhaps it was her, not Paul, with the commitment problem.

"Unlikely," Paul said. "They'd need to get in and out unnoticed, for a start."

Clarke conveniently ignored that issue. "I got accosted by some protestors on my first day at Carjon."

"You didn't tell me that. What happened?"

THE COVER-UP

Paul passed the half empty wine bottle back to Clarke, and she poured two glasses, handing him one. "They were demonstrating outside the main entrance. I had to walk through the group to get in. Things got a bit lively." The man with the curly black hair had certainly got quite heated. She imagined he might possess a violent streak. It wouldn't be far beneath the surface either. He had certainly scared her. Would he become violent enough to murder? He was passionate about his cause. Often, that was enough. That could easily turn into fanaticism, where he would stop at nothing to pursue his cause.

"It's a big step from waving a placard to murdering someone. In what way did it get lively?"

Clarke thought it was a very small step, once someone became fanatical about something, but she didn't want to argue the point and spoil the lovely atmosphere. "One of them wouldn't let me through. We got into an argument. It did get slightly scary." She played it down, not wanting to worry Paul. This was the first time she'd admitted to anyone that she'd been afraid.

"You didn't report the incident?" Paul asked.

"No, it didn't seem that bad."

"So, not bad enough to murder?" Paul stirred the sauce. It smelt good.

"You need to cook off the wine a bit more," she said. "No, it wasn't murderous, but it could easily have escalated."

"They would still need to access the building if they murdered Ollie." Paul pointed out again.

"Someone could have let one of them in the back way. Some of the protestors are very clever. They might have planned it in advance." Some of them were undoubtedly wasting their university education on something that, however morally correct, might one day land them in prison for a long time.

"It's unlikely," Paul said, draining the spaghetti.

"You might at least be open-minded."

"Who says I'm not open-minded?" Paul draped his arms around her and pulled her towards him.

Clarke looked up and smiled. Paul gazed at her like he used to when they first met, like she was the most amazing woman in the world, like he could never get enough of her. She stretched up and kissed him, her initial tiny peck on the lips turning into a full-on frenzy of passion. Finding out who killed Ollie would have to wait.

Chapter 27

"Hi, Erica, you wanted to see me?" Paul had received a message to come to Erica's office as soon as possible.

"Yes, I've got some results back." Erica scrolled down her computer screen.

"About time too."

"Not my fault. There's a huge backlog. You're lucky to get anything at all."

"Sorry." Paul didn't want to upset Erica. "So what did you find out?"

"The poison was in the coffee," Erica said.

"So why didn't Frank die too?"

"I don't know. You'll have to ask him. Did he drink the coffee?"

"No idea." Now that he recollected, there had only been one dirty coffee mug in the lab. That didn't mean Frank hadn't drunk any. He may have washed his mug before he left for the day.

Erica had her pensive face on. "Ollie's quite skinny." She looked through her notes on the computer screen. "Sixty-four kilos."

"So?" Paul didn't understand what Erica was getting at.

"So, how heavy would you say Frank is?"

Paul considered for a few moments. "He's got to be over a hundred. He's pretty big."

"So if he drank the coffee, he wouldn't react as badly as Ollie."

Or perhaps Frank poisoned Ollie, Paul reckoned.

"Are any of your suspects keen gardeners?"

"What?" Paul was puzzled. "What's that got to do with anything?"

"The poison was rhododendron," Erica said. "Easy to get hold of if you've got a bush in the garden. There are probably a few in Brackford's public parks too. Like I said, easy to get hold of."

"How would that get into the coffee?" It wasn't good news, that the poison was so easy to come by. It wouldn't narrow down the list of suspects.

"You can brew a tea with it," Erica said. "It's worth asking who made the coffee for Ollie. They could have slipped some of it into Ollie's drink and left the others alone."

"That would probably be Frank." Paul knew there was something wrong with Frank's original statement. Perhaps he'd been right about him all along.

"Or you could use honey from bees that have fed on the flowers. That wouldn't be so easy to find. You'd probably need to be a beekeeper and deliberately place the hive next to a rhododendron bush. That's definite pre-meditation, and anyway, you'd never be sure of the strength of it, and I'm not sure what honey would taste like in coffee. A bit sickly sweet, if you ask me."

"So, you're saying it's more likely that someone added rhododendron tea to the coffee."

"Maybe," Erica said, "but my guess would be that they dried the leaves, ground them to a fine powder, and mixed some into a jar of coffee."

"But that could have been anybody." Paul sighed.

"Anyone who had access, yes. That should narrow it down a lot. A laboratory would be a restricted area. Too many toxic substances." Erica laughed. "Funny that in a room full of poisons, someone picked a common garden bush to kill him off."

Paul didn't find it funny at all, but he understood Erica's sense of humour. She'd often told him that joking got her through the day, especially when the job got particularly gruesome.

"Thanks, Erica. At least now I've got the cause of death." It usually made his job easier, knowing the murder weapon, but that may not be the case this time. He couldn't even be certain now that Ollie was the intended victim. He would need to question Frank again. "And you're sure the time of death was late evening?"

"Pretty sure, but that won't help you much. The poison takes several hours to cause death, and the coffee may have been tampered with at any time."

Damn. That almost certainly ruled out Patrick Polkinghorne, which in turn ruled out any chance of a quick result on this case. "What are the symptoms of rhododendron poisoning?" Paul asked. He would need to check if anyone else at Carjon had been ill.

Erica counted off a list of symptoms on her fingers. "Nausea, diarrhoea, vomiting, and paralysis, for a start. The pulse slows down and blood pressure drops. Then you end up with seizures, coma, and death if it's not treated. He might have been lying on the floor for a few hours, completely unable to phone for help."

"Poor bloke." Paul felt ill just listening to Erica talk. "One more thing. Could it really have been in the coffee? Wouldn't that make it taste funny?"

"It's odourless, and I think also tasteless. Strong coffee would probably overpower any slight taste. And didn't you say that Ollie was a tea drinker?"

"Apparently, he hated coffee."

"Exactly. So, he wouldn't really notice anything. He'd already be expecting it to taste horrible." Erica clapped her hands. "Get out of my hair then. I've got work to do."

"Give me a call as soon as you find out anything else." Paul headed for the door.

"Don't I always?" Erica seemed annoyed.

"Yes, you do." Paul wondered why he'd said that. It always rubbed Erica up the wrong way. He should have learned that by now.

Chapter 28

Frank Varley had been in the police station for half an hour already. And they hadn't even started to question him yet. Technically, he had come in voluntarily, although it had taken a certain amount of coercion. Paul hoped he wouldn't decide to leave yet, as they didn't have enough evidence to arrest him.

"I don't understand what I'm doing here, Detective Sergeant Waterford."

"Please, call me Paul." Suspects always opened up more when they got on first-name terms with him. He'd seen a lot of female colleagues do that, with great results. They really empathised with the criminal. He wasn't so good at empathy, but he was trying because he desperately wanted the results his female colleagues got.

Frank fidgeted in his chair. Paul took his time, not saying anything yet. He wanted Frank to worry a bit. That way he might make mistakes, let things slip. The empathy thing only went so far, at least with him.

At last, he spoke. "Do you drink a lot of coffee, Frank?"

"Yes, white with two sugars, please."

"I wasn't offering," Paul snapped, annoyed that his question had been misinterpreted. *Empathy score down to zero. Must try harder.* He took a deep breath and recomposed himself. "I'll see what I can do." He got up and wandered around the room, trying to concentrate.

Frank started to twitch. Paul felt his gaze following him around the interview room nervously. *Empathy score minus one.* "Interview suspended at eleven hundred hours." He clicked off the recording. "Barry, get some coffee, please."

When Barry returned with the coffee, Paul made an effort to smile at Frank, hoping to put him at ease. "Sorry, it's only machine rubbish," he said.

"Thanks." Frank slid the plastic cup closer, hugging it with both hands.

"What about Ollie? Did he drink a lot of coffee?"

Frank shook his head. "No, he didn't really like it. Ollie usually drank tea. He loved his Earl Grey."

Paul had already heard that, but he'd wanted to hear Frank admit it. Erica had been adamant that Ollie had coffee in his stomach. "So, the day he died, did he drink any coffee?"

"No. I mean, yes," Frank said.

"Which? Did Ollie drink coffee, or didn't he?" Frank sounded as confused as Paul.

"Yes, he did. We ran out of tea bags, so Ollie had to drink coffee."

Paul smiled at Frank, remembering he needed to work on his empathy. "Did you have coffee too?"

"I always have coffee. Can't function without the stuff," Frank said.

Paul smiled again, this time to himself. A clear admission of guilt would be better, but this was a good start. "The thing is, Frank, Ollie was poisoned by the coffee."

Frank's mouth dropped open. He seemed like he was trying to talk, but no words came out.

Sod the empathy. Paul moved in for the kill. "So, how come you didn't get sick, Frank? Doesn't that seem a bit odd to you? It seems odd to me. Did you poison the coffee, Frank? Did you kill Ollie?"

"No, no, I would never do that. I loved Ollie like a son."

Paul smelt the sweat pouring off of Frank. He wondered if he should push him a bit more. That might cause him to really panic, followed by a confession.

"I want a solicitor," Frank said.

Damn. Paul still didn't have enough evidence to make an arrest stick but didn't want to risk Frank leaving until he'd checked out this new development thoroughly. He asked Barry to keep an eye on him while he organised the duty solicitor.

Frank was distraught. He'd only agreed to come into the police station to be helpful because he wanted the police to find out who had killed Ollie. Now that arrogant detective expected him to stay even longer and endure even more questions. Did the detective really think he'd poisoned Ollie? Frank wracked his brains. How could he prove he would never hurt him? The grumpy detective sergeant was pushing him for an answer. How come Ollie had been poisoned, but not him? It didn't make sense when he'd first found out about the coffee. But now Frank remembered he *had* been ill.

"I've been getting stomach pains all last week," Frank said. "Not really bad pain, but something was wrong and I couldn't work out what." He wondered if the coffee caused his dodgy stomach. But he'd had loads of coffee last week and Ollie had drunk one cup. It's possible the coffee only got poisoned that day. But the fact hit him like a thunderbolt. If the coffee was poisoned, nobody intended to kill Ollie. Not anyone who knew him well. Frank finally realised, they must have intended to kill him instead.

He should be dead now.

Who would want him dead?

"Ollie only ever drank tea. It's the first time I've known him to drink coffee, and that was only because we'd run out of tea bags. So the murderer couldn't have intended to poison Ollie." Could they? Frank wouldn't admit to the police officers that he was the one who'd forgotten to buy tea bags. They'd probably assume he'd done it deliberately so Ollie would be forced to drink coffee.

"We'd like to take a blood test," Paul said.

"What poison was it?" Frank possessed an encyclopaedic knowledge of toxins. If he knew what they were dealing with, he might be able to help. That would be a lot more productive than taking a blood test, which would be a total waste of time. By now, anything he'd ingested on the day of the murder would have already left his bloodstream. He had no way to prove his innocence.

"I can't release that information."

Frank didn't like not having all the facts. Were the police allowed to accuse him like this, whilst withholding vital information? Perhaps he should wait for the solicitor.

"When did you get ill? What symptoms did you have?"

"I felt sick. I threw up once, but I just felt sick all the time. It wasn't even that bad." The symptoms had stopped the day after Ollie had died. It explained everything.

Frank suddenly remembered something. "Deborah was ill too. She threw up in the office upstairs." He couldn't remember which day that had been. She rarely came down to the lab, and he didn't recall her ever drinking anything during any of her brief visits. Deborah normally couldn't wait to leave. Did that mean the coffee upstairs had been poisoned too, or had Deborah touched some trace of the poison elsewhere? It would be more useful if they told him the name of the poison.

"We'll look into that. Did you get on with Ollie?"

"Like I already said, he was like a son to me. He was just a kid. I would have never killed him."

"He's twenty-two. That's not a kid. That's old enough to be a threat. Did he threaten you?"

"What, Ollie?" Frank laughed. "He would never hurt anyone, not even a fly."

"So, what did he do to upset you? Not finish his work on time? Screw up some experiment? Did you get frustrated with him?"

"No." Frank shook his head. "Ollie was brilliant. He got a first-class degree from Cambridge. He could have worked anywhere. I never understood why he wanted to work at Carjon, when he could have got a job with one of the big pharmaceutical companies and been fast-tracked for promotion."

"So, let's suppose for a moment that someone wanted to poison you and not Ollie at all. Who would want to do that?"

"How should I know?" Frank wished he had some idea. It terrified him, knowing that someone wanted him dead, but not having a clue who he needed to be scared of. In the future, he'd certainly be a lot more careful about what he ate. He didn't like the direction this interview was taking. He hadn't done anything wrong, and he wanted all this to stop.

"So why would anyone want to kill you, Frank? Did you fall out with someone in the company? What about Henry? Did Henry want an easy way of getting you out of the company without paying you off?"

"No, that's ridiculous. I've been friends with Henry for years. We shared a flat at university. Patrick too. And I own a share of the company with the two of them. He can't get rid of me that easily." Henry had put up most of the capital to start the company. He and Patrick only owned ten percent each, nowhere near enough to ever outvote Henry.

"Precisely," Paul said. "He can't get rid of you. Unless you're dead."

"No, Henry would never do that." That was unthinkable. "And I haven't done anything to upset him. He's really excited about the new drug we're testing. The company can't function without me. I'm the lifeblood of the company." Without new products, new drugs, the company would stagnate. Suddenly, Frank began to wonder whether he might be replaceable, whether he had inflated his own importance. And what if someone wanted to ruin the company? An easy way to do that would be to get rid of the star research scientist.

Paul made a mental note to check with Erica whether Frank could have taken a mild dose of the poison himself deliberately, to allay suspicion. Or did he lie about the whole thing? Maybe he wasn't ill at all. It would be impossible to prove since he'd been too stupid to go to the doctor.

He realised he needed to talk to Clarke as well. The company hadn't brought in forensic accountants for no reason. There might be something in the work she was doing that would help him. Now he wished he'd paid more attention the other day when she'd been telling him about it. He'd better butter her up pretty damn well, or she wouldn't tell him anything. But how was he going to get any information from her without alerting her to the fact that her investigation might be connected to his? Because he knew Clarke well—once he planted that seed, she'd start investigating it further, poking her nose into places she shouldn't. He wouldn't just be planting the seed, he'd be watering it, putting plant food on it, and buying a new greenhouse to grow it in. He dreaded Clarke putting herself in danger like she did before. She needed protecting from herself.

Perhaps he should talk to Evan instead. He'd need to insist that Evan didn't tell Clarke. If she found out he'd gone to Evan behind her back instead of asking her, she would kill him, especially as she was already upset with him. Just because he didn't want to spread news of their relationship all over the police station, it didn't mean he didn't care. He cared a lot.

She did seem to be a bit oversensitive about it. Well, it was too late to do anything about that. If he admitted his involvement with her now, he'd be in big trouble, and he'd get chucked off this case for sure because she was a witness. Clarke was one of the first to find the body.

"Who else might want to kill you, Frank? What about your wife? How's your marriage?"

"My marriage is fine," Frank protested.

Paul made a note to interview Frank's wife. Frank had been a little too quick to deny any problems and rather too adamant about it. He wondered if things weren't all rosy in the Varley household. It was often the wife. And poison was a very female weapon because it didn't require any strength and because the perpetrator didn't have to wait around and see the dead body. Clean and easy. A woman's weapon.

He started wondering about other women in the company. "What about Deborah? Do you get on well with her?"

Frank hesitated. "Yes," he said.

"You're not sure?"

"Oh, Deborah doesn't get on with anyone. She's a bit touchy."

Frank looked like he regretted saying that. Paul would interview Deborah again first thing tomorrow. He couldn't imagine why she would want to kill Frank, but he might learn something more when he spoke to her.

"What about your other lab assistant?" Paul asked.

Frank looked confused for a moment. "Who? Carmen? She's not really a lab assistant. She cleans and helps care for the rats, stuff like that."

"But she has access to everything?"

"Yes, but... she would never hurt Ollie. Neither of us would. We're like a little family in the lab."

Paul silently agreed. Carmen de Silva wasn't a serious suspect. But he would talk to her, anyway.

Chapter 29

"We'll have to cancel our plans to work this weekend," Evan said. "I'd completely forgotten I'm meant to be going to a wedding. It's my girlfriend's brother. There's no way I can get out of going."

"No, of course not. You go and enjoy yourself. I'll get more work done on my own, anyway." Clarke had already cancelled her weekend plans when Evan asked her to work. She may as well come in. Otherwise, she'd only be sitting at home on her own.

"No," Evan said firmly. "You can't go in alone at the weekend, Clarke."

"Of course I can. If I get stuck on anything, I'll go home early."

Evan snapped the lid of his laptop shut. "No, I mean, it's too dangerous. Someone's just been murdered here. I don't want you to be the next victim."

"But Henry really wanted us to snoop around at the weekend while the building's empty."

"Well, it will have to wait until next weekend. I'm not putting you at risk."

"I'll be careful." Clarke didn't need Evan to look after her. She'd be perfectly ok on her own.

"No. Absolutely no. Ten times no. I've already had your other half on the phone worried about you."

"What? Paul phoned you?"

"Calm down. He only wanted to find out what we were working on, in case it might be relevant to his investigation."

"Then why the hell didn't he ask me?" She'd already discussed with Paul what they were doing at Carjon. Why would he go behind her back to talk to Evan as well? She took a deep breath. She admonished herself for becoming paranoid. Of course Paul would want to talk to Evan. He was in charge of the job they were doing. "Sorry," she said. "I didn't mean to bite your head off. I'm being stupid."

"Yes," Evan said. "Anyway, if you must know, he didn't want to discuss things with you because he's worried that you'll get too involved and put yourself in danger, which is fair enough, considering there's a murderer still on the loose."

"That's not fair," Clarke said. "I wouldn't do anything stupid. He can't tell me what to do."

"Maybe not, but while we're working here, *I* can. And I don't want you coming in tomorrow when the building's empty."

"I'm still going to kill him," Clarke said, angry with Paul for discussing her like that with her boss.

"Can you just forget I told you all that? Paul asked me not to tell you."

"He shouldn't interfere."

"He's worried about you. He doesn't want you to get hurt. I'm guessing because he loves you."

Clarke stayed silent for a moment. Evan was right. And she should be more grateful that Paul did actually care about her.

"Ok. I won't mention it to Paul." She'd have calmed down by the time she saw him next, anyway.

"And you won't come into the office tomorrow."

Clarke shook her head. If she didn't actually voice the words, it wasn't really a lie.

Clarke got up and walked over to the window, still annoyed that both Evan and Paul assumed she needed babysitting. They were totally overreacting. Just because Ollie had been murdered, it didn't mean anyone would want to kill *her*. She would be absolutely fine on her own.

She gazed out the window. The animal rights group marched wearily around the building's forecourt, a much smaller number of them than last week. Perhaps the murder, plastered all over the local news, had put some of them off. Certainly, they didn't appear quite as intimidating as previously, but then she was safely out of their reach this time, not in the thick of things trying to get past them. They still worried her a little, but at least they wouldn't be around at the weekend.

The demonstrators ambled up and down lethargically, carrying their banners like a burden, instead of waving them aggressively like they'd done before. Clarke searched for the curly-haired man who had accosted her last time, but he was nowhere to be seen. He seemed to be the leader. Was that why they'd lost their sense of purpose, because of his absence? She doubted they would have calmed down out of any sense of respect for Ollie.

"I'm off home now." Evan broke her thoughts. "It's a five-hour drive if we can avoid the traffic. We want to get a head start before the Friday afternoon rush."

Clarke looked at her watch. Nearly lunchtime. "Where's the wedding?" She hoped he hadn't already told her. She hadn't been paying much attention.

"Wales. Snowdonia. It's a beautiful location, but why can't they get married closer to home? Plenty of nice places in London."

"You'd better get on the road," Clarke said.

Evan transferred his bags to one hand so he could open the door. "See you Monday."

Clarke sat down. With Evan out of the way in the depths of Wales, she could do what she liked, with no chance of him walking in and surprising her. And she really didn't have anything better to do this weekend.

Chapter 30

Paul and Barry visited Carmen de Silva at her home, in a cheap block of council flats in Havebury. It didn't seem worth taking her to the police station, not yet. Easier to find out what she said first.

"This won't take long," Paul said. "Can we come in?"

Reluctantly, Carmen stepped aside to allow the two detectives into the dingy hallway. During his seven years in the police, Paul had become accustomed to negative reactions. No one ever seemed pleased when he showed up to question them, and certainly not when he came to arrest them. Even when they turned out to be innocent, people didn't like the police coming round their house, more so in places like this, which traditionally were hotbeds of petty crime. Things improved when he joined CID and ditched the uniform. But he was rarely made welcome. He'd developed a thick skin to deal with it. The unenthusiastic reception didn't bother him now. He barely even noticed it.

At least the shabby and sparsely furnished living room was clean. Barry sat on one end of the sofa. Paul waited for Carmen to sit down. He always liked to be ready in case the suspect tried to abscond, although he reminded himself that Carmen de Silva was very low risk, and not even a suspect.

"How long did you work with Ollie Jenner?" Paul resolved to adopt a softer approach with Carmen, who acted like a frightened mouse. This would be an ideal opportunity for him to work on his empathy skills.

"How can he be dead?" Carmen began to cry. "He's so young. He shouldn't have died."

Paul decided to ignore the fact that Carmen hadn't answered the question, not wanting to push her too hard. It must be difficult for her to process Ollie's pointless death. Because it didn't seem to have any point, not as far as he could work out.

"How did Frank get on with Ollie?"

Carmen wiped her eyes, sniffling loudly. "Frank put a lot of pressure on him. He expected everyone to meet his high standards."

"What sort of pressure?" Paul wondered if Frank could have been driven to murder if Ollie had persistently fallen short of his expectations.

"Ollie was inexperienced." Carmen blew her nose. "Frank didn't like it if he didn't get everything perfect. All Frank cares about is his work." She started to cry again.

"Barry, can you make Carmen a cup of tea?" Paul said, pointing towards what he assumed must be the kitchen.

"There's coffee by the kettle," Carmen sobbed. "And the cups…"

"I'll find them." Barry went to make the coffee.

Paul was confused. Carmen painted a very different picture than Frank. Frank had portrayed Ollie as some sort of genius golden boy. Carmen's take on things made Paul want to interview Frank Varley again, explore his real relationship with Ollie, find out whether Ollie might have screwed up enough to make Frank kill him.

Carmen continued to cry. If Paul was a female officer, he would put his arm around her and try to comfort her. But that sort of thing was a minefield these days, especially with Barry out of the room. She might accuse him of all sorts of things he had no intention of doing. He let her cry. Eventually, she would stop. He wondered if she was too overemotional to be a good witness.

Barry came back in, carrying three mugs of coffee. He set them down on the small table next to Carmen, sploshing coffee over the rims.

Paul hurried into the kitchen to find a cloth to wipe up the mess, cursing Barry. He grabbed a dishcloth from the draining board. While doing so, he automatically scanned the room for anything useful, anything that might tell him more about Carmen. A pineapple-shaped magnet pinned a photo of a very pretty girl to the fridge. Judging by her age and her resemblance to Carmen, Paul guessed it might be her daughter. A calendar hung by the door. Nothing much there. A doctor's appointment, the days she was working at Carjon marked up, and a big star on Saturday of next week, probably for her time of the month. He took a quick photo on his phone. It might be useful to check the days she'd been working.

Carmen had stopped crying and was sipping coffee when Paul came back into the living room. Barry hugged her as they chatted cheerfully. Paul made a mental note to discuss that with Barry in the car on the way back to the station.

Paul wiped up the coffee drips on the table and gulped a mouthful of coffee. Barry made rubbish coffee. That's another thing they would need to discuss.

They weren't going to get anything else useful out of Carmen. "We need to get back to the station," Paul said. "If we need anything else, we'll be in touch."

Carmen nodded and started to get up.

Paul signalled her to stay put. "We can let ourselves out."

"So, what did we learn from that?" Barry asked as Paul steered the car out into the road.

"You make crap coffee," Paul said.

"Sorry, Guv."

"We need to interview Frank Varley again." Paul slowed down for the corner before firing the powerful Audi out of the bend. "His version of happy families in the chemistry lab doesn't tally with Carmen's take on things."

"I noticed that too," Barry said.

"Let's go straight to Carjon. He'll probably still be at work."

Frank was about to go home when Paul and Barry came into his lab.

"We need a chat," Paul said.

Frank sighed. Didn't he answer all their questions last time? "Sit down." He pointed to a couple of empty chairs. He'd only been allowed back into the lab this afternoon and he'd hoped to have some time to himself to start tidying up the mess that the forensic team had left it in.

"No, not that one." Frank intended the detectives to sit on the other side of him, but they'd headed one to each side. "That's Ollie's chair," he said lamely. He didn't want anyone sitting there. It didn't feel right.

The detective sergeant, Paul, didn't move. Frank wondered if they were deliberately trying to upset him. He realised it might not be personal. How could they possibly realise the gut-wrenching sorrow that still gripped him every time he even looked at Ollie's desk? He turned towards the younger detective, trying to ignore Ollie's violated chair.

"Tell me about Ollie's work. Did he have any problems with it?"

Frank was forced to look at the detective sergeant, Paul, to answer him. *It's just a chair*, he told himself. Except it wasn't. "No, of course he didn't have problems. Ollie was outstanding and hardworking too."

Paul stared at him. "Was he so outstanding that you put extra pressure on him to succeed, to see how far he could go?"

"I didn't have to." Ollie's ambition and drive reminded Frank of himself at that age. "I couldn't possibly have pushed him harder than he pushed himself." Frank wished he understood what Paul was getting at. Surely, he didn't think Frank might have driven Ollie to suicide or anything like that. They'd already stated he'd been murdered, hadn't they?

"And he never once got anything wrong or upset you?"

"No." No way would Frank tell him about Ollie's error in the calculations. He would take the blame for that himself, wouldn't sully Ollie's good reputation, wouldn't implicate himself in a murder he didn't commit. He hadn't even discovered the error until after Ollie died—yet another thing he wouldn't be able to prove.

Paul stood up and walked across the room. "So, you're saying that Ollie was a freaking genius and never once got anything wrong."

"No, that's not what I'm saying. But he was exceptionally good. He didn't make mistakes." Frank tried to say the words with confidence, hoping Paul wouldn't detect any hint of a lie. He felt his cheeks flushing and wiped his hand across his face, hoping Paul wouldn't notice. Weren't detectives trained to spot everything? Frank didn't understand why he felt so guilty, when he really hadn't done anything wrong. He needed to stop worrying.

"If you've finished, I'd like to go home," Frank said.

Paul nodded. "That's all for now, but we'll be back."

Frank remained seated while he watched the two detectives leave. When Paul said they'd be back, it sounded like a threat. He wondered why they were taking this sudden renewed interest in him. What did they know?

Chapter 31

Clarke got up early on Saturday. She would go into the office for a couple of hours, snoop around, then take the rest of the day for herself.

The building was eerily silent. Clarke shut the staff entrance door from the car park behind her, waited for the automatic lock to click, then headed straight upstairs to the boardroom. There were no other cars in the car park, so she expected the building would be empty, but at least if she got her laptop out, she could pretend to be working rather than snooping if anyone showed up unannounced.

She set the coffee percolator going and started in Henry's office. Why Henry would call in a team of forensic accountants to investigate if he himself was the guilty party, Clarke simply couldn't fathom. She would probably be wasting her time. But this might be the only chance she got to rummage around his office. And people's minds worked in mysterious ways. No one should be above suspicion.

Henry had provided her with a complete set of keys but, to her surprise, most of the internal doors were unlocked.

She found nothing of interest in Henry's office. Henry seemed to take the paperless office concept seriously. Apart from a couple of trade magazines, Clarke found no paperwork at all. Her younger brother, Rob, would be useful here. He was a genius with computers. He'd be able to access everyone's computer, even recovering any recently deleted files. That would be where Henry stored everything. She would suggest to Evan on Monday that they should bring in a computer expert to check Carjon's network for further evidence.

The aroma of freshly brewed coffee drew Clarke back to the kitchen. She poured herself a cup and sat down to make a plan.

She'd got another letter from the prison yesterday. It was a request to visit. If only she could talk it through with Paul, but he'd been working silly hours on this murder case and she'd barely seen him.

Clarke shook herself. It was no good wallowing like this. She needed to focus on the job and plan where to search next.

Hopefully, not everyone in the office embraced the paperless ethos as much as Henry. She'd certainly seen piles of documents on Patrick's desk before. And Frank's lab was a treasure trove, assuming the police forensic team hadn't taken away everything of interest.

Clarke took her coffee into Patrick's office and sat at his desk, overjoyed to find stacks of paperwork. She got stuck into a heap of papers in his out-tray, immediately pouncing on several invoices. Perhaps she should take them back to the boardroom to check if any of them matched the lists of year-end creditors on her laptop. But when she looked at them more closely, they all seemed to be for drugs of some sort, or perhaps ingredients to make drugs, and all were addressed to Patrick Polkinghorne personally.

Why would Patrick be buying drugs? Were they for his wife's cancer? Surely the hospital would prescribe drugs for her. Evan had a pharmacist friend. Perhaps he could check what the drugs were used for.

She turned on the photocopier to warm up while she finished her coffee and washed up the mug. Her laptop wasn't connected to the company network. Pity. It would have been much easier to scan the invoices. Never mind. Copies would do the job.

As soon as she'd done her photocopying, she headed to Deborah's office.

Deborah's desk was cluttered with photos and ornaments. The photos were mostly of herself. Various exotic paperweights seemed to be decorative, rather than functional. A small vase of half-wilted flowers sat precariously close to the desk's edge.

At the back of one of her drawers, tucked behind a pile of business magazines, Clarke found an unused pregnancy test. Was Deborah pregnant? Nobody bought one of those tests unless they believed they were pregnant, in which case, why hadn't she used it? Unless she'd bought a second test as a backup. If she was right about Deborah having an affair with Henry, then she could be expecting Henry's baby. That changed everything. It would certainly give a powerful motive for Deborah to alter the accounts to help the company. Clarke counted the months in her head. Deborah wasn't showing any outward signs of pregnancy yet. There was no way she could have been pregnant when the accounts were altered. It was all supposition, in any case.

Clarke found nothing particularly exciting in any of the offices. Perhaps a trawl through the computer network would throw up something, although no doubt anything incriminating would have been long since deleted.

Suddenly, Clarke thought she heard a door slam. She froze for a moment. The building was silent. She'd probably imagined it. Empty buildings were full of creaks other and strange noises. *Ignore it and focus,* she told herself. Only one place left to search. The sooner she got on with it, the better, then she could get out of here and go home. She was beginning to think that Evan might have been right: she shouldn't have come here on her own.

She grabbed one of the paperweights from Deborah's desk and went out into the corridor, shutting the door behind her.

The most interesting place in the building was Frank's lab. The police had searched it thoroughly, but a fresh pair of eyes might unearth something they might have missed.

She walked down the stairs, rolling the blue glass paperweight in her hands until she found a good grip. It was just a precaution, she told herself. It made her feel better, not as helpless. But, honestly, she was being stupid. Whoever killed Ollie—they must have wanted something specific. They wouldn't want her.

Frank's lab was locked. It seemed to be the only place in the whole building that was. Of course, he kept drugs there, hence the enhanced level of security. Clarke turned the key and crept in.

A bang from the other end of the lab startled her. It was closely followed by a piercing scream.

"Who's there?" Clarke clutched at the paperweight, lifting it up, ready to throw it and run if need be. She hadn't expected anyone to be here, not with the door locked. "Who's there? Come out."

"Clarke. You frightened me." Carmen appeared from behind the rat cages.

Immediately, Clarke relaxed. She dropped the paperweight. It crashed onto the floor and shattered.

"I'm so sorry, Carmen. To be honest, I was a bit surprised myself. What are you doing here?"

"I came in to feed the rats and clean out the cages," Carmen said. "There's no one else to do it. I normally share the job with Frank and Ollie." Carmen walked over to Clarke. "Ollie used to do weekends most of the time. He liked the extra money."

They both looked at the mess on the floor, the fragments of blue glass catching the light and glittering like sapphires.

"I'll get a dustpan and brush?" Carmen said.

"Thanks. It's Deborah's. She's going to kill me." Clarke would have to admit it to her on Monday. She'd offer to buy her another one. She only hoped it didn't have sentimental value.

When she had swept up the mess, Clarke sat down and pointed to the chair next to her. Carmen perched on the edge of it, as if she wanted to be ready to flee at any moment.

"I'm sorry, it must be hard for you having to keep coming in here, under the circumstances." Clarke wondered why Carmen locked the door behind her just to feed the rats. She supposed Ollie's death may have made her nervous about being alone in an empty building.

Clarke almost suggested making some coffee. Just in time, she remembered that the coffee in the lab had been poisoned. Although the poisoned coffee would have been removed by the police, she still wouldn't want to risk it, even with a new jar. She should really play safe and bring in a jar of instant for herself and Evan, but the fancy Costa Rican blend tasted too good. She didn't want to give it up that easily.

A loud squeak came from the far corner of the lab. Both women turned towards the noise.

"I need to finish feeding them." Carmen got up from her chair.

Clarke followed her. "I suppose you must get attached to the rats, same as Frank."

"I'm just here to do a job." Carmen took a bag of feed out of the cupboard next to the cages. "The rats have a job to do too. We need to test drugs thoroughly before risking them on people. It's more important not to risk people dying." She poured some feed into each of the hoppers attached to the sides of the cages.

Clarke assumed it would be a more scientific process, weighing out each rat's feed to the nearest gram. Carmen's feeding method seemed somewhat haphazard, but Clarke didn't like to say anything.

"You're not a fan of those animal rights protestors then. I've had a couple of run-ins with them. They're a bit scary."

Carmen shrugged. "They're ok," she said. "Just a bit misguided."

Clarke wondered what the man with the curly black hair would say to being called *misguided*. She guessed there would probably be a lot of F-words involved.

Carmen replaced the bag of feed in the cupboard, slamming the door shut. She checked her watch. "I need to go." She seemed flustered. "I've missed my bus."

"I can give you a lift home," Clarke said, regretting the offer almost as soon as she said it, even though she was to blame for Carmen being late. "I need to pack up my stuff. I'll be ready in ten minutes."

"Thank you. That's very kind."

"I'll see you in reception." Clarke raised her voice to be heard over the sound of running water, as Carmen washed her hands vigorously in the sink further along the wall.

Carmen stood waiting when Clarke came down the stairs. They exited into the staff car park. Clarke's VW Polo was still the sole occupant.

"Where do you live?" Clarke asked, regretting she hadn't found that out sooner.

"Havebury. Are you sure this is ok?"

"Of course." Havebury was out of her way, so it would take her an extra thirty minutes to make the detour. She felt responsible for Carmen missing her bus. If she hadn't got her talking for so long, the poor woman would probably be halfway home by now. Taking her home was the least she could do.

Forty minutes later, Clarke pulled up in front of a tired-looking block of flats in South Havebury.

"Thank you." Carmen smiled weakly. "This is very kind of you."

Clarke gave her a big smile back. Carmen looked so worn down. Clarke was sure she'd aged in the few days since they'd first met, hardly surprising, with such a close colleague in their small team being murdered. It must be devastating for her. As Clarke accelerated down the road, she renewed her resolve to keep an eye on Carmen to make sure she was coping.

It was late by the time Paul came over.

"Sorry," he said. "We're working all hours, trying to solve this murder."

Clarke gave him a hug. She was well aware of the pressure his job put on him. "I'm glad you showed up, eventually." She poured him a beer.

"Thanks. I wanted to ask you about Carmen de Silva. Have you met her?"

"Yes, she works with Frank in the lab." She hoped Carmen wasn't one of Paul's suspects. The woman had enough issues without him adding to her stress.

"What do you know about her?"

Clarke paused for a moment, realising how little she did know about Carmen. "She's devastated about Ollie," she said. "She had a daughter who died, and she's a widow. I think she's very lonely."

Paul took a gulp of his beer. "Yes, judging by her calendar, she doesn't have a wild social life. All she's got marked on it is her work days and a big star for Saturday next week, which I'm guessing is for her time of the month, rather than any wild social outing."

"Paul, that's really none of your business. Leave the poor woman alone." She felt so sorry for Carmen. She didn't deserve to have Paul joking about her bodily functions to his mates at the station.

"Sorry." Paul looked sheepish. He draped his arms around Clarke's neck and kissed her.

"Have you found out anything else?" Clarke asked.

Paul gazed into her eyes. "You know I'm not supposed to tell you stuff."

"But I'm expected to help you, right?"

"That's different."

Clarke didn't think it was so very different. She poured him another beer, wondering how much alcohol she would need to ply him with to get more answers. She gave a big yawn. It was getting late. Making Paul talk to her might just have to wait until another day.

Chapter 32

Clarke arrived at Carjon Pharma's offices on Monday morning well before Evan. She wanted to be sure she hadn't left any incriminating signs of being in the office on Saturday. Evan was generally pretty easy-going, but he did give her specific instructions not to go into the office on her own. She didn't want to find out the hard way how he might react to her blatant disobedience.

She needn't have got up quite so early. After the long drive home from Wales the previous day, Evan showed up quite late.

"How did the wedding go?" Clarke asked.

"Great," Evan said. "I brought you a piece of wedding cake." He delved into his briefcase and pulled out a small box.

Clarke smiled. She liked cake. "Thanks."

"We need to start collating all the evidence we've accumulated so far," Evan said. "Can you write up everything you've done by the end of the day and we'll see what's left to do?"

"No problem." She'd organised most of it already, so she would easily finish the task today.

"I can't do this anymore," Kerry said. "I'm sure Patrick suspects."

"That's rubbish. Patrick only cares about his wife right now. You must have noticed that. He hasn't got time to worry about anything else." Carmen shut the door to the kitchen, obviously worried that someone might overhear.

"But I feel bad about lying to him." Much more than that, Kerry admitted to herself. It seemed traitorous lying to Patrick.

Carmen shrugged. "He'll never find out. Not if you don't tell him."

Kerry ignored her. "What were you doing on Saturday?" she asked. "I saw you getting into Clarke's car. Did you tell her anything?"

"No, of course I didn't."

Kerry didn't completely believe her. It would be so easy for Carmen to drop a few hints deliberately. Clarke was an outsider, with no loyalties to anyone in the company, least of all her. From what she'd observed of Clarke Pettis so far, Kerry was certain she wouldn't ignore anything like that. It would be Kerry getting into trouble, not Carmen. All the proof led back to her, and she had absolutely nothing to show Carmen's involvement. Kerry shook her head sadly. She'd been an idiot to agree to do this. Carmen had blackmailed her into it, making her feel guilty over Annie.

"You can't say anything," Carmen said. "You'll go to prison."

"It's not my responsibility. You shouldn't have made me do it." Kerry didn't like that threat hanging over her. At least Carmen didn't pick up on her being outside the office on Saturday. She hadn't meant to let that piece of information slip out. Luckily, Carmen was so concerned with saving her own skin, she'd completely ignored the fact that Kerry had been snooping on her. She hoped Carmen wouldn't recall it later and start interrogating her again. She'd need to make up some reasonable excuse for being here, like a shopping trip to Brackford.

"They won't see it like that," Carmen said.

"Is that why you got me to do your dirty work? So I'd suffer? Do you still blame me for Annie's death? Because that's not my fault."

"Of course it is. The drug trial was your idea. If you hadn't suggested it, Annie would still be here." Carmen turned away from her, too late to stop Kerry from seeing a tear roll down her cheek.

"She wanted to do it." Did Carmen think she wasn't already wracked with guilt over Annie's death? Annie had been her friend. And even after two years, she still missed her. And she still felt responsible, even though Annie's death wasn't her fault at all. "I didn't realise it would be dangerous. Anyway, they always explain the risks to everyone." Kerry knew that for a fact, from when she'd done a drug trial herself. It was easy money. Annie needed to fund her South American trip, the one she sadly never got to take, so of course Kerry suggested the drug trial. She'd been doing Annie a favour. "They don't just let anyone take part. They always do loads of health checks." Annie was young and fit. She shouldn't have died. Kerry knew Carmen thought the same thing. That was why Carmen would never accept Annie's death.

She deeply regretted getting Carmen the job at Carjon because now Carmen could pressure her every day. Kerry needed to find a way out of this situation. Carmen was right. Kerry could go to prison. Worse still, she would always be at Carmen's beck and call, and she would dig herself in deeper and deeper to avoid Carmen dropping her in it. "I can't do anything else for you," she said, wondering if she was wasting her breath uttering the words. She needed this to stop. She needed to get her life back.

"That's ok. I'm not going to ask for anything else."

Kerry didn't believe anything Carmen said now. She'd said exactly that the first time, but then she still came back for more. Why couldn't she just accept that Annie's death had been a tragic accident? That's what the coroner said. It really wasn't Frank's fault. Kerry liked Frank, and he was good at his job, meticulous in everything he did. There's no way he would have made a mistake, or not triple-checked every last thing. The truth was, she knew for certain that Frank didn't make any mistakes.

On the third day of the drug trial, Annie had told her that a few of the participants had swapped drugs. They thought it would be a laugh to screw up the trial. Three grand they'd been paid, and they wanted to screw things up. Kerry didn't approve one bit, but if she said anything, she'd get her friend into trouble, so she kept quiet. Annie told her how much she wanted to visit South America and explore the city her mother came from. She'd needed that money. So, some of the people in the placebo group got the real drug, and some of the people who should have received the real drug got a useless placebo. That must have really messed up Frank's results. Although not very many of them got involved in the swap, Kerry still felt guilty about not telling anyone. She should have told the coroner during the inquest. The other girls involved should have said something. Kerry waited for one of them to confess, but they didn't.

It was too late to admit it now. Besides, how would she prove it? Equally, she couldn't admit what she'd done to falsify the accounts. She laughed suddenly.

"What are you laughing for? It's not funny."

"I'm sorry. I didn't mean..." Kerry took a step back, away from Carmen. It was kind of funny, though. Carmen had actually asked her to make the accounts appear much worse. She wanted the whole company to suffer for Annie's death. Carmen would be delighted if Carjon went bankrupt and everyone lost their jobs. But Kerry couldn't do it. She couldn't do it to herself. But she particularly couldn't do it to Patrick. So she'd turned the tables completely on Carmen. Instead of making the accounts appear worse, she'd made them seem very much better. She'd laughed about that after she'd done it too. Then she'd started to worry that one day Carmen would find out. Perhaps when the accounts were published.

The accounts looked great, but Carmen never questioned it. She assumed they would have been even better without Kerry's tampering. Carmen accused her of not doing enough, told her she should have done more to make them appear much worse. She never even guessed that Kerry actually did the polar opposite of what she'd wanted. Kerry allowed herself another smile.

"What are you laughing at?" Carmen said.

"Nothing." If Carmen wanted things done right, she should have done it herself. Kerry was glad she hadn't hurt anyone. It might even help. It might help Patrick's wife, although the only reason Kerry wanted to help her was because Patrick would suffer so much if Martina died, and Kerry would hate to watch him go through that. Martina would probably die eventually, anyway. She'd overheard Patrick talking about her to Frank. So, Kerry simply had to be patient, and one day Patrick would notice her. She'd be there for him when he needed her.

"Do you want me to make coffee for you?" Kerry was washing up some cups in the small staff kitchen when Clarke came in and started to take the old grounds out of the coffee machine.

"No, it's fine," Clarke said. "It's a nice chance to take a break." She could do without having to clean the percolator. Really, why didn't people throw their old coffee grounds in the bin when they finished? Why would you leave them in the percolator all night? But she needed to talk to everyone in the company. Kerry might let something useful slip.

"The grounds go in the tiny bin in the corner." Kerry pointed, her fingers covered in washing up liquid bubbles. "They get recycled. Compost, or something."

Clarke headed in the direction Kerry indicated, tipping the paper filter, full of old coffee grounds, into the small recycling bin. "How long have you worked here?"

Kerry paused for a moment, the mug in her hand proclaiming Best Dad Ever. Clarke guessed that one didn't belong to Kerry. "A couple of years," she said.

"Do you like it here?"

"Oh, yes, I love it. I'm learning so much from Patrick. He's great." Kerry blushed. She turned back to her washing up.

"He seems all right," Clarke said casually.

"He's brilliant," Kerry said. "And he's so helpful and so nice. He's definitely the best boss ever."

Clarke smiled, wondering how many bosses Kerry could compare Patrick with. She looked barely old enough to be out of school. Clarke realised that Kerry might just have a giant crush on Patrick. Clarke wondered if he was aware of it, and if perfect Patrick really appreciated his devoted assistant. She rinsed out the coffee percolator and filled it with water.

"How much longer will you and Evan be here?" Kerry asked.

"I'm not sure." Clarke smiled at Kerry, relieved that she seemed much friendlier now than she was a few days ago.

"The percolator takes fifteen minutes," Kerry said. "I prefer instant. It's quicker."

Clarke protested. "This stuff is fabulous. It's worth the wait."

"If you go back to the boardroom, I'll bring it in when it's ready."

Clarke beamed at her. "Yes, please." She really didn't have time to wait around, although she kicked herself for passing up the opportunity to stay and chat with Kerry some more while she was relaxed and off guard. She would somehow need to engineer another opportunity. She'd learned a lot from Kerry in those few minutes. Especially about Kerry's feelings for Patrick. How far would she go to help him?

Chapter 33

Frank left work early. He'd spent much of the day cleaning and tidying up after moving the rat cages back in on Friday. All weekend he'd been dreading the task, especially as he'd given Carmen the day off. So now he'd had to do all the work himself. Another pair of hands would have made everything so much easier.

Anyway, by the time Frank got round to doing any proper work, well into the afternoon, he was exhausted. By three o'clock, he decided to pack up and go home. He'd get some rest, then he'd be fresh and rearing to go tomorrow.

The car park was deserted at this time of day. Jam-packed with cars, but not a single soul in sight. He'd just reached his car when he remembered that Kas asked him to pick up a loaf of bread on the way home. Annoyed, he dumped his briefcase in the car boot and walked back towards the building.

Frank took the shortcut round the side of the building to an alleyway that would get him into Brackford within five minutes. Everyone at Carjon used the alleyway at lunchtime. At this time of day, it was completely empty. He walked briskly, despite his tiredness, keen to get home and relax in front of the TV. He would love to have gone straight home, but Kas would give him hell if he showed up without the bread. In any case, he didn't fancy forgoing his toast for breakfast in the morning.

Brackford's best bakery was close to the other end of the alley. More expensive than the supermarket, but a much quicker walk. He breathed in deeply, almost able to smell the freshly baked bread from here.

A cat screeched further down the alleyway behind him, making him jump and turn around quickly. A ginger tabby ran across the path and climbed up the fence on the other side. Frank laughed. Ollie's death was making everyone a bit jumpy. He needed to relax more.

THE COVER-UP

Frank bought a large granary loaf and, as an afterthought, a baguette as well. He'd skipped lunch and really fancied a nice crusty piece of baguette with a hunk of cheese and some pickle. Perhaps he'd treat himself to a beer with it when he got home.

Within a few minutes, he got back to the alleyway. The aroma of the freshly baked bread in his arms urged him on. As he walked, he fished his keys out of his pocket to speed things up.

He turned the corner towards the end of the path. Suddenly, he felt a massive pain on the side of his head.

Frank dropped to the ground, sending bread and keys flying. A hand reached out in front of him, scooping up the keys, and the sound of running footsteps pounded in his head. That was the last thing he remembered.

Chapter 34

Clarke had forgotten some vital shopping at lunchtime. "Do you mind if I pop into Brackford for ten minutes?"

Evan glanced up at the clock on the wall. "Sure," he said. "What are you going for?"

"I meant to get some prawns and a bottle of wine at lunchtime," Clarke said. "Paul's coming over later and I promised him I'd cook his favourite prawn risotto."

"Everything's Paul's favourite."

Clarke laughed as she went out the door. Yes, Paul certainly appreciated her cooking. It was true that the way to a man's heart was through his stomach. In Paul's case, the way to his heart was via a spicy prawn risotto and a lemon meringue pie.

As she walked, she dialled Paul's number. For once, he answered immediately.

"Hi, darling."

Clarke felt better already, hearing his voice. "It's these letters from the prison," she said. "I don't know what to do. They're asking me to visit."

"I assume you don't want to."

Clarke stopped walking. "Do you think I should?"

"No, absolutely not. It's upsetting you too much even thinking about it. Ignore them."

"I can't." Clarke knew if she did, the letters would keep coming.

"Yes, you can. I'll talk to the prison governor. She can make the letters stop."

"Can she really do that?"

"Yes," Paul said. "I'll make sure of it. I want you to feel safe."

"Thank you." Clarke felt better already. She would try to forget, but it wasn't easy. She glanced at her watch. Evan would be expecting her back, so she needed to hurry. She'd found a shortcut into Brackford

THE COVER-UP

when she'd been wandering around at lunchtime a couple of days ago. Quickly, she headed for the alleyway on the other side of the building. Hopefully, Evan wouldn't actually be timing her because this would take double the amount of time she'd suggested it would.

She turned into the alleyway. Immediately, she realised something was wrong. Someone lay sprawled on the ground part-way along the path. He looked like he may have fallen, landing in a crumpled heap. Clarke ran towards him. He wasn't moving.

As soon as she reached him, she grabbed his wrist and found a faint pulse. Quickly, she rolled him towards her into the recovery position.

"Frank? Oh my God, Frank." How on earth did he end up here, and in this state? Clarke searched her handbag for her phone.

"Ambulance, please, and police." She added the latter on seeing a nasty wound on the side of his head. This didn't look like a fall. She glanced around, worried in case anyone was still in the vicinity, before leaning over him to check him more closely. His hot breath warmed her cheek. Good, maybe placing him in the recovery position had helped him. She was grateful that her former fire brigade training kicked in automatically. After spending over five years in the service, in an emergency she acted instinctively, despite the long gap since leaving. Her ankle started to throb, reminding her why her firefighting career ended. Running to help Frank aggravated her old injury. She ignored it, focusing on the task at hand.

"Frank, can you hear me?"

Frank's lips moved and Clarke bent her head towards him to try to distinguish his words, but none came out.

"What happened, Frank? Who did this to you?" Clarke noticed a trickle of blood now, pooling beneath his head. Quickly, she took off her scarf, folding it up and using it to put pressure on the wound. He couldn't have fallen. This looked much more like someone had hit him.

Again, he opened his mouth a fraction but made no discernible sound.

Clarke took his wrist again and searched for a pulse. Thank God, it was stronger than she expected.

"Come on, Frank, stay with me. The ambulance is on its way. Everything's going to be all right."

As if in answer, Clarke heard sirens approaching. She wondered if they would find them here, if she had explained their location well enough. Quickly, she phoned Evan.

"You're late," he said as soon as he answered.

"Evan, it's an emergency. I need some help. Frank's hurt. We're in the alleyway behind the building. Someone needs to show the paramedics where we are."

"What happened?"

"Never mind that, just get some help down here, fast."

"What happened?" Patrick hurried along the alleyway in the wake of the two paramedics. Evan followed close behind.

Clarke ignored him. "He's got a pulse," she said, addressing one of the paramedics. "I put him in the recovery position and checked that he was breathing. But there's a nasty wound on his head. Someone may have hit him."

"Ok. We'll take over now. How long has he been here?"

"I'm not sure." Clarke checked her watch. "I found him about twenty minutes ago." It seemed like hours.

"Clarke, what's going on?" Patrick asked again before addressing the paramedics, as they rolled Frank onto a stretcher. "Will he be all right?"

"We'll know more when we get him to the hospital." The paramedic put an oxygen mask over Frank's face, then lifted him onto the trolley. Within seconds, they were wheeling him along the alley towards the ambulance.

"Has someone phoned Frank's wife?" Clarke asked Patrick.

THE COVER-UP

"Henry's gone to collect her and take her to the hospital."

Clarke looked at Patrick quizzically. That seemed a bit above and beyond, for a colleague.

"We're like a family at Carjon Pharma," Patrick said, by way of explanation. "What happened?"

Clarke remembered that the three of them, Henry, Patrick, and Frank, used to flat-share at university. "I don't know," Clarke said. "I found him lying on the ground. It looks like someone hit him over the head."

"Thank God you found him."

Evan came back into the alleyway with DC Kevin Farrier in tow.

"You found the body?" he asked Clarke.

"Body? Is... is he dead?"

"No. Not yet anyway. Sorry, I meant, did you find the victim?"

"Yes. I think he got hit over the head."

"Are you ok, Clarke?" Evan looked concerned.

Clarke nodded.

"Did the victim say anything?"

"No." Clarke wished she'd heard him. Frank wanted to say something. Probably to tell her to phone his wife. Or maybe nothing important. He probably didn't even see his attacker. If he did, he wouldn't have been taken by surprise, would he? "He tried to say something, but he couldn't get the words out. He was struggling to breathe." Poor Frank. He didn't deserve this.

For a moment, Clarke wondered if her guess about Frank being the intended target all along, instead of Ollie, might be correct. It certainly seemed more likely now. She should probably tell Kevin Farrier. Except that he was a moron, and it wasn't his case, anyway. She would tell Paul later.

Clarke suddenly burst into tears. She'd completely forgotten about the prawns. By the time she finished with the police, the shops would be shut and she'd have to make a long detour to the supermarket, Except she wouldn't. If Frank died, MIT would get called in and Paul would be working half the night, yet again.

"Clarke?" Evan put a hand on her shoulder. "Are you ok? This must be a big shock for you. Come back to the office and I'll make you a nice cup of coffee."

Clarke pulled herself together. She was being ridiculous. Frank might actually die, and here she was worrying about Paul not being able to come round later, about Paul not actually caring enough about her to admit to his colleagues that he'd been seeing her for the past few months. He didn't even realise how much that hurt. A whole raft of emotions welled up inside her. Was it any wonder that it had all got too much? Paul hurt her once before, badly. But, she admonished herself, even if he did it again, that paled into insignificance against a man's life being in the balance. But she knew only too well, at times of stress, it only took the tiniest thing to tip a person over the edge.

"I'm ok," she said. "But sitting down with a cup of coffee would be good."

She held back as Evan very assertively told DC Farrier that, if he wanted to talk to them, he would have to come to the office. For once, she appreciated not having to take charge and be the strong one. It probably would never happen again.

Chapter 35

By the end of the following day, Clarke still hadn't heard any news about Frank, so she was quite pleased to see Carmen.

"Hi." Clarke was on her way out as Carmen came down the stairs. She hoped she wouldn't expect another lift home. It took much longer than she'd expected to drop Carmen off on Saturday. Anyway, she couldn't. She needed to go into Brackford first and pick up a couple of things from the shops.

"Is there any news on Frank?" she asked. If anyone knew anything, Carmen certainly would.

Carmen shook her head. "I phoned the hospital, but I'm not family, so they won't tell me anything."

"I'm sure Henry will give us an update as soon as he finds out. Let's hope it's good."

"Anyway, I'm on my way home now," Carmen said.

Clarke nodded, willing her not to ask for a lift. The shops would shut soon, so she needed to hurry. And one thing was for certain, she would walk the long way round into Brackford this time. No way would she use that alleyway as a shortcut again, not anytime soon.

The two women walked towards the front entrance. As they got closer, Clarke saw that the usual protestors were demonstrating again. The local animal rights group seemed to be targeting Carjon heavily at the moment. Clarke wondered why.

"I'm going out the back way." Carmen turned abruptly, putting a hand up to her face as she pivoted.

"They're ok," Clarke said. She wanted to avoid the longer walk into Brackford from the other side of the building. After her run-in with the protestors on her first day, everyone told her they were harmless. If they tried to intimidate her again, she was perfectly capable of standing up for herself.

"Best not to get involved with them." Carmen headed back towards the staff entrance.

Clarke wondered if Carmen had clashed with the demonstrators before. Given her views on the rats in Frank's lab, she could imagine things would get heated if they got into a debate. Much as Clarke didn't want to walk the extra distance, it did occur to her that perhaps Carmen knew best. Reluctantly, she tagged along behind her. She ought to face her demons, but perhaps she wasn't ready for that yet.

"Have they given you trouble before?" Clarke asked.

Carmen shook her head. "I don't like fighting through crowds."

Clarke reached the dry cleaners two minutes before closing time and managed to drop off a couple of work jackets. Her ankle started to ache from having to walk further and faster, so she slowed down a lot on the way back to the car park. She cursed herself for listening to Carmen.

Carmen was so full of contradictions. One minute she swore the animal rights activists were harmless, the next minute she went out of her way to avoid them. She didn't seem to care that much about animals. Had she got into an argument with one of them? Right now, Clarke didn't really care. She would make up her own mind about the protestors.

Chapter 36

The following day, the demonstrators were in full flow outside the building at lunchtime when Clarke set out from the office to collect her dry cleaning. She decided to walk straight through them. Her ankle still pained her from yesterday, and Carmen hadn't given her any real reason to worry about them. She needed to do this. She didn't want to be running away from them forever.

The front door was locked, as usual.

"Best to go out the back way," the receptionist advised. "We always keep it locked when the protestors are outside, just in case they try to come in."

Clarke wondered if there was any point in having someone sitting in reception all day when no one could actually enter the building. "Couldn't you let me out and lock the door behind me?" She really didn't want to walk that extra distance.

The receptionist hesitated. "Henry doesn't like me unlocking the door."

Clarke smiled at her. "Please. I'll take full responsibility if it's a problem. I've got a bad ankle. It's too painful to walk all the way round the building."

The receptionist fumbled under the desk for the key. "I suppose I can make an exception. You'll need to slip out really quickly."

"Of course." Clarke hated using her old ankle injury like that. She usually tried to hide it from other people. Even Evan wasn't aware of her problem. But needs must. She waited while the receptionist sorted out the key.

"Let's do it quickly, while they're not too near the door," she said. Within seconds, she unlocked the door and ushered Clarke out.

The door slammed behind Clarke and the click of the key turning in the lock informed her she wouldn't be able to get back in that way.

Outside, the demonstrators sounded threateningly loud. From inside, she hadn't heard a thing. The doors and windows must have great double glazing. They shouted slogans, more angrily than they had on her first encounter with them. They seemed to have grown in numbers too, perhaps because it was later in the day, or perhaps the notoriety of a murder attracted more people now. They'd certainly expanded their numbers hugely from the tiny group that showed up the day after Ollie's death. Clarke took a deep breath. The only option was to walk straight through the middle of the group, and that option didn't go well on her first day here. She took a deep breath and started walking, trying to appear more confident than she felt.

The group of demonstrators parted for her to go through. Clarke relaxed. This was much easier than expected. But, as she got nearer to the road, a wall of people suddenly closed up in front of her.

"Can I come through, please?"

None of the demonstrators moved. None of them looked friendly. Clarke wondered if she could make a run back to the door, if the receptionist would let her in, because now there was a very real risk of being followed inside. She glanced over her shoulder before turning around to find herself surrounded on all sides by a wall of people. As she turned, they closed up, leaving no way through.

"Still working here?"

Clarke turned around again. The curly-haired man she'd spoken to on her first day stood right in front of her.

"Can you let me through, please?" Clarke hoped he hadn't noticed the slight waver in her voice. She regretted saying *please*. It made the request sound less assertive, less of a demand, weaker somehow. The last thing she needed right now was to appear weak.

"Why are you still working here?" His words came across as more of an accusation than a question. "They're scum." He put his face right up close to Clarke's. "And it's not just the animals that suffer. They kill people too," he said ominously.

Clarke shrank back. He'd made it sound like a threat. The demonstrators surrounded her more tightly now. The receptionist wouldn't notice anything. She wondered if anyone upstairs would be able to see. How often did people look out the windows? They were usually too busy. Surely no one would be stupid enough to hurt her here right outside the building. The wall of people had become two or three deep, completely blocking her from view. No one would see anything.

"I'm just trying to earn a living. I love animals." Should she say she loved people too? She didn't imagine the curly-haired bloke was really concerned about poor Ollie. He probably saw the story in the news and decided to use it against her. "I don't make any decisions here."

"You're part of the corporate scum," Curly-Hair spat at her. "Whatever you do, you're feeding the machine. You're enabling them to exist. You're an accessory to murder."

Clarke assumed he meant the animals when he'd mentioned murder, not Ollie. On either count, she wasn't responsible.

"Let me go. You can't keep me here." Clarke didn't understand why they were singling her out for intimidation. Wasn't there supposed to be a police presence at demonstrations like this? She wondered if she might be able to get her phone out of her bag and speed dial Paul, or Evan, but they were hemming her in too tightly. The best she could do was to hold her ground and try not to show any fear, even though, in reality, she was petrified.

"Go on then, go." The curly-haired man didn't budge. Neither did any of his friends.

Clarke couldn't see how to leave without pushing one of them out of the way, and that might give them an excuse to get nasty. "I haven't done anything," she said. "Why are you picking on me? You're just a bunch of bullies."

The curly-haired man laughed. "See how bad it feels to be completely helpless, with someone much stronger than you controlling your every move. Like those animals."

"But I love animals," Clarke protested. "I agree with everything you're saying. So why are you being so horrible?" Why had she been so stupid? She really regretted not leaving the office by the back entrance. She should have learnt from her first encounter with the demonstrators and stayed well away.

In the distance, the sound of sirens distracted them both for a moment. Clarke prayed that someone had called the police to help her. The sirens were coming closer, so it was possible.

The curly-haired man clearly got the same idea. He stepped aside. "Get out of here, scum," he said.

Clarke didn't need telling twice. As she barged through the gap, the curly-haired man kicked out, catching her bad ankle. She wanted to scream in pain but didn't dare. Instead, she headed towards Brackford town centre as fast as she could walk.

Tears streamed down her cheeks as soon as escaped the group. As she reached the corner, two police cars headed along the road towards Carjon. She paused for a moment to watch, but they kept going past the building, sirens still blaring. No one was coming to rescue her. She'd had a lucky escape.

Drained from her encounter, she forced herself to keep walking quickly, keen to put some more distance between herself and the protestors. Clarke couldn't stop herself from limping now. Why did that horrible man pick that ankle to kick? But it was nonsense to assume he'd deliberately aimed for her weak spot. With everyone so tightly packed together, he could have never seen where his kick would land, and certainly would have never known that her ankle was a problem. She'd been unlucky. The curly-haired man seemed to dislike her for some unfathomable reason. Surely not simply because she worked in the Carjon offices? He scared her more than she wanted to admit. It wouldn't take much for his playground bullying to turn into something more serious. Clarke wondered, not for the first time, if he had anything to do with killing Ollie.

Paul dismissed her theory when she'd first mooted it to him, adamant that the animal rights protestors weren't involved. Clarke resolved to talk to him again. Did he have new information he hadn't told her? Perhaps they all had alibis. She would make him tell her now, if only to put her mind at rest.

After all that, when she arrived at the dry cleaners, her jackets weren't ready. She would have to come back tomorrow. If she could face it. If the protestors had gone. Today really wasn't going right.

Clarke walked slowly back to the office, taking an extra-long detour to the staff car park so the protestors wouldn't see her. She didn't intend on getting caught like that again.

Chapter 37

Clarke's ankle was killing her. She'd taken two paracetamol but still was in no fit state to drive home. Reluctantly, she decided to leave the car and get the bus.

Evan would probably give her a lift if she wasn't too stubbornly proud to ask him. Since the accident, when she'd slipped off a ladder and badly broken her ankle back when she was still in the fire brigade, she'd been determined not to let the injury affect her. After two operations, which hadn't completely fixed her and ended her firefighting career, she couldn't bear other people pitying her. Often her ankle felt fine. But when she did too much walking, or running, or when she got deliberately kicked in the ankle, like today, it took all her mental strength not to walk with a limp. She didn't want any disability defining her. It didn't stop from her doing what she wanted. So, Evan didn't have a clue about her problem. It would take too much explaining to tell him now, and Clarke knew it would make him treat her differently, and she didn't want that.

Luckily the bus stop wasn't far away.

The bus was almost empty. Clarke sat near the doors so she wouldn't need to walk any further than necessary.

Her ankle already felt a little better when she arrived at her stop to change buses. The paracetamol must have finally kicked in after all. She stepped off the bus, taking care to land on her good leg, and sat in the bus shelter to wait for the number 52 bus that would take her all the way to her flat.

A young man sat on the other end of the bus shelter bench. She'd noticed him get off the bus behind her. Clarke ignored him and started checking emails on her phone. A few minutes later, she glanced up to see the same man glaring at her. She avoided eye contact and pretended not to have noticed, but it unnerved her, the way he looked at her constantly. Clarke kept glancing at him out of the corner of her eye. There was something about him, something familiar. Finally, she remembered where she had seen him—right outside the Carjon building, demonstrating with the animal rights protesters. Was it simply a coincidence that he'd showed up here, and that he stared at her so intently?

Clarke looked along the road and saw the number 52 approaching. If the man changed buses here, he surely would get on the 52. He was probably going the same way as her. She shouldn't take things so personally. Why would he have any interest in her?

In a split-second decision, Clarke got up just as the bus pulled into the bus stop. She started to walk in the other direction. As soon as the man got on the bus, she would go back to the bus shelter and wait for the next bus. Because, even if he turned out to be totally innocent, she didn't fancy being stuck on the same bus as him. And she certainly didn't want to risk him finding out where she lived when she got off the bus near her flat.

The bus quickly passed her and Clarke turned around to head back to the bus stop. As she turned, she saw a shadow duck into a shop doorway. She took a deep breath as her imagination ran wild. Surely the man must have got on the bus. Why didn't she turn around to check when the bus pulled up at the stop?

She decided to play safe. It wasn't worth taking chances. The way he'd been looking at her really scared her. Clarke carried on walking. She glanced over her shoulder a couple of times but couldn't be sure. Something didn't feel right. There was definitely someone following her. Her ankle started to hurt again, and she cursed herself for leaving the car at work.

Clarke spotted a good gap in the traffic and started to cross the busy road. She would try to shake off her pursuer. As she crossed, she spotted him crossing the road fifty metres or so further down. In a split-second decision, Clarke turned round and retraced her steps to the same side of the road. Further along, she saw the man over the opposite side of the road, trying to find a gap to cross back again. That wouldn't give her much time. She started to run. It would kill her ankle, but she must get away while she had the chance. She turned into a side road. Thankfully, she was familiar with the area. Further down this road, a footpath would take her to the other side of the park, exiting next to a cab company. She ducked into the pathway and ran.

Visions of Frank, lying on the ground in the alleyway near the Carjon building, played in her head as she hurried along, spurring her to go faster, despite the pain in her ankle. At the end of the footpath, she looked back. She couldn't see anyone following her, but it would be too risky to slow down now. If he'd seen which road she'd gone down, he might work out how she'd disappeared from view so fast. The park was completely empty today. No one would help her. As soon as she got her breath back, she set off towards the exit at a steady jog.

She only allowed herself to relax when she was sitting in a cab, being driven the last couple of miles home. Not that *relax* was the right word. Her ankle pain was excruciating and running in her work shoes had rubbed at her heel on the other foot. She couldn't wait to get home and put her feet up on the sofa.

She wondered why that man had followed her. Did the protestors plan on intimidating her some more? Was it just bullying or something more? Perhaps the curly-haired man had smelt her fear. The recent events at Carjon, with Ollie's murder and Frank's attack, would be enough to make anyone a bit fearful. Perhaps she didn't hide that as well as she imagined. She took her phone out of her handbag and sent a quick text to Paul, inviting him over this evening. She would prefer not to be on her own, and perhaps he would help her make sense of this.

Chapter 38

"You've got a nerve," Deborah said. The last person she'd expected to see when she opened her front door was Henry. After the way he'd reacted when she'd told him about the baby, she didn't even want to see him at work. But, bold as you like, he stood on her doorstep, expecting to be invited in. At least this time he'd bothered to bring flowers.

"I'm worried about you." Henry fidgeted from foot to foot, his usual confidence seeming to dissipate rapidly. "Can I come in?"

Deborah considered slamming the door in his face. Except that probably wouldn't do her career prospects any good, especially after the trouble she'd gone to in order to secure her position in the company. She gritted her teeth and stood aside for him to pass. One cup of coffee, then she'd throw him out.

"How are you?" Henry pulled out a chair in her kitchen, not waiting for her to ask him to sit down. "We wondered whether you might be ready to come back to work soon."

Deborah spooned coffee into two mugs, deliberately putting an extra heaped spoonful into Henry's mug, knowing he didn't like his coffee strong. "Yes, I'm planning to come back on Monday."

The relief on Henry's face was evident. Deborah considered whether he needed her more than even she realised. She was still a bit shell-shocked at discovering Ollie's body. Added to that, the morning sickness was hell. And, despite having a few days to herself to mull over the problem, and despite Henry making his opinion pretty clear, she still needed to make a decision about the baby. But she couldn't afford the luxury of taking more time off work. It wasn't just the money, with the crippling mortgage payments where she'd over-extended herself buying a big house that she really didn't need. If she stayed away for too long, Henry would find a way to get her out of the company, especially now that they were no longer on the best of terms.

Her glittering career might fade into obscurity all too quickly if she was forced to find another job, when her performance at Carjon Pharma would be judged by the company's success, or lack of it, during the very short time she'd been in charge. Although, with the murder on top of the financial problems, Carjon might not survive for long. Trying to find an equally well-paid position elsewhere while pregnant would be tricky. Best to get back to work and do whatever it took to ensure the company soldiered on for another year, then search for a better job.

Henry sipped at his coffee, making a face as he realised it was much too strong for his taste. "And the baby? What's the plan?"

Deborah looked at Henry's worried face. Was that worry that Sarah would find out? She knew now that Henry would never divorce his wife. She'd been naïve to imagine he might. Sarah had inherited a great deal of family money, as well as their huge house. Without his wife, Henry's lavish lifestyle would be severely curtailed. No, he would never divorce her. But *she* might divorce *him*. That would be highly likely if she found out that Henry had not only been unfaithful but also fathered an illegitimate child. She decided to make him sweat.

"I'm keeping it," she said. As soon as the words left her mouth, she decided she must be mad. Being a single mother was never in her game plan. How would she find the time to care for it? She wondered if Henry would stomp up some money for a nanny.

Henry's face crumpled, bringing Deborah instant satisfaction. For a moment, she wondered if he might cry.

"Are you sure?"

Deborah nodded, not trusting herself to actually voice the words. She'd never been less sure of anything in her life. She put her hands over her womb. In that moment, she realised, yes, she did want to keep it. She really did. Something good would come out of Ollie's tragic death. A brand-new life grew inside of her. Perhaps, if the baby was a boy, she'd call him Oliver.

"Have the police found out anything about Ollie yet? Do they know who did it?" Deborah asked, eager to change the subject, although they would need to talk more about the baby soon if she wanted that nanny.

Henry seemed equally happy with the change of subject. "They don't seem to have progressed much yet. They suspected Frank, of course, and Patrick."

"Frank's the obvious suspect."

"Nonsense. Frank isn't capable of killing anything. He cries every time one of his lab rats gets killed off."

"I didn't know that." Secretly, Deborah didn't think that precluded him from being a murderer. Frank always seemed to prefer animals to humans.

"There's a lot you don't know about Frank. You should talk to him more."

Deborah shifted in her chair, finding it difficult to get comfortable. She supposed she would get several more months of this. "I can't afford to support this baby on my own." There, she'd said it. May as well get straight to the point. Henry got her into this mess. He owed her.

"Really? We're paying you a generous salary. Whatever are you doing with it?"

"That's none of your business." He'd tell her to sell her house and buy a smaller one. She loved her house. And the baby would love it too. "It's your baby too, Henry. You should contribute."

"It's *your* baby. How did it even happen? Aren't you supposed to be on the pill?"

"Of course I was. I would have never done this deliberately, if that's what you're suggesting?"

"Yes," he said. "I'm beginning to wonder if you cooked up this whole idea to get money out of me. Well, I don't have any, so you'll get nothing. I can't afford it any more than you can. You should get rid of it."

"Really!" Deborah parodied him. She stared at Henry, questioning what she ever saw in him. She once thought him good-looking and kind. Now all she saw was the face of a baby murderer. That's all he wanted—to get rid of her baby. Well, she would definitely keep it. The more she looked at Henry, the more determined she became.

"Yes, really. I've invested everything in the company. I only draw a small salary. You would know that if you read the accounts."

Deborah did know. She'd forgotten. "Carjon's worth millions. Give me a share in the company. Then when the company floats on the stock exchange, I can afford to resign and you need never see me again if that's what you want." If Henry was going to push for an abortion, then she would get as mercenary as possible.

Henry laughed.

"What?" Deborah said. "What's so funny about that?"

"I'm not selling the company."

"You are, Henry. That's why you've got those people in, Evan and Clarke, to do a full report on the company and produce a brochure for the stock-market. So don't lie to me."

"I'm not lying, Deborah. Even if I wanted to sell, which I don't, the company's not worth nearly as much as you seem to think."

"It's worth plenty." No way would she back down now. She wanted her baby to get what was his by right, not have to struggle to make ends meet while Henry and his family swanned around in the lap of luxury.

"Don't be so naïve, Deborah. The company's in financial trouble. No one would buy it. Not right now. Evan and Clarke aren't producing a brochure for stock-market floatation. They're investigating the finances, trying to find out if anyone's embezzled any money out of the company. If we don't get to the bottom of this, Carjon is finished."

Deborah kicked herself for not realising all of that much sooner. If Henry was telling the truth, she would need to do something to protect her future, her baby's future.

"You need to keep that information to yourself," Henry said. "Everything may be all right. We don't want any key people jumping ship on the strength of rumours. Let's wait until we find out for sure what's going on."

Deborah opened her mouth to speak, but Henry cut her off.

"It's in your contract. You can't divulge confidential company information. I won't hesitate to sue if I find you've leaked any of this."

"Then why didn't you tell me all of this before?" It shocked Deborah that Henry had kept such a massive secret from her. Until very recently, she would have said they were close. Was she under suspicion?

"You didn't need to be told."

"Of course I did. I'm the managing director. You recruited me to run the company. And you don't tell me something this big?" She shook her head. Henry was unbelievable. If only she could afford it, she would resign on the spot.

Henry took another sip of his coffee before placing the almost full cup on the table and stood up. "I should go," he said. "I've got work to do."

Deborah didn't bother to answer. Henry clearly wanted to escape before the subject returned to the baby. Whatever. She was pleased to get rid of him, hardly able to bear the sight of him anymore. She didn't know yet how she would cope on Monday, when she would be back to working with him every day.

"I'll see you in the office on Monday." Henry headed towards the door.

"Yes." Deborah wouldn't be looking forward to it. She considered telling him to see himself out. But that wouldn't give her the satisfaction of slamming the door behind him. She followed him along the hallway, keen to ensure he left as quickly as possible, wondering if he would go back to the office immediately or if he would go home instead. Or had he replaced her already? Was he on his way to his new mistress's house for an illicit romp? She shook the scenario from her head. She didn't care anymore. From now on, her relationship with Henry Carver-Jones would be strictly business.

Chapter 39

Frank was getting bored at home. He had nearly recovered from the attack. Thankfully, it was just a mild concussion and a head wound. It annoyed him that he couldn't remember much about the attack, although that might be a godsend. At least he wouldn't get nightmares reliving the incident. He sat on the sofa, wracking his brains, trying to work out what to do and how to get everything back on track, when Kas came in, followed by Patrick.

"I wasn't expecting you," Frank said, wondering what Patrick wanted. He didn't hear the doorbell, but perhaps Kas spotted him coming up the drive. Maybe she'd been expecting him.

"Sorry." Patrick sat down next to Frank. "Henry said you'd left the hospital. I wanted to make sure you were ok."

Frank twisted round to face Patrick. "How's Martina?" He always dreaded asking that question. Nevertheless, he felt obliged to inquire, particularly as Martina was undoubtedly the main reason for Patrick checking up on him.

Patrick looked serious. "That's why I'm here. Martina's getting worse."

Frank sighed quietly, hating to be right about this. He always got the impression these days that Patrick cared about him only because he wanted his damned drug for Martina. They were supposed to be friends. That didn't seem to count for much anymore. "I'm really sorry," he said.

"She's dying, Frank. She needs the Fexizon. I can't lose her. I can't."

"Patrick, I'd do anything to help Martina, but my hands are tied. Henry's stopped the trials." He was glad of the chance to blame Henry. The truth was, when he'd recalculated the test results, the effectiveness of the drug came out below average, certainly not the wonder drug Patrick expected. It wouldn't save Martina's life. And, if Patrick and

Martina were putting their faith in it, in him, they would be extremely disappointed.

"Henry need never find out."

Frank stared at Patrick. He'd aged noticeably in the last few weeks, the lines crossing his face etching out bigger and bigger wrinkles. He shut his eyes for a few seconds, trying to take in what Patrick wanted him to do. "I can't," Frank said. "What if it all goes wrong? If it's unofficial, the company's insurance won't cover it."

"We'll sign something, absolve you of liability."

"Patrick, that's not the only issue." How could he tell him the real issue: that the drug wasn't effective, that Martina would almost inevitably die, that the drug probably wouldn't even act to slow down nature's course? How could he tell him something that would rob them of all their hope? "If Martina takes the drug, she'll need proper medical monitoring." They normally hired a doctor to supervise the trials. That didn't come cheap, and the logistics of even doing something like that without Henry being aware would be impossible.

"I'll pay."

"It would cost a fortune. And these people get booked up months in advance. You can't simply drag a consultant oncologist off the streets. I already cancelled the one we booked. He's no longer available." Frank didn't have a clue if that was true about his availability, but he needed to get out of this impossible situation. He couldn't start administering a drug to Martina that wasn't ready for testing. Now he wished he'd come clean and confessed everything to Patrick about the error in the test results, instead of digging himself into this deep, dark hole.

"Frank, please. You must help us. If you don't, Martina's going to die. Please, you're our only hope." Patrick got up. "Please," he said, his voice wavering as if he was about to start crying. "I'm begging you."

Patrick turned towards the door, but not quickly enough, so that Frank saw an escaping tear trickle down his cheek.

As soon as Patrick left, Frank slumped back onto the sofa. If only he could find an easy answer. On the one hand, he needed to get out of this predicament. No way would he allow Martina to have the drug. It wouldn't work and with no medical supervision and no insurance cover, when she inevitably died, he would be finished.

On the other hand, he really wanted to help Martina and Patrick, and he found it upsetting that he couldn't. If only he were able to find a solution.

Chapter 40

Clarke peered out of the upstairs window in the Carjon kitchen. The animal rights protestors were back again today. They seemed to be ramping up proceedings lately. She spotted the curly-haired man at the front. He definitely seemed to be the ringleader.

He looked up and Clarke ducked back quickly.

"Are you ok?" Henry asked.

Clarke hadn't noticed him come in. She nodded. "I didn't want the protestors to see me watching them."

"Don't worry." Henry laughed. "It's one-way glass. We can see out, but they can't see us." He came over to the window.

Clarke stepped forward again and stood next to him. Henry waved enthusiastically at the protestors with both hands. A couple of them were looking in their direction, but they made no reaction to Henry's waves.

"We've got so used to them, we completely ignore them now," Henry said. "I gather you had a run-in with them yesterday."

"Yes." So, someone *had* seen her having problems. Why didn't they do anything to help her? "They got a bit intimidating, actually."

"They're pretty harmless. Just a bit of a nuisance."

Clarke's ankle twinged, reminding her how wrong Henry's opinion was. "Who is he?" Clarke asked. "The one with the black curly hair." She pointed him out to Henry.

"He's their leader, Timmo Macintosh. Fancies himself as a major political anarchist, but he's a small fry. We did consider getting an injunction against him, but he's never done anything violent, and a piece of paper isn't going to keep him away. Like I said, they're pretty harmless. It's touching that they care about Frank's rats so much, but no one could care about them as much as Frank does. He cries when any of them die."

"I can imagine." Clarke remembered how Frank acted with Delilah. "How is Frank?"

Henry moved away from the window. "He's doing well. He's out of the hospital. We're hoping he'll be well enough to come back to work any day soon."

"That's great news." Clarke was genuinely happy. At one point, while they were waiting in that alleyway for the ambulance, she worried Frank might not survive.

"It will be good to have him back. He's a huge asset to the company, a really great scientist. Do you realise, if our new drug works out as well as expected, he may be in contention for a Nobel Prize."

"Wow." Clarke didn't know. That was huge. Was it possible that someone wanted to steal Frank's drug formulation? Something so good might be worth millions. Perhaps another pharmaceutical company was responsible for Ollie's murder. She must mention it to Paul, in case he hadn't followed up that line of inquiry yet.

The day passed quickly, and at 5:00 p.m., Evan insisted, for once, that she should leave on time. Clarke knew she should use the staff exit to the car park and go straight home. But there was something she must do first.

"Timmo," Clarke called to her curly-haired nemesis. She must be mad doing this, venturing out into the crowd of demonstrators after what happened yesterday. But she needed to confront him. If she didn't face her fears, he would have won. Someone followed her yesterday, and she wanted to find out why.

Timmo sauntered over. "Well, look who it is. Didn't think you'd have the nerve to come back so soon."

"I want a word with you," she said.

"Oh yeah?"

Clarke looked him in the eye, determined not to show any fear. "Someone followed me yesterday when I left here. One of your people." Clarke looked around. She couldn't see the man who'd been at the bus stop. Was she wrong? She was so sure yesterday.

"Really?" Timmo met her stare with a contemptuous look. "So, who would that be then?"

Clarke scanned the crowd again. But she knew, from the confident tone of Timmo's voice, from the sparkle in his eyes, that she wouldn't find the man. "He's not here today."

"You're imagining things, love."

Clarke stretched up to her full height, although that still didn't match up to Timmo. "Why would you have me followed? Why are you trying to intimidate me? I haven't done anything."

"No idea what you're talking about," he said. "But you're right about not doing anything. You pretend to be an animal lover, but you still work for a company that tortures animals. So let me ask you a question. Why would you do that?" He tossed his head, making his curls bounce.

Clarke hesitated. The truth was, she'd asked herself the same question more than once. Evan had asked her if she had a problem with it, right on day one. She'd put her career first. And, since meeting Frank, seeing how much he cared and listening to him explain the legal requirements to test drugs on animals, and that ultimately, it saved millions of lives, she had become much more relaxed about the entire process. But it still didn't sit right with her.

"Well."

"Well, I don't believe you're ever going to change anything parading up and down out here," she said. "I can do more good by being part of it, talking to people, finding out exactly what the issues are, and trying to improve things from within." Clarke cringed inside, not knowing why she'd said that. She'd opened her mouth and her tongue had run away with her, virtually offering her services as an inside mole, if

Timmo chose to interpret it differently. The words just popped out. She wasn't even fully aware of having those thoughts before. But now that she'd said that, it did make perfect sense. Except she would never help anyone like Timmo, not if she wanted to keep her job, and especially not after his behaviour towards her so far. She didn't want to get involved with the likes of Timmo Macintosh. He was bad news.

"If you want to do some good, we should collaborate."

Damn. He had read between the lines. No way could she get involved with these activists. It would be career suicide, as well as probably bordering on illegality. "I'll think about that," she said, "if you tell me why I was followed yesterday."

Timmo smiled at her. "We both need to do some thinking."

"I need to go." Clarke glanced back towards the main entrance door. The receptionist had gone for the day. She headed towards the end of the building, to go the long way round to the car park, walking quickly, eager to put as much distance as possible between her and Timmo Macintosh.

Chapter 41

Frank paused at the door of Patrick's house. He really didn't want to be here. Undoubtedly, Patrick only invited him in order to put more pressure on him to test the new drug on Martina. Ironic that, the last time he visited, Patrick wouldn't even let him into the house, much less allow him to see Martina. He should turn around and go straight home. Steeling himself, he rang the doorbell.

"Come in." Patrick ushered him in. "Martina's in the living room. Go through. I'll get you a scotch."

Frank headed along the hallway. He admonished himself for arriving empty-handed. He should have bought Martina some flowers. Bit late for that now. He tapped on the living room door and opened it.

"Frank. Do come in."

"Good to see you, Martina. How are you?" Frank tried hard to hide the shock he felt at the massive deterioration in Martina. He'd not seen her for several weeks. She'd never been big, but she seemed to have shrunk into a fragile structure of skin and bone, who could have been mistaken for someone nearly twice her age. The chemotherapy was causing her hair to fall out, and it was at that in-between stage where it looked raggedy and patchy. Again, he wished he'd brought flowers. It would have provided a distraction—for both of them.

"I was about to ask you the same thing." Martina smiled. "Patrick says you've recently come out of hospital. He told me about the attack. It sounded awful."

"Oh, don't worry about me. I'm fine. Just a bump on the head." Martina was propped up against the arm of the sofa, with her feet up, using it like a chaise longue. Frank selected an armchair opposite her. He was relieved when Patrick appeared with two glasses of whisky.

Patrick waited until Frank was about to step out of the front door before he broached the subject Frank had been dreading. Frank almost believed he'd got away with it. If only he'd hurried out the door that bit quicker. But he hadn't.

"I told you Martina's got much worse. We're relying on you, Frank."

"Patrick, I'm sorry. Of course I'd help if possible, but I've already explained, there's nothing I can do at the moment." Frank felt bad. He'd been friends with Patrick for over twenty years. He owed him the truth—that Fexizon wasn't nearly as effective as he'd previously convinced them.

"Martina's dying. You're our last port in the storm." Patrick sounded so desperate. "She's given up. She needs something to hope for, some beacon of light at the end of the tunnel to make her fight. You're our beacon, Frank."

Frank didn't know what to say. He wasn't a beacon. He was a flickering candle, the size of candle you get on a birthday cake, and a damp, half-burned-down candle at that. He noticed the deep worry lines on Patrick's face. Martina was his whole life. Frank understood perfectly what losing her would do to Patrick. "Let me think about it," he said.

"Please, Frank."

Patrick gripped his hand, clinging on as if not only Martina's life, but his life too, depended on him. Frank smiled weakly, hating that the best he could offer was to consider it, with probably nothing useful at the end of it.

Frank was over halfway home when he decided to take a detour and go into work. He simply couldn't let Patrick down without at least trying. There must be something he could do to help Martina. As he drove into Carjon's car park, he realised what bothered him. Yes, the calculations of the final testing were flawed. But the results of the earlier testing were phenomenal. He rarely made mistakes. In fact, he was obsessive about checking and double-checking his work. What were the chances that he'd made mistakes in analysing the results of both rounds of testing? There must be something else he'd missed. He would check every last thing, a million times if need be, until he found the answer. If there was the slightest chance of being able to help Martina, he would pull out all the stops to try.

After five hours of checking every single figure, Frank was still no further towards finding an answer. He decided to go home to eat. He didn't even dare drink a cup of coffee at work since he found out about Ollie being poisoned. If he ate something and got a few hours of sleep, he could get in really early tomorrow and start again.

Frank woke up in a sweat. He rolled over and peered past Kas at the luminous alarm clock. 4:05 a.m. *Formula.* That one word buzzed around his brain. The answer lay in the formula. If the initial calculations were correct, the formula must be the issue. Something must have changed between the first and second rounds of testing. Nothing else explained it.

Kas was still sleeping soundly. Frank rolled towards the edge of the bed and quietly sat up. He didn't want to risk waking her this early. Yesterday's clothes still lay in a heap on the bathroom floor. He would wear them again. If he opened the wardrobe to find clean clothes, he'd need to put the light on, then he would wake Kas for sure.

He slipped out the bedroom door, closing it carefully so as not to make any noise. Five minutes later, he was in his car, heading to the Carjon building.

Chapter 42

Four hours later, Frank was convinced he'd found the answer. The formula hadn't changed, but they'd swapped to a new supplier for three of the components. He remembered five or six months ago, a problem at the factory of his regular supplier meant several weeks of delay, so Frank had sourced a new supply.

Frank ran some tests on the component chemicals and found a small amount of contamination in one of them. He set up some more tests to try to pinpoint exactly what it was, but they would take another twenty-four hours to show a result.

In the meantime, he put in an order with his old supplier, express delivery. With luck, he'd get it tomorrow and could reformulate the whole drug. He was certain that would make the difference.

Adrenalin coursed through his veins, making his earlier tiredness completely disappear. He was thrilled to be back on track.

His stomach rumbled, and he realised he hadn't eaten. Still reluctant to drink coffee in the lab, he walked up the stairs to the kitchen. They had much better coffee up there anyway, and he may be able to borrow some bread to make toast for his breakfast.

As he opened the kitchen door, his mind buzzed with the list of things he needed to do in order to make a new batch of the drug as quickly as possible. He didn't notice Patrick coming out, carrying two mugs of coffee. The door swept into Patrick's hands, knocking the coffee flying. The mugs clattered onto the hard-tiled floor as Patrick shouted out.

"Frank, you bloody idiot." Patrick went straight to the sink and ran his hands under the cold tap. "You've burnt my hands. Why don't you look where you're going?"

"Sorry." Frank sidestepped around the delicious smelling puddle in front of him. "Let me see."

"I'm fine," Patrick snapped, wincing as he wriggled his fingers in the stream of cold water. "There should be some cloths in the cupboard. If you want to be helpful, clean up the mess before someone slips on it."

Frank found a bucket and some cleaning cloths. He carefully picked up the broken pieces of china and put them in the bin. He craved coffee now. The aroma had weakened rapidly as the puddle of coffee on the floor cooled, but it still tantalised him, crying out to his taste buds and his empty, rumbling stomach. He mopped up the puddle with one of the cloths and tried to dry the floor with a clean one.

"Patrick, I've been thinking." Frank paused. He must be a bloody idiot to offer this, even to his oldest friend, but he'd never forgive himself if he didn't at least try. And now that he'd totally pissed off Patrick by showering him with coffee and scalding his hands, he felt doubly obliged to reach out and offer him something.

"Yes, what?"

"I may be able to help Martina." There, he'd said it now. There was no going back. He only hoped his theory about the formula stacked up.

Patrick's face lit up. "That's wonderful. Thank you so much."

Frank smiled weakly, pleased to see Patrick so happy, but terrified that if things didn't go to plan, it could turn into a nightmare for both of them, all three of them, Martina included.

"So, when can we start? I've burnt my hands. I need to go home. And you look like you've spent the night in a doss-house. No one would blame you for taking the morning off too. We could start right away." Patrick's enthusiasm was running away with him.

"Tomorrow evening." The new chemicals should arrive tomorrow morning, giving him most of the day to produce a new batch of the drug.

"Frank, you don't understand. Martina hasn't got long. Even a short delay could make all the difference."

"I need to prepare properly," Frank insisted. "It will give Martina the best chance. I need to work out exactly how we're going to do this, without anyone finding out and without putting Martina at any risk. She's going to need a lot of monitoring." It was tempting to give in and start Martina on an existing batch of the drug today, simply to keep Patrick happy. He willed himself not to relent. Frank believed in the placebo effect for some things, but Martina's illness would never be helped by that. And giving her the wrong formulation might actually shorten her remaining lifespan, instead of prolonging it.

"Are you sure?"

Frank wasn't sure of anything. He must be insane. In all probability, it was already too late for Martina, and even Fexizon wouldn't be able to save her. At best, it might simply prolong her agony for a few more weeks. So he wasn't at all sure about doing this, without even going into the ethics and legality of the plan. But he had promised, so that no longer gave him a choice.

Chapter 43

"We know exactly what happened with the company's accounts." Evan Davies sat down and powered up his laptop.

"Yes, but we're still nowhere near to finding out who did it." The final creditors' and debtors' confirmation letters had come back earlier this week. Large numbers of invoices had been altered. By changing the dates of the transactions on either side of the company's financial year end, to include more income before the year end, and put all the suppliers' bills after that date, it painted a completely different picture of the company's financial position, a much rosier one. Of course, it would make the next financial year appear correspondingly worse but, whoever did it, would have a whole year to try to sort out that problem.

"We should really go back to head office now and write up our report," Evan said.

Clarke knew that. As far as T&C was concerned, they'd fulfilled their brief. Their remit didn't include finding out the *who* or the *why*. "Do you have any idea who might have done it?"

Evan sighed. "There are a few possibilities. Why don't you make a list." He took off his jacket, hanging it on the back of his chair. "What about Henry?"

"I can't see it," Clarke said, typing his name into her laptop, anyway. "Why would he call us in? It's drawing attention to the problem and spending extra money that he doesn't have. If he'd left it alone, probably no one would have noticed anything for months, if at all."

"Agreed. How about Patrick? He's the obvious suspect."

"Yes. He's the most qualified, with all the technical knowledge to pull this off. And his wife's dreadfully ill. He wants Frank to help her. So, if the company is in dire financial straits, he'd be keen to cover that up to keep it going."

"Agreed. Oh, and I forgot to say, my pharmacist friend checked out those drug invoices you gave me that were addressed to Patrick."

"Were they cancer drugs?" Clarke caught up with typing her notes.

"No. I thought they would be too, but they're anti-depressants. Pretty strong ones too."

"Are they for Patrick or his wife?" Clarke still believed that Patrick's wife would be prescribed anything like that by her consultant at the hospital. She wouldn't need to get it off the internet.

"Don't know, but my friend says whoever's taking them would probably be in la-la land half the time. They're part sedative and part happy pills. If Patrick is using them, he wouldn't be functioning anywhere close to the top of his game. No wonder the company's finances are in a mess."

"Wow. That would explain a lot. The thing is, I'm pretty certain it wouldn't be in his best interests to try to kill off Frank and Ollie."

"Who said anything about that?" Evan stood up and paced across the room. "Let's stick to the financial problems."

"We can't," Clarke said. "We've got huge financial irregularities, a murder, and an attempted murder, all in the same small company. What're the chances of that?"

"Coincidences happen."

"No, they don't," Clarke insisted. "Not ones like that. Not often. Almost never."

"If they're connected, it's a conundrum," Evan said. "On the one hand, you've got the accounts manipulation, which is in the company's favour, then the murder, which most definitely is not."

"Did Ollie know something detrimental to the company?"

"It's possible, but how would we ever find out?"

"Just putting a few things out there. Something for the genius of Evan Davies to ponder." Evan possessed a brilliant analytical mind. He might come up with something Clarke hadn't considered.

"What about Frank? Could he be the killer?"

Clarke laughed. "Nothing's impossible, but I really can't see it. Can you?"

"No. I don't think he's the murdering type."

"I'm not sure what is," Clarke said. "In any case, he couldn't have attacked himself."

"Good point." Evan laughed.

"What about Deborah? Poison's supposed to be a woman's weapon, isn't it?"

"That's a bit sexist," Evan said. "It's a coward's weapon if you ask me. Like leaving out rat poison. No need to confront the victim or do the deed. It removes the perpetrator from the equation, when it comes to the actual death."

"But Deborah would gain indirectly if she manipulated the accounts in the company's favour. It might be good for her career."

"Only if she was planning to leave fairly soon," Evan said, "before the brown stuff hits the fan."

"Maybe she is." Clarke still had a hunch that Deborah and Henry might be having an affair. It may be making things tricky for her.

"Is this the kind of thing you talk about with Paul?" Evan asked. "Serial killers and psychos before bedtime?"

Clarke ignored the comment. Paul's last conversation with her went more along the lines of *stop trying to do my job, or you'll get hurt*. She already was getting hurt, not physically, but hurt nonetheless. She still hadn't got over Paul omitting to tell his colleagues about her, and it was making her extremely insecure about their relationship.

"I suppose Deborah does possess the expertise. She's got an MBA."

"I'd forgotten that," Clarke said. "Ok, she's definitely on the list."

"Who have we missed?"

"Kerry." Clarke was sure that Kerry had a massive crush on Patrick. If he asked her to help him, she would never be able to refuse.

"Is she knowledgeable enough to pull off that kind of accounts manipulation? Those replacement invoices were expertly done. They looked like the real thing."

"Evan! She probably learnt enough to do that in her first year of accountancy exams. And, as for the invoices, my brother could have produced them easily by the time he was eight years old." Clarke wondered if Evan underestimated Kerry because of her relative youth.

"That's an unfair comparison. Your brother's a computer genius."

"True," Clarke said. Rob's awesomeness with computers had led him to run his own successful company inventing computer games. "But the point I'm making is that lots of teenagers can do clever stuff on Photoshop. They learn that in school. They're not old relics like you."

"Ok. I'm not completely past it. I'm twenty-eight."

"And I'm pretty certain that Kerry is in love with Patrick too. That's a motive."

"He's old enough to be her father," Evan said. "Are you sure?"

"You've only got to listen to her talk about him. It's obvious."

"Not sure it's a motive, though. I mean, she couldn't tell him she'd done it, could she?"

"Love can be philanthropic. Maybe it would be enough to see Patrick happy, or he may even have taken advantage and asked her to help him."

"I still don't buy it, but leave her on the list. I'd hate to be accused of being ageist." Evan made a face at her. "What puzzles me still is how the auditors managed to miss this. They would have done the same thing as you did, sending debtors and creditors confirmation letters."

"Could someone have bribed them to ignore it?" Clarke asked.

"That would be risky. Unless one of them was related to someone here. Can you ask Paul to investigate that?"

"I'll mention it." Paul might be able to help. She hoped so. It would bug her intensely not to get to the bottom of things. "So, what do we do now?" Clarke realised their task was nearly complete, but it concerned her that there was still a murderer out there somewhere. "Can we stay here while we write up the report?"

"Exactly what I planned to suggest. Except, I'll write the report. You can talk to people. You're good at that. See if you can wheedle any more secrets out of them."

"Not much chance of that." Clarke laughed. "But I'll try to find out who may have had the opportunity. See what else I can discover too. Just don't write too quickly."

Chapter 44

Frank pounced on the parcel containing his drug components, keen to start work on the new formulation. It was nearly 11:00 a.m. already, and he had promised to visit Martina this evening.

He had the lab to himself. Carmen fed the rats and cleaned out the cages earlier. Henry wanted her to help out upstairs for the rest of the day, cleaning the offices while the usual cleaner took a holiday and making tea and coffee. Henry often borrowed her like that. Some weeks she spent more time working upstairs than she did for Frank. He must talk to Henry about that. With Ollie gone, he needed the extra help in the lab. He remembered the budget cuts. No way would Henry let him recruit anybody else yet. Until then, it would just be him and Carmen.

He spent the next hour meticulously checking the exact list of ingredients he needed, then began weighing them out.

Deciding the process was too critical to leave anything if he popped out to buy a sandwich, Frank skipped lunch. Kas frequently nagged him to go on a diet anyway, so it wouldn't do him any harm. He didn't fancy using the shortcut alleyway into Brackford either, not after the attack. Best to keep working. He got out his mini tablet-press machine, sterilising it to ensure nothing got contaminated. He needed Carmen. She could have done jobs like this, freeing his time to do more important stuff.

By 5:00 p.m., forty-eight perfect tablets lay on a stainless steel tray in front of him. That would be enough for a twenty-four-day supply for Martina. Quite honestly, if they didn't make a significant difference by then, they were wasting their time. He vacuum-sealed the tablets and boxed them up.

His hands shook as he put the last tablets into the box. The enormity of his actions, both the testing that might prove the brilliance of his drug and the illegality of doing uncontrolled testing on a person, terrified him.

Chapter 45

This was the second time this week that Clarke had given Carmen a lift home. She hadn't meant to offer, but she couldn't bear the sight of a bedraggled Carmen waiting at the bus stop in the rain.

"I'll see you in the office tomorrow, shall I?" Clark said as she dropped Carmen off outside her block of flats.

"No, I'm having a day off tomorrow."

Clarke smiled. Well, at least that would be one day she wouldn't feel obliged to drive Carmen home. Probably the only day. Clarke simply couldn't say no. Since Carmen had told her she'd lost both her daughter and her husband, she hadn't been able to get that out of her head. Ollie's death on top of that must be unbearable for her. Every time she saw Carmen, Clarke put herself in her shoes and imagined how awful life must be for her. And Carmen carried around an air of tragedy. Even though she spent a lot of time trying to smile and be friendly, she exuded an underlying current of unhappiness, so the simple act of smiling became an effort, not a pleasure. Clarke felt desperately sorry for her. So how could she ever say no?

She turned the car around to go out of the housing estate where Carmen lived and started driving slowly towards the exit road. At least the rain had stopped now. A little way up the road, suddenly her head snapped around, as if drawn by a huge magnet. She instantly recognised the mop of curly black hair. Timmo Macintosh. What was he doing here?

In a moment of madness, Clarke pulled the car up onto the kerb and got out, curious to find out where Timmo might be going. Did he live in this area, or was he visiting? Either way, Clarke guessed he'd be up to no good. Something about him made her suspicious every time she saw him.

She followed him at a distance, ducking behind parked cars to keep out of sight whenever possible. Although she shouldn't be worried about being seen. She had every right to be here. If he questioned her, she'd tell him she was visiting a friend, as if it was even any of his business. But at least it would be the truth. Giving Carmen a lift home gave her a good reason to be here.

Timmo sauntered along without a care in the world, except that his saunter proved faster than Clarke's walk. Those long legs ate up the distance effortlessly. Clark would have preferred to walk slower, although, so far today, her ankle was standing up to the strain. Perhaps all the recent stress on her ankle was strengthening it. She gave herself a reality check. It hadn't got stronger in what, four years, five years? So there really wasn't much hope. She must learn to live with it. And she had. She made the best of what she'd got and got on with life. No point in being miserable, pitying herself all the time.

Before long, Timmo turned a corner, and for a few moments, Clarke lost sight of him. She jogged a few strides in an attempt to catch up. But when she rounded the corner, she'd lost him. She wondered where he might have gone. This was Carmen's block of flats. The only logical place to go from here would be through the communal entrance. She scanned the area again for any sign of Timmo, but he'd vanished. Had he already entered the block of flats? Could he have covered that distance in those few seconds? She found that hard to imagine. She conceded it might be possible if he ran fast enough. Clarke wondered if he knew Carmen, or if he simply lived in the same block of flats. Plenty of people must live in that same block without knowing each other. Timmo and Carmen were hardly likely to be well-acquainted.

Something struck her as odd. The day when she'd been going out the front entrance with Carmen. Carmen had suddenly noticed the protestors outside and decided to go out the back door, putting her hand up to her face. Clark had ignored it at the time, but the oddity of it stayed in her head. Carmen had been trying to hide her face. Perhaps she did know this Timmo character. Perhaps more than she admitted to.

She looked around, still not seeing Timmo. He'd magic-ed himself away without even a puff of smoke. Clarke decided to go home. She would ask Carmen about him next time she saw her, find out if she and Timmo were acquainted and how well.

Clarke started to walk back to the car. Suddenly, a hand clamped over her mouth from behind her, taking her by surprise. Her body was pulled backwards, causing her to nearly lose her balance. The large, rough hand pressed hard against her face, ramming her backwards against her assailant and muffling her attempt at a scream. She struggled and tried to pull the hand off, but she was no match for her attacker's strength. If he was trying to mug her, she had nothing to give him. She'd left her handbag in the car. Clarke frantically wracked her brain for some way to get out of this. She hoped he wouldn't hurt her when he discovered she was empty-handed.

"What are you doing here?" he asked.

Clarke couldn't answer, not with his hand still clamped over her mouth. She struggled again, but his free hand snapped up to grip her arms.

"You need to stay out of my business, bitch."

Clarke recognised his voice, sure it was Timmo Macintosh. Instinctively, she lifted her good leg and smashed her foot backwards as hard as she could, making contact with his leg, right on his shin bone. He loosened his grip on her, just enough for her to wrench her arms out of his hold. Then, before he could react, she whacked her elbow back into his stomach. He let go. She grabbed her chance and ran.

She was aware of running in the wrong direction, with no clue where to find her car, but all that mattered right now was getting as far away from Timmo as possible. She ran faster, ignoring the pain in her ankle. It was several minutes before she dared to turn around. No sign of Timmo, but that didn't mean anything. This housing estate was a rabbit warren of random alleyways. That must be how Timmo had managed to come up behind her in the first place.

Clarke wasn't sure how to find her car, kicking herself for ever getting out of it. She shouldn't be getting involved with people like this. Timmo Macintosh seemed dangerous when she'd met him that first day. And she hadn't changed her mind about him now, no matter how much Henry tried to reassure her. The way Timmo bristled with anger scared her, and she didn't trust him one bit. Henry was wrong. And why was Timmo threatening her like that? She tried to remember what she'd done that might have affected him in any way, but drew a blank. What business of his did he want her to stay out of? She really hoped that Timmo wasn't in any way involved with Carmen because he was bad news. She would warn her next time she saw her.

Clarke kept walking, too scared to go back the way she'd come in case Timmo might be waiting for her. She turned left. If she tried to walk in a huge circle, eventually she would end up near her car. There were alleyways everywhere. There must be one that would give her a shortcut back to the car, although the idea of being stuck in an alleyway with Timmo frightened her. Her mind flashed back to finding Frank unconscious in the alley near the office. If Timmo cornered her down one of these paths, she wouldn't come off well. He wouldn't make the mistake of letting her go twice.

A little ahead of her, Clarke spotted a woman walking her dog, a pretty little brown Yorkshire Terrier.

"Hi," Clark called, careful not to come right up behind her and startle her. Although anyone who lived in this area probably didn't get scared too easily—definitely not a good area to be lost in. "Excuse me," she said. "I'm not sure where I am. How do I get back to the road with the supermarket on the corner?" She wished she'd taken note of the road name.

The woman seemed to realise exactly where she meant. "You'll need to go back the way you came," she said. "You can't get through if you carry on in this direction." She pointed back down the road behind

Clarke. "Go around the corner of that building. Take the next right turn and you're there."

Clarke thanked her. Her heart sank at the prospect of retracing her steps and possibly running into Timmo Macintosh again. She would really need to keep her wits about her. And if he came anywhere near her, she'd scream the place down and run. There must be lots of people around. Not that any of them would take any notice. If they were indoors, they would probably turn the TV up louder if they heard screaming. They were probably used to it around here.

She considered going to Carmen's flat but didn't actually know the flat number. She started walking back, marching stridently as if she owned the place, as if no one would ever dare to come up and accost her. They'd better not anyway. Constantly, Clarke scanned her surroundings for any sign of Timmo. Thank God, she didn't see him. He might be anywhere by now.

She hoped this wouldn't give her further problems getting into the Carjon office. Next time they were protesting, she resolved to be extra careful, to avoid running into Timmo again. She couldn't even call for help because she'd got out of her car so quickly to follow that awful man and left her phone behind. Whatever was she thinking? Now the fear was starting to subside, leaving Clarke feeling pretty stupid. The hunter had become the prey. How on earth did she let that happen?

Clarke turned the final corner and now she could see her car not too far away. What a huge relief. She reminded herself not to let her guard down yet, in case Timmo still lurked somewhere. No relaxing until she was safely in the car with the doors locked. She certainly didn't intend to come back here, ever. Let Carmen take the bus next time. It wouldn't kill her. She'd been doing exactly that ever since Carjon had employed her. Havebury was out of Clarke's area, anyway.

At last, Clarke got back into the car. She clicked the central locking button as soon as she slammed the door shut and fumbled to put her seat belt on. As she accelerated out onto the road, she allowed herself a tiny sigh of relief. She'd be much happier once she put a couple of miles between her and Timmo Macintosh. Even happier when she got back home.

She wondered if Timmo was on Paul's radar. He must have a police record, given all his animal rights activities. Surely, he'd been arrested for something by now. Paul probably wouldn't be permitted to tell her, but if she told him Timmo was harassing her, he'd at least be able to keep an eye on things. On the other hand, Paul had just given her a lecture about keeping out of trouble. So maybe she wouldn't tell him anything about this. She'd made a stupid mistake, and she didn't intend to do it again. Paul didn't need to know.

Hopefully, Paul would come over tonight, if he didn't have to work too late. That would make her feel better. She could quiz him on the murder case. She hoped he was making more progress than her.

They'd questioned Frank more than once, but surely Frank would have never poisoned Ollie. She'd seen them together. Frank had so obviously been really fond of Ollie. Clarke simply didn't believe Frank would ever hurt him. He had no reason to. Which meant that someone must have wanted to poison Frank. That was the thing about poison. It was like leaving a mousetrap out. Hardly a well-targeted murder weapon. Much too hit and miss. Perhaps whoever did it wasn't very clever. That might narrow down the list of suspects, but there still had to be a reason why. Who would want to kill Frank? He seemed like a nice bloke, but you could never tell, could you? She'd only met him a few times. He could have a whole lot of secrets up his sleeve. Stuff that he didn't want people to find, so you would never guess what lay behind the mask. People hid so many things. She really wanted to talk to Frank again.

Chapter 46

Frank had been worrying about this all day. Now that he was finally here, at Patrick and Martina's house, about to break the law and almost certainly commit career suicide, he struggled to stop himself from shaking.

Patrick opened the door before Frank even got the chance to ring the doorbell. Patrick must have been watching for his arrival. Immediately, he felt even more pressured. He fingered the box of tablets, which were burning a hole in his pocket. It wasn't too late to back out. One look at Patrick and he knew he couldn't change his mind.

"Come in." Patrick closed the door behind him. Martina's upstairs. She's waiting for you in the bedroom.

Frank headed for the stairs. Patrick followed closely behind.

"Second on the left."

The door was ajar. Frank knocked anyway.

"Come in, Frank."

Martina sat up in bed, reading. She looked much more relaxed than Patrick did, and certainly miles calmer than Frank felt right now.

"Shall we get on with it?" Patrick moved to Martina's side. "What do you need to do?"

Martina interrupted before Frank could compose his thoughts. "Paddy Bear, perhaps you should give us some privacy. Let Frank concentrate on what he's doing."

Patrick took Martina's hand. "I wanted to be here to support you."

"I'll be fine. It's not as if Frank's a stranger. Why don't you make a start on cooking dinner? We don't want to be eating too late." Martina smiled at Patrick and pulled her hand away. "Go on, I'll be fine. I'm in capable hands."

Frank was relieved not to have an audience. Even so, he remained torn between the knowledge that he shouldn't be doing this and the excitement of finally being able to prove what Fexizon could do. Did

Martina understand what a huge risk he would be taking for her? He took the box of pills out of his pocket and set it on the bedside table. Seeing them made it more real and more terrifying on so many levels.

As soon as Patrick shut the door, Martina put her Kindle on the pillow next to her. "Frank, can I rely on you to keep patient confidentiality?"

Frank hesitated. She wasn't really a patient. He wasn't her doctor. He wondered what she wanted to keep hidden from Patrick.

"Yes, of course," he said, wanting to put her at ease, although he certainly didn't feel at ease himself.

"Good. Because Patrick mustn't find out any of this."

"Any of what? What's the problem, Martina?" He sat down on the corner of the bed, worried now. He didn't want to keep secrets from Patrick.

"I don't want the new drug," Martina said firmly.

"But Fexizon is a real breakthrough. It might really help you." It might be the only thing that would help her.

"And it might not."

"Martina, you need to try the Fexizon. It really might make a difference." Correcting the formula had restored his confidence in the drug. If Fexizon didn't cure Martina, nothing would. "Think of Patrick." Patrick would fall to pieces if Martina died. Frank couldn't bring himself to point out the obvious, that she would die without the drug. Surely, she knew that already.

"I'm dying, Frank. It's too late. All you'll be doing is prolonging the agony, and I'm tired of trying treatments that make me feel dreadful and don't work."

"But..." Frank stopped himself. Martina seemed very sure of this. And she was giving him an *out* from this impossible situation that Patrick had put him in.

"I understand. How are you going to tell Patrick? He'll be devastated."

"I'm not, and neither are you." Martina fumbled in her dressing gown pocket, pulling out a small packet. "They're vitamin tablets. I bought them on the internet. We'll put them in your packaging, and Patrick will never know. I can't tell him, Frank. He doesn't understand. All he sees is a chance to keep me forever. He won't accept the inevitable like I have. Trust me, I've had plenty of time to come to terms with this and it's for the best. It's what I want."

"But when..."

"When I die," Martina finished the sentence for him.

"Yes. Patrick will be heartbroken. And he'll assume my drug killed you."

"Frank, I never wanted to drag you into this in the first place, and I'm sorry. I've written Patrick a letter. My sister will give it to him after I die. It explains everything, including that I'm not taking your drug and absolving you of all blame. You've got nothing to worry about. But I need your help."

Frank nodded. He really hadn't expected this. A few minutes ago, he'd been worried sick about what he was going to do. Now he was experiencing a mixture of enormous relief, together with deep concern over how Patrick, his friend, would deal with this, and a tinge of regret that he wouldn't get the chance to test out Fexizon yet.

Chapter 47

This was Clarke and Evan's final Saturday at Carjon Pharma. Evan would probably be ready to present his report to Henry on Monday, then their work here would be complete. So this would be Clarke's final chance to snoop around the building, her one remaining chance to find some concrete evidence to prove who manipulated the accounts. She was sure Evan only agreed to it because they were being paid overtime.

"I've got a brilliant idea." Evan handed Clarke a coffee. Instant. Clarke craved Henry's Costa Rican blend, but they were both wary of the Carjon coffee since Ollie's poisoning, so they made do with Evan's jar of instant coffee.

"What?" asked Clarke, already wary. Evan's brilliant ideas often involved her doing extra work.

"How about if *you* present the report to Henry on Monday? You only need to give a twenty-minute presentation. It will be good for your career development."

"Me? No." Clarke was by no means shy, but giving a presentation, when she didn't consider herself an expert on the subject, terrified her, even if she would only be addressing an audience of one. Two, if she counted Evan. "I don't know enough about it."

Evan laughed. "Rubbish. You discovered the issue. You understand exactly what you're talking about. All you need to do is explain what's happened, how that affects the accounts, and quantify the size of the error."

"Maybe," Clarke said. Evan made it sound so easy. "But what if he starts asking questions I can't answer?"

"Ok, so we'll do a joint presentation," Evan said.

"Yes, that's a much better idea." Clarke happily agreed to that much less scary proposition. She saw Evan smiling and suspected that he intended to go with that scenario all along.

"We can rehearse it," Evan said. "After you find out who the guilty party is. Then you can present that to Henry too. Get Paul to stand by with some handcuffs for a grand finale."

"Don't even joke about that. Whoever did it will probably end up in prison." Clarke didn't want to actually name anyone, in case she got it wrong. Being wrongfully accused could be catastrophic for them. She downed the last dregs of her coffee and stood up. "I'll go and search the offices while you finalise the report, then you can coach me through the presentation."

Clarke went straight to Kerry's desk. She'd already searched the offices and found nothing. She'd not given much attention to Kerry as a suspect. Evan was right. Kerry didn't have anything to gain. And Clarke considered her too intelligent to risk going to prison for the sake of a schoolgirl crush on Patrick. But she wanted to be thorough. At least they might be able to rule Kerry out.

Kerry's desk was bare, apart from a purple orchid and a tub full of pens, arranged to either side of her computer monitor. Clarke thought of Rob, wishing she had her brother's computer expertise. Perhaps she would ask T&C to send her on a computer course for cybercrime. Although the truly paperless office didn't really exist, almost everything of use got stored on computer, so it made sense to become an expert.

She leant down and switched on Kerry's computer, on the hard drive located under her desk. It whirred into action, quickly showing a login screen. Clarke typed in Kerry's username. They were all standard, surname plus initial. She pondered for a moment. Three guesses before the computer locked her out. If that happened, it would be obvious to Kerry on Monday morning that someone had attempted to access her computer. Clarke and Evan would be prime suspects for that. So that meant only two guesses at the password. In reality, one guess, as she had no clue what Kerry might have used as a second choice.

Carefully, Clarke typed in *Patrick123*.

No one could have been more surprised than Clarke when the computer logged her in. She started searching through Kerry's files, opening up anything with a likely looking name. This might take forever. She would need to speed up.

Some time later, Evan came in and plonked another cup of coffee on the desk.

"Thanks," she mumbled, not looking up from her task.

"Looks promising," Evan said.

Carmen de Silva sat in her kitchen, gazing at the big star against today's date on her calendar. She'd been looking forward to today for the last couple of weeks, but now that it was here, she was starting to have doubts about whether she actually wanted to go through with it.

She picked Annie's photo off the fridge door. "My darling girl," she said, kissing the photo before putting it neatly back in its place. Carmen realised now how much she did want to do this. She was doing it for Annie. Her young life had been so cruelly snuffed out, and now it was time for everyone to pay.

For a minute, she stared at her daughter's photo, then plucked it off the fridge and put it in her coat pocket. Carmen checked her watch. The bus was due in less than ten minutes. Taking a deep breath, she picked up the bag Timmo had given her last night and walked out of her flat.

An hour later, Clarke finally found something interesting. She printed it out before taking a sip of her coffee. Stone-cold. She forced herself to swallow it. After a bit more digging, she quickly logged out of Kerry's computer and went back to Evan.

"Look at this." Clarke pushed the piece of paper she had printed in front of him.

"A journal?"

"Yes."

"And..."

"And that's Frank's research cost centre. That's a ton of spend being moved out of it. It's relevant spend that probably should be in there. I looked up the current position. He's hugely underspent, and I mean HUGELY. Kerry moved the spend."

"Really? Why would Kerry do that?" Evan looked as puzzled as Clarke. "Did she do it to help Patrick? His wife's seriously ill. He needs Frank to be able to spend more money on research."

"That doesn't really make sense," Clarke said. "Yes, I'm sure now that she's in love with Patrick. Her password is Patrick's name."

"Wow," Evan said. "That's obsessive."

"Anyway, firstly, any research that Frank does now will take years to get to the stage where it can help Patrick's wife. Frank explained it all to me. It's a slow process."

"And secondly?"

"Yes, secondly, how would it benefit Kerry to save Patrick's wife? She's more likely to want her to die, isn't she? With the wife out of the way, Patrick would be free for Kerry to make a move."

"Good point. So maybe somebody told her to do it."

"If it's anything dodgy, surely Patrick would do it himself, rather than involve Kerry," Clarke said.

Evan laughed. "You've got so much to learn. When you're young and at the start of your career, you learn all these things, like how to input journals. Then, the higher up you get, the more you get used to delegating, and all you do is go to meetings all day and talk. Then, eventually, you forget how to work the computer system, or you never bother learning how to work a new one properly because you've got people to do the work for you. Then when you actually need to do a dodgy transaction, like this one, you find you don't have a clue how to load it onto the system. Patrick probably needed Kerry to do the job for him."

"And if Patrick asked Kerry to do it, her name goes against the transaction on the computer system, not his. He doesn't get implicated."

"Good point," Evan said. "So, either Patrick or Kerry want to show that Frank's underspending his budget, so it appears there's plenty of money left. And they also manipulate the accounts, so the company looks much healthier financially than it really is."

"So, the question is, why would they want to kill Ollie and attack Frank? It doesn't make any sense."

"No. The question is, how can we prove which one of them manipulated the accounts? Solving a murder case is not in our remit."

Evan sounded very firm, so Clarke decided not to argue. If they got to the bottom of the accounts cover-up, they would likely be one step closer to discovering who murdered Ollie and attacked Frank. Clarke still found it hard to accept that there would be so many completely separate incidents in the same small company, in such a short space of time. But Evan may be right in this case. Clarke still wondered if Timmo had anything to do with the attacks. He'd already shown her his violent streak.

"I need to talk to Kerry on Monday," Clarke said. "We can prove she did the technical bit of loading the transactions onto the system. If I can get her to open up, she might tell me who told her to do it."

Evan agreed. "I'm not going to finish my report today anyway, so we'll probably be here until Tuesday at this rate. It's gone three o'clock. Why don't you go home? I'll stay for another couple of hours. I'm meeting some friends in Brackford at five, so there's no point in me going home first."

"Thanks." Clarke closed up her laptop. It would be nice to get an extra couple of hours to get the flat clean and tidy before Paul came over later. Not that he would appreciate that. "I'll see you Monday."

"Don't be late. We'll start going through the presentation."

Clarke resolved to be mega-early on Monday. She hoped she wouldn't spend the rest of the weekend worrying about this presentation. It was a good opportunity, but scary. Clarke smiled at the irony. In her previous career as a firefighter, she frequently had gone into dangerous burning buildings, yet public speaking, even to only a couple of people, made her wobble at the knees. She supposed she would need to get used to it.

She was still worrying about the presentation when she rounded the corner towards the staff exit and almost knocked Carmen flying. She hadn't even realised anyone else was in the building.

"I'm so sorry. I was miles away," she said as soon as the initial shock wore off.

"It's ok." Carmen picked up the bag she had dropped.

"Can I at least offer you a lift home after I nearly flattened you?" Clarke asked. She'd promised herself she wouldn't give Carmen a lift home again, not after her run-in with Timmo near Carmen's flat, but how could she not offer? Hopefully, Carmen would say no.

"Thank you, that's very kind. That would be lovely."

Clarke gritted her teeth and smiled. "You're welcome. Here, let me carry that." Carmen's bag looked heavy. Still feeling guilty in case she had hurt Carmen, Clarke at least wanted to try to help.

"No." Carmen hugged the bag towards her. "I can manage."

Clarke wished she hadn't bothered asking. Carmen was a bit touchy today. Perhaps she had that same independent streak in her that Clarke herself had. She understood that. Even so, she could have refused a little more politely. She hoped Carmen would lighten up, or it would seem an eternally long journey to her flat.

Clarke opened the car door for her, standing aside, not daring to offer any more help as Carmen hoisted the bag inside.

"You must work a lot of weekends now," Clarke said after a long silence. They were nearly halfway to Carmen's house, and Clarke had been regretting her offer for the entire journey so far. Carmen was definitely in a mood today. Clarke hadn't dared speak until now.

"I went to feed the rats," she said. "Frank and I share the work between us now that Ollie..." she trailed off, not needing to actually put into words the fact that Ollie was dead.

After another minute of silence, clearly Carmen wasn't going to say anything more. "Evan and I were trying to finish things up, ready for next week," Clarke said. "We won't be here for much longer."

"That's a shame working on Saturday."

"Yes, it absolutely is, but the job needs to be done. At least I get to go home early. Evan is working until five."

"Evan is still in the building?"

Did she detect a hint of worry in Carmen's voice? Clarke ignored it. She was good at imagining things that weren't there, reading things into situations that didn't actually exist. She needed to relax more. The traffic lights turned amber. Clarke accelerated across and moved into the outside lane of the dual carriageway. The sooner she dropped Carmen off and got home, the better.

Chapter 48

"Are you ok?" Carmen was very fidgety and Clarke noticed her checking her watch for at least the fifth time.

Carmen hesitated, so Clarke assumed she intended to keep up the silence. "Do you need to be somewhere?" The way she kept looking at the time, she must be seriously late for something.

"We need to go back," Carmen said.

"Back?" They weren't far now from Carmen's flat. Clarke just wanted to get home.

"To the office."

Clarke looked across at Carmen. Sweat dripped down her face and her hands trembled. "Are you ok? You don't look well."

Carmen shook her head. "Please, we must go back." She looked at her watch again. "We don't have much time."

Clarke turned off the dual carriageway and pulled up at the side of the road. "What the hell's going on, Carmen?" Carmen's odd behaviour was really worrying her.

"Please, we need to go back, quickly." Carmen reached for the door handle, but the central locking prevented her from leaving.

"Yes, you keep saying that, but why? What's the problem?"

"Please," Carmen begged.

Clarke stared at her. "We're not going anywhere until you explain."

Carmen avoided her gaze. "Evan," she said almost inaudibly. "We have to get Evan out of the office."

Without waiting for further explanation, Clarke pulled her phone out of her handbag and hit Evan's name in her contacts list. The phone rang twice before diverting to voicemail. Clarke growled at it in frustration. Knowing Evan, he'd probably switched his phone off so he wouldn't be disturbed.

Carmen snivelled in the passenger seat. Clarke ignored her. As fast as possible, she turned the car around and put her foot to the floor. The clock on the dashboard said 3:35.

Something clicked in Clarke's brain. Carmen had told her last week that she'd had her daughter when she was thirty-five. The daughter who was around Ollie's age. That would make Carmen very late fifties. She must have gone through the menopause by now.

"How long have we got?" Clarke demanded.

Carmen continued to cry.

"How long?" Clarke was shouting now. She would get an answer from Carmen even if she had to beat it out of her. A lorry started to pull out in front of her. She swerved around it, thrusting her foot down hard on the accelerator and blasting past it.

"Four fifteen." Carmen cried more violently now, her whole body shaking with sobs.

Bloody hell, if the return journey took as long as it had to get out here, that gave her five minutes to get into the office, find Evan, and get out. She would need to be very much faster on the return drive.

The star on Carmen's calendar. The one Paul had told her about. Something big was happening, something she didn't want to spell out, and it was today. And it sure as hell wasn't her time of the month.

She needed to get Carmen talking. "Is it the animal rights people? What have they done?" She glanced down at Carmen's bag, lying in the footwell of the passenger seat, and wondered what was in it.

Carmen continued to cry. Clarke shot her questions at full force. "Is it a bomb?" *Please God, let her be wrong about that.* "For pity's sake, Carmen, give me some answers."

"Yes." The answer came out as a tiny whimper.

Clarke glanced at the clock. 3:50 p.m. They had nearly reached Brackford already, but the roundabouts and traffic lights would slow them down now. The traffic was starting to build up—shoppers going home from their Saturday outings.

She ought to phone the police, but she didn't have hands-free on her phone and, if she told them about the bomb, they wouldn't go into the building until all the necessary expert teams arrived. That would be far too late. She would phone for help as soon as Evan was safe. Clarke dropped the car into second gear and blasted across the roundabout in front of her as she spotted a gap in the traffic.

Four p.m. Nearly there. There was a no-right-turn sign into the office car park from this direction. You were meant to carry on past Carjon, go round the roundabout, and come back up on the other side of the road. No time for that. Checking for any approaching traffic, Clarke spun the car right-handed across the road. The traffic camera would snap her and she'd get fined. Right now, she didn't care.

As soon as she got into the car park, Clarke slammed on the brakes, abandoning the car as far away from the building as possible. Grabbing her phone and her entry pass, she sprinted across the tarmac. As she raced towards the building, she speed-dialled Evan. He still didn't answer.

The staff entrance door opened as soon as she zapped it with her pass. Quickly, she headed for the stairs. Evan had to be somewhere on the first floor, probably in the boardroom, with his phone on silent. She screamed his name, again and again. "EVAN."

Clarke slammed open the boardroom door. Evan looked up, puzzled.

"Quick, we..." Clarke cut herself off as she saw Evan remove his earbuds. "There's a bomb. We have to get out."

Evan seemed frozen for a minute. Clarke pulled at his arm. "Come on," she shouted.

He pulled himself together. "Where?"

"I don't know, but we need to get out fast."

A couple of seconds seemed like forever before Evan fully understood the urgency. They ran along the corridor. "I think it's the animal rights protestors," Clarke said. She would be willing to bet that Timmo

Macintosh had something to do with it. No doubt Carmen would be able to tell the police more.

"Oh my God," Evan said, puffing from the exertion. "Aren't they supposed to be peaceful?" He grabbed the door, pulling it open. "Wait. Did you see Frank leave?"

"Frank?"

"I saw him in the kitchen ten minutes ago. He came up for some coffee. Said he was going to the lab."

"Get out and call the police," Clarke said, turning abruptly. Of course, the bomb must be in Frank's lab. She needed to find him, fast.

"No, Clarke, wait." Evan tried to grab Clarke's arm, but she was too quick.

"Just get out, Evan. I'll be ok. And find Carmen," she shouted.

Chapter 49

Clarke raced down the stairs to the lab. There was no time to check her watch. She just hoped there was enough time left to get out. "Frank," she screamed. "Frank, where are you?"

She opened the lab door. "Frank."

He sat at his desk, coffee in one hand, a big white rat in the other.

"Frank, we need to get out of here, fast. There's a bomb."

Frank was a good deal quicker than Evan to cotton on, like he'd done this before. He jumped up, dropping the coffee, but keeping hold of the rat. "There's a fire exit," he said as Clarke turned back the way she'd come. "It'll be quicker."

Clarke followed him, running to the back of the lab. Frank threw himself down on the exit bar on the fire door. Nothing happened. He pushed the bar down again and shoved the door hard with his shoulder.

"Somebody's locked it," he said. "Out the other way. Quick."

Clarke beat him to the door and raced up the stairs two at a time, her heart pounding in time with Frank's heavy footsteps behind her. She ran to the staff entrance. It didn't need a staff pass to open it from inside. She thumped at the exit button. The door didn't move. The realisation hit her like a thunderbolt. Someone had locked them in.

"How do we get out?" Clarke didn't dare look at her watch. Surely it must be nearly 4:15 by now.

"There's another fire exit upstairs," Frank said.

"We don't have time." If the upstairs fire exit was locked too, they would stand no chance. She spotted a fire extinguisher on the wall near reception and ran over and pulled it off the wall.

"That isn't going to help with a bomb," Frank yelled at her. "I'm going to try upstairs."

"No." Clarke thrust the fire extinguisher towards him. "Use this as a battering ram and break the glass." The full-length windows fronting the reception area loomed ahead of them. "Run at it and put all your strength behind it." Frank was much stronger than her. If the window was made of toughened glass, he would need some strength to stand any chance of breaking it.

Frank hugged the extinguisher under his arm.

"Hurry," Clarke screamed. She watched, terrified, as Frank ran at the window, ramming the extinguisher into the window with as much force as he could manage.

The window cracked. Frank bounced backwards as he hit the glass, struggling to keep his balance.

Clarke's heart plummeted. They were going to run out of time.

Frank charged at the window again. This time he angled the extinguisher, making a sharp edge to bash against the glass.

The window cracked much more, and some shards of glass broke away. Frank grabbed at the remaining glass shards, frantically pulling them out of the way to make a gap.

"Go on," he said.

Clarke stepped through the hole easily as Frank pulled out some more pieces and, seconds later, they were both outside.

"Run," Clarke shouted. "Get away from the building." If a bomb exploded now, at worst it could kill them if they were too close. At best, the windows would get blasted outwards, sending broken glass flying everywhere.

They sprinted across the car park. Clarke was surprised by how fast Frank ran, especially for such a big man, but fear either froze you, or it gave your feet wings. Frank's feet were flying.

Evan stood by Clarke's car, still talking on the phone when they reached him. "Thank God you're ok," he said. "The bomb squad are on their way."

Frank leaned against the car, breathing heavily. "What's going on?" he asked.

"It's the animal rights activists," Clarke said. "Carmen told me." She looked around. "Where is Carmen?" She'd disappeared. Clarke hoped she wouldn't do anything stupid. She had been extremely stressed. Had Carmen been coerced into helping the animal rights group? Their leader, Timmo, lived in the same block of flats as Carmen. Clarke knew first-hand how intimidating Timmo could be. She scanned the car park, wondering if Timmo was here somewhere. Had he locked them in the building?

"Carmen? What, our Carmen? How would she know?" Frank looked perplexed.

Clarke suddenly realised there had been no explosion. She checked the time. Four twenty-six. "The bomb should have gone off eleven minutes ago." Had this whole thing been a hoax? Why would they do that?

Frank took the rat out of his jacket pocket, making Evan jump back. "It's ok, Delilah. Nothing bad's going to happen. You can go back to your friends now." He turned to Clarke. "There is no bomb. They've done this before, made empty threats. Trouble is, we always have to take it seriously. Bet one of them is hiding somewhere, filming us. It'll be on YouTube later."

"Frank, your hands are bleeding." He must have cut them when he pulled the glass out of the window. Pink patches stained Delilah's perfect white coat.

"It's nothing. Just a few scratches," he said.

Clarke sighed. She opened the car door, desperate to sit down and take the weight off her bad ankle. With all that running, she could hardly stand up, and she almost certainly wouldn't be fit to drive home safely today, assuming she didn't get instantly banned for speeding and making a prohibited right turn. She wondered if rescuing someone from a non-existent bomb would count as a valid excuse to get out of paying a fine. She closed her eyes for a moment, trying to breathe through the pain.

When she opened them again a few seconds later, Evan was sitting in the passenger seat next to her. She looked around. "Where's Frank?"

"He's gone back inside. Needs to feed the rats," Evan said.

Clarke jumped out of the car. "You shouldn't have let him go." She knew a little about bombs from her years in the fire brigade. Sometimes the first device failed, but often there would be a secondary device, timed to go off a bit later, to cause maximum destruction.

Frank was already halfway across the car park. Clarke shouted to him. He ignored her, so she ran towards him, limping like crazy. She needed to stop him. It wasn't safe to go inside. What if it wasn't a hoax? Carmen had seemed really upset. Had she been forced to plant the bomb? Did she know it was real? Is that why she told Clarke to come back, so that Evan wouldn't die? She wouldn't have done that for a hoax bomb. Besides, if it was a hoax, wouldn't they have phoned to let people know, so they could cause the maximum disruption when the building was evacuated? No one put a hoax bomb in an empty building. What would be the point?

Chapter 50

Frank must be twenty metres from the door now. Clarke was still much further away. She kept shouting at Frank, her yells getting eaten up in the open space of the Carjon car park.

She felt the blast almost before she heard it.

The force of the explosion knocked her off her feet even from a good distance away. Immediately, she propped herself up, looking for Frank. He lay sprawled on the ground nearer the building, completely motionless. Clarke pushed herself up off the tarmac. Still a bit shaky and dazed, she went over to Frank and bent down next to him.

"Can you hear me?" She couldn't even hear her own words with the blast still ringing in her ears. She reached for Frank's wrist and found a pulse. Drops of blood speckled his face. Debris littered the surrounding ground. Something must have hit Frank.

Clarke surveyed the damage. Part of the front wall had been blown out, and the ground was strewn with broken glass and bits of rubble. Across the car park, Evan remained by Clarke's car. She strained to focus better. It looked like Carmen was standing next to him. That was good news. Carmen would have a lot of questions to answer. At least she hadn't run away.

She forced herself to concentrate on Frank, leaning over him to check his breathing. He needed an ambulance. Hopefully, one would arrive soon, together with the explosive experts.

A moment later, she looked over at Evan again. Even from this distance, Clarke could tell that something was wrong by the way Evan stood so tensely, and neither he nor Carmen moved, like they were frozen to the spot with fear. Perhaps she should expect that. After all, witnessing a bomb going off in the building Evan had been sitting in a few minutes earlier would make anyone tense, wouldn't it? She shouted at him and waved for him to come over. He still didn't move.

She needed to stay with Frank. Pulling her phone out of her pocket, she dialled 999.

"Ambulance," she said as soon as they answered her call. Even though Evan had said he'd called the emergency services earlier, she refused to take any chances. "And police, and fire brigade." The whole scene was a disaster. She needed everybody.

"Frank, can you hear me?" She tried again to get a reaction from him, but still nothing. His pulse was getting weaker.

Suddenly, she felt a presence behind her.

"Clarke." Evan's voice. "Clarke, be careful."

Clarke glanced around.

Carmen was clutching Evan's arm. Something felt desperately wrong.

"Clarke, she's got a bomb." Evan's voice came out in short gasps. "It's a suicide vest. She's threatening to detonate it."

Clarke immediately remembered Carmen's bag. Was the suicide vest in it? She cursed herself for not looking earlier, after she'd found out about the bomb.

"Carmen? What's the problem?" Clarke spoke softly, not wanting to aggravate her. "I'm sure we can help. You don't have to do this."

"Is Frank dead?" she asked.

"He's not looking good." Maybe if Carmen thought he might die, she'd let Clarke help him.

Carmen didn't answer.

"Who made you do this?" As soon as the words escaped her mouth, Clarke regretted them. She didn't want to antagonise Carmen. Not while Carmen was clinging on to Evan with a bomb strapped around her torso.

Chapter 51

Evan looked terrified.

"Why don't you let Evan go, and we can talk about this. Everything will be ok. We can work things out. Evan hasn't done anything." Carmen had made her come back to save Evan. Why would she want to hurt him now? But she was too much of an emotional mess to think straight, so Clarke worried about what she might do. She tried again. "Evan doesn't deserve to get hurt. He's got a wife and children," ~It was a lie, but Carmen wouldn't realise that. She hoped Evan wouldn't correct her. Clarke hadn't risked her life to get Evan out of the building only to get him blown up now.

"It's all gone wrong," Carmen said. "There's nothing left for me now. I may as well press the button."

"No," Clarke said. "Think about it. How will that solve anything?"

"It would solve what I'm feeling now. I've made things worse. I don't know what to do."

"There's an answer for everything." Clarke willed herself to stay calm, even with her heart beating at a million miles an hour, threatening to fly out through her chest at any moment. "You don't need to do this. We can make it ok."

"Nothing can ever be ok again. There's nothing left for me to live for. My daughter died, and it's his fault." Carmen pointed at Frank, waving her arm angrily at him while holding what looked like a remote device.

"I don't understand," Clarke said. She needed to pacify Carmen before that detonator went off by accident. "Tell me about it."

"It's his fault. His drug trial killed her."

"Why don't you tell me exactly what happened." The soft, soothing tone of Clarke's voice belied the panic that coursed through her whole body. She wondered where she got the sound from, certain it couldn't have come from anywhere inside of her. Not right now.

Carmen lowered her arm. "My daughter signed up for his drug trial two years ago."

"Tell me about your daughter." Clarke was keen to get onto more neutral ground, something that would make Carmen less angry.

"Annie. Her name was Annie. She was a lovely girl, beautiful and kind, the best daughter a mother could wish for." A tiny smile flickered across Carmen's face. "Annie wanted the money to go on holiday with her friends from university. They planned to tour South America and visit Rio de Janeiro, where I come from. She was so excited about it."

Carmen sighed, relaxing her grip on Evan. Clarke hoped Evan wouldn't try anything stupid. She glanced at him, but from the blank expression on his face, she guessed he was in deep shock.

"She needed money, and Frank paid three thousand pounds to each volunteer. Me and my husband could have never given her so much money. That murderer promised her it would be all right. He said there was no risk." Carmen began to cry. "Annie signed up for the testing because she believed him. But she was perfectly healthy. She shouldn't have died."

"If Frank was to blame, he should go to trial. You need to get justice." Clarke wondered what Frank would have to say about it, assuming he survived. Had he really been negligent? He seemed so meticulous. She found it hard to believe, although it occurred to her that, if he had been responsible for Annie's death, that might have been what made him become so painstakingly thorough in everything he did.

"We can't afford justice. I can't afford justice. There's only me now. Tony, my husband, killed himself because his heart was broken. That man..." Carmen pointed at Frank, waving the remote control dangerously. "That man took everything from me. What do I have to live for now? He should die, like they did."

"I'm sure Frank didn't want your daughter to die. I'm sure he tried his best to save her." Where was that ambulance and the police? Carmen was becoming more unstable all the time, despite Clarke's best efforts to calm her, and Frank needed urgent medical attention. "You should let the courts deal with him. I'm sure you could get legal aid for the cost." Clarke really wasn't sure if the state would pay for a private prosecution, when the coroner had already declared Frank innocent. Probably not, but she'd say anything if it meant Carmen would let them all go.

"She took his drugs, and she died. That makes it *his* fault."

Clarke wondered what to do for the best. Carmen's fixation on the idea that Frank caused her daughter's death meant she wouldn't listen to anyone, which made her extremely dangerous. And, indirectly, Frank had been responsible. Clarke couldn't argue with that. Thoughts of her mum and dad, her brother, Rob, and Paul flashed through Clarke's mind, together with the very real feeling that she might never see them again. Even during her firefighting years, when she faced danger almost every day, she never once experienced this emotion.

"He lied," Carmen spat out the words like venom. "That man lied. At the coroner's inquest, Frank told them Annie was in the placebo group. But then how did she get ill? Why did she have the same symptoms as the others, the others who took the drug and got ill? The others were all lucky. They didn't die. Why her? My angel, my darling daughter. Why not someone else?" Carmen's sobs tore at Clarke's heart. It must be dreadful to lose a child.

"I'm so sorry," Clarke said. She felt completely inadequate. No words could ever be enough. Carmen needed professional help. "I'm really sorry," she said again, as if repeating the words would make them sound less trite. "But more deaths won't solve anything." Clarke steeled herself. No matter how much sympathy Carmen deserved, Clarke needed to concentrate on somehow making sure Carmen didn't blow them all up.

"It will make me feel better," Carmen sobbed.

"No, it won't. And if Evan and I die, it will make you feel much worse. Please, can you at least let Evan go? He hasn't done anything."

Evan's face was ghostly white. He opened his mouth, immediately closing it again as if he didn't trust himself to speak, didn't trust himself to say the right thing.

"Carmen, how did you feel when Ollie died? I know you didn't mean that to happen, did you?"

"It should have been Frank." Carmen waved her hand angrily at him.

Clarke worried she would drop the detonator. She shouldn't have mentioned Ollie, but she needed to know. It must have been Carmen who poisoned the coffee. Carmen had access, but Clarke hadn't been able to understand why she might do it, until now. She was willing to bet that Carmen had attacked Frank in the alleyway too, but it would be madness to ask her that right now, and it would be no consolation to find out she was right.

Behind Carmen, a police car pulled into the car park. That would really make Carmen panic if she turned around and saw it. Clarke wracked her brains for something she could say that might pacify Carmen. Two police officers got out of the vehicle and started walking towards them. Clarke put her hand up to signal them to stop, doing it quickly in the hope that Carmen wouldn't notice.

"What are you doing?" Carmen grabbed Evan tighter and twisted them both round. The police officers had split up, so Carmen would only be able to see one of them. "Get away from me," she screamed.

"Stay back," Clarke shouted. "She's wearing a suicide vest."

The officer came to an abrupt halt and pressed a button on her radio.

"Turn that off," Carmen screeched.

The other officer skirted around the outside of the group to approach Carmen from behind. Clarke shivered. If he wanted to be a have-a-go hero, Carmen only needed to touch that button in her volatile state and they would all be dead. They were too out in the open here, so Carmen got a great view of everything around her. There was no way for anyone to sneak up on her unseen. Clarke wondered how she could persuade Carmen to move, to give the paramedics a chance to tend to Frank.

"Don't come any closer," Carmen shouted to the female officer. "I'll detonate it if you come any closer."

Carmen trembled visibly. It would be so easy for her to lose control and hit that button by accident.

"It's ok," the female police officer said. She held both hands in the air in a gesture of surrender. "We're not going to hurt you. Just put the detonator down, please, before someone gets hurt. I'm sure you don't want that."

Clarke wondered when the bomb squad would show up. They must be on their way, but they were taking their time getting here. At least, it seemed so. It seemed as if they'd all been here for hours. Realistically, it must have only been a few minutes.

"What was Annie like? What did she like doing?" Clarke hoped that talking about her daughter might distract Carmen and relax her a bit.

"She loved animals." A faint smile flickered over Carmen's face as she recalled her daughter. "Annie loved horses most. She wanted to learn to ride, but we couldn't afford lessons."

"I love horses too," Clarke said. "And my parents couldn't afford lessons either." Clarke remembered going for riding lessons every week for a couple of years. She wouldn't tell Carmen that.

"Annie volunteered at an animal rescue centre instead, to be around animals."

"That's a brilliant thing to do. Annie sounds like a wonderful person." Very slowly, being extra careful not to make any sudden moves, Clarke knelt down, deliberately putting herself between Carmen and Frank.

"What are you doing?"

"It's ok. I need to sit down," Clarke said. "I hurt my ankle." She didn't dare say she wanted to check on Frank. Carmen would never allow that, wouldn't allow anything that might help him to live. To her, Frank was the enemy, and she wanted him to die. Clarke wondered if they would send in armed police and shoot Carmen. She hoped it wouldn't come to that. It might not be safe for them to shoot, anyway. If Carmen dropped the detonator, it would probably go off. Suddenly, Clarke realised how much trouble they were really in, how slim their chances of survival. She took a deep breath. If she didn't hold it together, their slim chance would become no chance at all.

"How long have you worked at Carjon?" Clarke asked.

"Over a year," Carmen said. "Kerry got me the job when I found out Frank worked there. He didn't even recognise me. All those days we attended the coroner's inquest, and he didn't even recognise me. Like he didn't care. Annie was just another number to him. He should pay for what he did."

Clarke wished she hadn't asked Carmen that. She worried that Carmen's obsession with avenging her daughter's death had gone on for so long. Had she been planning this for a year? "I'm sure Frank's really sorry. I'm sure he didn't do anything deliberately. He must have tried very hard to get everything right. I'm sure Annie's death was an accident. Killing Frank won't put that right."

Clarke glanced across the car park, quickly so Carmen wouldn't notice her doing so. The second officer stood in the shadow of the building, talking into his radio. Clarke allowed herself a brief moment of relief. At least he didn't appear about to do anything stupid. At least he would get the experts here to deal with this. The relief moment was short-lived. This was unlikely to end well for all of them, and she didn't know how to get out of this situation. But she would keep trying because she sure as hell didn't want to get blown up.

"That's nice of Kerry to get you the job. How do you know her?" Clarke had been insisting all along that the accounts and the murder must be connected. Was Kerry the connection?

"She was Annie's friend." Carmen moved closer to Frank, pushing Even in front of her. "Kerry encouraged Annie to do the drug trial. She is nearly as bad as him." Carmen pointed angrily at Frank. "Except that at least Kerry felt guilty, so she tried to help me every time I asked."

Clarke wondered if Carmen had asked Kerry to alter Carjon's accounts. She didn't dare ask. "You need to do the right thing, Carmen." Through the booming in her ears, Clarke heard sirens. She hoped it was an ambulance.

With years of training and practice, Clarke excelled at emergencies. Being threatened by an unstable, emotional woman with a bomb strapped to her differed hugely from putting out fires, but it still very much counted as an emergency. She began to prioritise, counting things off in her head. Frank was number one priority. If he didn't get medical attention soon, he would probably die. She needed to settle Carmen, somehow to make her think logically and listen to reason. And Evan. He didn't deserve to be here, and he really wasn't coping with the situation well. Clarke worried that Evan might crack under the strain if they were here for much longer.

"Carmen," Clarke spoke softly and sympathetically, despite longing to slap the woman round the face and bring her to her senses. "What would your daughter tell you if she saw you here now? I'm sure she wouldn't want you to do this."

"I need to make Frank pay. Can't you see I'm doing this for her?"

"But I'm sure your daughter would never want *you* to die."

"I'm doing it for her."

"Of course you are, but why don't we let the paramedics take Frank. If he dies, you'll never get the real truth from him. You deserve to be told the truth. We'll make him tell you."

Carmen was silent, but she seemed to be considering it. Clarke hoped she'd finally got through to her. Carmen's eyes glazed over, like she'd gone to a private place in her head. If only she wasn't holding that damned detonator, this would be a perfect opportunity to overpower her. Clarke took advantage of the situation and quietly pushed her fingers against Frank's wrist. His pulse point still throbbed faintly.

"You need to find out the truth, Carmen." Clarke still had hold of Frank's wrist. She felt a wiggle of his arm and glanced at him without moving her head. It would be dreadful timing on Frank's part if he woke up now.

It wasn't Frank moving his arm. Clarke caught a glimpse of Delilah peeping out at the end of his sleeve. Poor Delilah. She would be yet another casualty in this disaster if Clarke couldn't talk Carmen round. She wondered if Delilah might be of some use, but Carmen was neither frightened of rats like Deborah, nor did she love them like Frank.

Across the car park, the paramedics were preparing for action. They wouldn't be able to do anything until Carmen put that detonator down.

"Carmen, you don't need to make Evan pay," Clarke said quietly. "He hasn't done anything. Why don't you let him go? He's an innocent party who's got caught up in all of this. Carmen, please let Evan go, I'm begging you."

Carmen didn't answer. She looked shell-shocked now, almost catatonic, and Clarke wasn't sure how to get through to her.

Clarke did consider that the vest may be fake or not functional. Carmen may have thought she'd wired everything up correctly, but she wasn't an electronics expert. Clarke looked at the state of Frank and glanced across at Carjon Pharma's ruined offices. The bomb in the building hadn't been a fake.

How had Carmen learnt how to make bombs? Were the animal rights activists tied up with this, or was it all her doing? Would she have gone along with the animal rights protestors because it gave her a way to punish Frank? Or was she manipulating the activists, not the other way round? Clarke didn't know. She did know that if Carmen hit that detonator button, they might all die.

"Carmen, why don't you take the vest off and we can talk about this. I'm your friend. I can help you. Your daughter wouldn't want you to die, would she?"

Carmen shook her head slowly.

Clarke wondered if she was getting through to her in some small way. She hoped that the police officers or Evan didn't screw things up at the last minute.

"Tell me more about Annie," Clarke said.

Carmen smiled weakly. "Annie was really clever, the first person in our family to go to university."

"You must have been so proud of her."

"Yes, we were incredibly proud."

"Carmen, make her proud of you. Do the right thing now. Put the detonator on the ground." Clarke tried to make eye contact, establish more of a connection, but Carmen was shedding so many tears, Clarke doubted she could see clearly.

"She studied chemistry. Annie wanted to be a research scientist too, and she would have been brilliant. She wouldn't have killed people." Carmen's voice changed instantly from wistful to bitter. "She just wanted to help everyone."

"I know," Clarke said, picking up on the mood change and trying her best to stay calm. "She would want to help you too, wouldn't she? She sounds like a lovely girl. She would never want you to die."

"No." Tears streamed down Carmen's face.

"Give the detonator to Evan," Clarke spoke quietly, but firmly. She didn't expect Carmen to do as she asked, but she had to ask, anyway. For a moment, Carmen appeared to move her index finger closer to the button. Clarke screwed her eyes tight shut, bracing herself.

When she opened them a few seconds later, Carmen was extending her hand towards Evan. Clarke scarcely dared to breathe. Carmen's hand shook as she passed the detonator to Evan, and Clarke worried that Evan might be so terrified that his hand would shake too and he might drop the detonator and set it off. Evan closed his fingers round the deadly device and ran.

"Walk!" Clarke shouted, concerned that he might trip and fall. She went over to Carmen and hugged her. "Well done," she said. "Annie would be very proud." She held Carmen close to her as the paramedics moved in on Frank. Carmen broke down in floods of tears, and Clarke wasn't surprised that her own tears started falling down her cheeks as she held on to Carmen. The woman police officer headed towards them. In a few more seconds, Carmen would get arrested and taken away. Her life as she knew it would be over, and nothing that happened from here on in would ever take away her pain.

"What happened, Carmen? How did you get involved with the animal rights people? You did know them, didn't you? Timmo lives near you, doesn't he?"

"Timmo started harassing me when he found out I worked here," she said, struggling to get the words out through her sobs. "He lives in the same block of flats as me."

"You must tell the police that. You can use it as a defence," Clarke tried to reassure her. She would undoubtedly still be looking at a hefty prison sentence.

She shook her head. "Timmo thought he could use me, but he wasn't clever enough. I used him. It's all my fault. If only Evan hadn't stayed in the office today, everything would have worked perfectly."

Carmen looked over at Evan as if she hated him. Clarke was relieved she couldn't hurt him now.

Clarke let go of Carmen as the police officer snapped her handcuffs around Carmen's wrists.

"What's your name?" the officer addressed Carmen.

Carmen didn't answer. She continued to stare blankly ahead. Clarke assumed she must be in shock. Maybe the enormity of her actions had hit her now.

"Her name's Carmen de Silva," Clarke said. "She works here." She looked at Carmen, not wanting to set her off again by telling the police officer things about her, even though she couldn't blow them up now. "She's upset because her daughter died on a drug trial. Frank's a research scientist. He develops new drugs. I'm sure it wasn't his fault that Carmen's daughter died. He takes a lot of care over his work.

"Anyway, the building blew up. Frank's been hurt." She was relieved to see two paramedics already tending to Frank. "Carmen's wearing a suicide vest," she continued, "but Evan has the detonator."

"It's ok," the officer said. "My colleague took charge of that. The bomb squad will disable it." She started to lead Carmen towards the police car.

Evan came over and put a comforting arm around Clarke's shoulders. "Are you ok?"

Clarke nodded. "I'm fine." She was pleased to see that Evan seemed none the worse for his ordeal, although she could feel him shaking a little, or maybe that was her. "I'm more concerned about Frank."

"Is he alive?"

"Yes, but he's in a bad way," Clarke said.

"What the blazes was Frank doing, going back?"

"He wanted to save his rats," Clarke said. Evan wasn't much of an animal lover. He would never understand that Frank probably loved his rats enough to risk his life for them.

Evan shook his head in disbelief. "I'll phone Henry. He'll want to know about this. And he can phone Frank's wife. The second time this month. Poor woman. Unbelievable."

Chapter 52

Clarke watched as the ambulance pulled away, hoping they'd got to Frank in time. Carmen had already been taken away by the police. Clarke felt bad for Carmen. She would end up with a lengthy prison sentence for sure, which wouldn't help her one bit. She needed counselling, not prison. Years in prison would make her pain fester all the more. The whole thing was tragic. It should have never come to this. If only someone had spotted Carmen's suffering and reached out to her earlier.

She walked with Evan across the desolate car park, where two female police officers were waiting next to her car.

"Clarke, you were amazing. I thought we were all going to die. You saved my life," Evan said, staring at her in awe. "I've always wondered what you were like as a firefighter. I've never been able to imagine it before. You must have been brilliant."

"I was ok," Clarke said modestly. Evan seemed to be back to normal, thank God. No doubt by tomorrow, he'd be in the pub, recounting the whole story to his friends.

"Why ever did you give it up?"

"Oh, just because," Clark said casually. She still missed the brigade sometimes, especially the camaraderie with her colleagues. She would have never given it up voluntarily, but she wouldn't tell Evan that. If she did, then she would have to tell him about the accident and her injured ankle. No chance. She didn't want him feeling sorry for her or making allowances.

"You really were wonderful," he said. "How did you stay so calm? I couldn't have done what you did. To be honest, I was absolutely bricking it when I saw Carmen had a bomb."

Clarke smiled. She didn't need Evan to tell her how terrified he had been. "I've had a lot of training." In a minute, Evan would probably start calling her *brave*, and Clarke hated that because she wasn't brave, not really. She was simply well-trained.

"Well, I have massive respect for you now. You wouldn't believe how much. You're so brave."

There, he'd said it. Clarke cringed. "You could always give me a pay rise then," she said, trying to change the subject.

"That might be a bit trickier," Evan said. "Anyway, how did you find out about the bomb? However did you get Carmen to admit that?"

"I gave her a lift home," Clarke said. "And when I mentioned that you were still in the office, she got very upset. She obviously likes you a bit because she didn't actually want to kill you. Maybe she still felt guilty about Ollie."

"She killed Ollie?"

"Yes, it had to be her. Once Frank got attacked, I knew it couldn't be him, and Carmen was the only other person, apart from Henry, who had keys to everything. She thought poisoning the coffee would be safe as Ollie only ever drank tea." Clarke realised how lucky it was that she'd turned down Frank's offer to make her a coffee that day.

"Wow. So how did you work out there was a bomb?" Evan asked.

"Eventually, her conscience got the better of her and she told me to come back. I couldn't even get you on the phone. Why don't you ever answer your phone?"

"I was listening to music and didn't hear it ring."

"You were lucky." Evan could have been killed. Clarke suspected Evan wouldn't be listening to music at work for a long time to come.

"It hasn't sunk in yet. So, you agreed to come back. How did you know it was a bomb?"

"Let's just say a little star told me." If Paul hadn't mentioned the star on Carmen's calendar, she may not have added everything together to guess that something big was happening.

"Anyway, everything ended up all right. And they think Frank will recover."

THE COVER-UP

"I certainly hope so," Clarke said, relieved that Frank would survive. That meant Carmen hadn't won.

"I thought he was dead," Evan said. "What an idiot, trying to go back in."

"The bomb didn't go off at the time Carmen said it would, so he probably assumed she'd messed up and not managed to get it working." Clarke wondered if he didn't think Carmen capable of rigging up a bomb. Just goes to show, never underestimate anybody.

"It was a risky thing to do, whatever he believed. Why would anyone endanger their life for a bunch of rats?"

"They are quite cute. He must have got very fond of them." Clarke had always loved animals. She understood Frank's attachment.

"That's what seems so odd," Evan said. "Surely proper animal rights campaigners would save the rats before they blew up the lab. I'm sure some of these activists are more interested in causing trouble than they are in saving animals."

"I'm sure a lot of them do genuinely care. They just don't always go about it the right way." Clarke wanted Evan to be wrong. If nobody cared, who would look out for animals like these? But she didn't think Timmo Macintosh cared that much about the animals. He seemed to have his own agenda. The police were on their way to arrest him and promised to investigate him thoroughly.

They had nearly reached the car and the police officers. Clarke longed to sit down. She was struggling to walk now and progress across the car park had been slow. She turned to take a final look at the building. Frank's lab was on fire, but the bomb squad wouldn't allow the firefighters near the building yet. A group of them waited some way back across the car park. Clarke knew they would be itching to tackle the blaze before it got completely out of control. Part of her still wished she could be with them.

The corner of the building started to collapse, listing to one side before imploding, almost in slow motion. With the lab being situated in the basement, Clarke guessed the explosion must have damaged the foundations. The entire building would be unsafe now.

"I wonder how long it will take to get everything repaired," Clarke said.

Evan sighed. "A long time, I would guess. There's a great deal of damage. I'm no expert, but it probably needs demolishing and completely rebuilding."

"I hope they're well insured."

"The Carjon Pharma's in a mess now, anyway. They may have to dissolve the company."

"What about Frank's new drug?" Clarke asked.

"I suppose it might be possible to sell it to another company. It all depends. With luck, he's got all his research backed up safely in the cloud. If he hasn't, that's years of work wasted."

"Let's hope so. I'm pretty sure Patrick's wife was counting on his latest drug."

"Well, Frank won't be around for a while, not the state he's in, so she might have to find something else," Evan said.

Clarke felt sad. All of Carmen's actions had consequences. All of Carjon's employees would now be out of a job. Frank was seriously injured. He may have lost all his research, and he'd be devastated about the rats as well. Patrick's wife would probably lose her battle with cancer. Henry would almost certainly lose the company, although apparently his wife was rich, so he'd be fine, even if he lost all of his own money. Clarke hoped he hadn't invested too much of his wife's money in the company.

They both turned and headed towards her car. Further across the car park, Paul was striding towards them. Even after all this time, he still looked as cute as when Clarke had first met him, way when she was still a firefighter, and he was a lowly police constable.

"Are you ok?" he asked as soon as he got close.

THE COVER-UP

"I'm fine." Clark wasn't exactly sure about that right now, but she would be ok.

"Was this another attempt on Frank's life? That's the third failed attempt. He's got more lives than a cat," Paul said.

"Yes, he is kind of lucky," Evan said.

"Not that lucky," Clarke reminded him. "He's going to be in the hospital for a while, but he was fortunate not to be killed."

"We can't interview Carmen until the doctors have checked her over. She's an emotional wreck. She won't stop crying. It could take ages time to calm her down before she can talk properly," Paul said. "Did she say anything to you?"

"She did all this for her daughter," Clarke said. "Her daughter, Annie, died two years ago in one of Frank's drug trials. Carmen blamed him for her daughter's death, even though the coroner didn't."

"Wow, did Frank have no idea who she was?"

"I don't suppose he recognised her, and he wouldn't have connected Carmen to her daughter. Carmen used her maiden name, De Silva, when she joined the company."

"I'm surprised she wanted to work with Frank," Paul said.

Clarke stopped for a moment, taking her weight on her good leg to rest her bad one. "I don't suppose she did." She'd been trying to puzzle things out as she'd been talking to Carmen. "I reckon she got the job here deliberately so she could get her revenge on Frank. She obviously planned it for a very long time, then when Timmo Macintosh showed up, she saw how she might do it."

"Timmo Macintosh? Is he involved with this? He's just been arrested for breaking into Frank's house. We found one of his fingerprints at the scene."

Clarke nodded. "He's up to his neck in this. He'll have far bigger problems than burglary charges to worry about."

"Let's hope we can prove it. I don't think Carmen will be the most reliable witness."

"You should talk to Kerry as well. She works here. Kerry was friends with Carmen's daughter and encouraged her to do the drug trial in the first place. So, Carmen blamed Kerry nearly as much as she blamed Frank." It really wasn't Frank's fault that Carmen became obsessed, and now she'd screwed up her entire life because of it. Clarke found that so sad.

"But where did she learn how to make a bomb, for Christ's sake?" Paul asked.

"She got in with the animal rights protestors. That's where Timmo fits in. He's one of Carmen's neighbours. They probably egged each other on to blow the place up. He must have got hold of the bomb or learned on the internet how to make one."

"Timmo Macintosh has an electronics degree," Paul said. "He'd be very capable."

Clarke nodded. "That figures. I can't really see Carmen making bombs. But I can see her agreeing to help as a way to punish Frank. But that was probably after the poison attempt went wrong. Carmen never planned on killing Ollie."

"Wait a minute. Carmen killed Ollie?" Paul looked surprised.

"Yes. She must have thought that poisoning the coffee would be a safe bet because Ollie only ever drank tea. That's why she was so devastated about Ollie. She treated Ollie a bit like a son. I guess that was to make up for losing her daughter. They must have been a vaguely similar age. And not only did she lose her daughter, but her husband committed suicide a while later because he couldn't cope with their daughter's death, leaving Carmen to manage all on her own." It was hardly surprising that she'd cracked under the stress of all that.

"But how did you find out about the bomb? Is there anything you don't know?"

Clarke smiled. "Well, I don't know where you're taking me for dinner tonight."

"Not much chance of that," Paul said. "I'll be working late. Anyway, how did you find out?"

"I gave Carmen a lift home." Clarke repeated the story for Paul's benefit.

"Lucky you did, isn't it," Paul said. "It saved Evan, and it probably saved Frank as well. It looks like the bomb was in the lab, so Frank would have really got the full blast of the explosion."

"What will happen to Carmen?" Clarke asked.

"She obviously needs psychiatric help, but she'll end up in prison. It wasn't a one-off. Three times she tried to kill Frank, and she's been planning it for a long time too. I don't imagine the courts will let her off of that too quickly. And she did succeed in killing Ollie, even if it was by mistake."

"And there's one other thing," Clarke said. "The way the accounts were manipulated was down to Carmen as well. Not directly. She got Kerry to do it for her, except that Carmen didn't understand what needed to be done. I think Kerry did everything the wrong way round deliberately. She made the company appear to be in a better position, not a worse one." Kerry could go to prison for what she did, despite her good intentions. Would she get off if the courts knew how much Carmen had intimidated and blackmailed her?

"Carmen wanted to bring the company down because Frank owns shares in it. But Kerry wanted the accounts to look much better. I'm assuming she intended to help Patrick and probably also to stick two fingers up at Carmen."

"And I found out how it got past the auditors," Paul said. "The reason the auditors didn't pick up on it is because one of them went to school with Kerry. It seems he's still sweet on her."

"She did an amazing job, but that explains a lot." Clarke had forgotten she'd asked Paul to check that out. The auditor must have been seriously sweet on Kerry to take such a huge risk for her.

"And Carmen never suspected that Kerry did things the wrong way round?"

"Carmen wouldn't even have guessed. She might have assumed that, without Kerry's intervention, the accounts would have appeared even better than they did. But sadly, the company was on shaky financial ground anyway, and it still is. This bombing will probably make the company go under, what with the bad publicity and the time it will take to get the building rebuilt. And we're not even sure how well Frank's got all his research backed up. Let's hope Henry's got a good contingency plan, but it will probably need a miracle."

"There's another thing I really don't get," Paul said. "Why did Ollie drink that poisoned coffee if he never drinks coffee?"

"I know the answer to that one. I was with them at the time. Frank ran out of tea bags. He felt a bit guilty because he knew Ollie didn't like coffee. But he didn't have time to go out to buy more tea because I'd arrived to interview him. So it's my fault, I guess. Frank offered me coffee too."

"Wow, that was a lucky escape," Paul said. "I assume you didn't drink much."

"I didn't have any. Thank God I'd only just finished one upstairs, so I turned it down."

"Well, that wouldn't normally put you off having another."

"No, you're right," Clarke said, well aware of her coffee addiction. Normally, she couldn't get enough of it. Like she couldn't get enough of Paul either. She still needed to get around the issue of him not telling his colleagues about her. Maybe if he left it a while until this case was over, he could finally tell them. She would probably forgive him for the moment, as long as he put things right as soon as possible. She didn't want to be hidden away, as if he was embarrassed by her or something. Clarke realised she had a complex about her injured ankle. She never told people about it because she didn't like being judged. She didn't like people assuming there were things she couldn't do. Paul shouldn't be embarrassed by something like that. She'd meet him halfway on the colleague issue. As long as he told them eventually, then perhaps they would have a future together. She realised now how much she really wanted that.

Clarke stared at the ruined building. At least the one good thing about this was that Timmo Macintosh and his animal rights cronies wouldn't be able to hang about outside the entrance for a long time to come. It would stop them from intimidating people trying to go in and out. Doubtless they would go somewhere else, find some other pharmaceutical company to demonstrate at instead, if Timmo didn't get sent to prison, which he probably would. There were always other places. Perhaps they wouldn't come back. It didn't really matter to her because she and Evan had been planning to move on to another job in a couple of days, anyway. She guessed they would need to give their findings to Henry somewhere else. But something told her Henry wouldn't really care very much now.

Clarke guessed the three friends, Henry, Patrick, and Frank would go their separate ways now, and the company would be dissolved. It looked like the end of the road for Carjon Pharma. She turned away from Paul, not wanting him to see the tears that had started rolling down her cheeks.

If you enjoyed this book, scroll further to download a FREE prequel to the Clarke Pettis series, THE THEFT. But first...

THE PAYBACK

Book 3 in the Clarke Pettis series

Two years ago, Clarke Pettis helped to convict a work colleague for murder and fraud. Now, forensic accountant Clarke, is tasked with finding out what happened to the stolen millions. Reluctantly, she visits the offender in prison.

The prison visit goes badly, leaving Clarke wracked with guilt about ruining her ex-colleague's life. She vows not to visit a second time.

Minutes later, Clarke's old colleague kills again, and escapes from prison.

Locating the stolen money just got harder, and Clarke finds herself in serious danger when the fugitive becomes obsessed with revenge.

Clarke becomes tangled up in a cat-and-mouse game as she searches for the escaped prisoner, who holds the key to the missing millions. How can she track them down before she becomes their final victim?

The Payback is the final book in the Clarke Pettis series.

THE THEFT

Find out what Clarke did in her previous career as a firefighter. This action-packed book is a prequel to The Fraud and The Cover-Up. It's **FREE** to download when you sign up for my author newsletter.

This was twenty million pounds' worth of dangerous...
   Firefighter Clarke Pettis' priority was saving lives, not possessions. But, when she discovers the painting that disappeared during the rescue of an injured man in a house fire was worth a fortune, Clarke couldn't leave things alone.
   She puts herself in serious danger when she crosses paths with art thief, Antonio Balleri.
   Can Clarke save herself from Balleri and find the stolen painting?

Be the first to find out about new releases, special offers, and other interesting stuff. Download the free book and sign up at https://BookHip.com/ZFKSLZQ.

Also by Christine Pattle
SECRETS NEVER DIE

Would you risk your life to save a baby?
Would you do anything you could to protect her from harm?
Even if that meant taking her and never giving her back?

Twenty-five years ago, Dan Peterson risked his life to rescue a baby from a dangerous cult, the Seventh Heavenites. That baby grew up to be the well-known model Pagan.

When Pagan gets the chance to be the face of a new perfume, she must spend a week working on the beautiful island of Jersey, the one place she will never be safe.

As Dan digs deeper into the past, he endangers both Pagan and her young daughter.

Can Dan protect Pagan from the Seventh Heavenites, and a secret that she knows nothing about?

A Letter to the Reader

Dear Reader,

Thank you so much for reading this book. Readers are by far the most important people in an author's world. Of all the millions of books you could have chosen to read, a massive THANK YOU for giving my book a chance. I really hope you enjoyed it.

I loved writing THE COVER-UP. If you loved reading it, please would you leave a short review on Amazon. Reviews are so important to raise visibility and help other readers find my work.

Take Care
    Christine

About The Author

Christine Pattle writes mystery-thrillers with interesting characters and plenty of action. Her aim is always to write a good page-turning story that readers will love.

When she's not writing, she's busy scaring herself silly, riding big, feisty horses, or walking round the countryside dreaming up exciting new plots.

You can contact Christine at christine@christinepattleauthor
Or visit her Facebook page https://www.facebook.com/ChristinePattleAuthor

Acknowledgments

A HUGE thank you:

To my brilliant editor, Emily at Laurence Editing.

To my wonderful launch team. I couldn't do this without you. While I was in the middle of writing The Cover-Up, I asked members of the team if they would like to name some of my characters in the next two or three books. So, thank you to John O'Regan, who chose Patrick's pet name, *Paddy Bear*, and to Neil Weston, who named *Evan*.

To my cover artist, Get Covers.

To all the authors who have ever inspired me.

To my parents for bringing me up to believe I could accomplish anything I wanted to in my life.

And to my fabulous friends who have encouraged me on my author journey.

Copyright

Copyright © Christine Pattle, 2022

Christine Pattle has asserted her right to be identified as the author of this work in accordance with the Copyright, Designs and Patents Act 1988.

All rights reserved. No part of this book may be reproduced, stored in any retrieval system, or transmitted, in any form or by any means, electronic, mechanical, photocopying, recording or otherwise, without the prior written permission of the author.

This book is a work of fiction. Names, characters, businesses, organisations, places and events other than those clearly in the public domain, are either the product of the author's imagination or are used fictitiously. Any resemblance to actual persons, living or dead, events or locales is entirely coincidental.